CAFFEINE N

CW00670746

INCISIONS

CUT 2

Shaun Hutson

Fiction to die for…

Published by Caffeine Nights Publishing 2023

Published in Great Britain by
Caffeine Nights Publishing
Amity House
71 Buckthorne Road
Minster on Sea
Isle of Sheppey
ME12 3RD

caffeinenightsbooks.com
British Library Cataloguing in Publication Data.
A CIP catalogue record for this book is available from the British
Library
Available as a paperback
ISBN: 978-1-913200-30-5

Cover design by
Ria Fend

Everything else by
Default, Luck and Accident

WARHOL'S PROPHECY
WHITE GHOST

Hammer Novelizations
TWINS OF EVIL
X THE UNKNOWN
THE REVENGE OF FRANKENSTEIN

INCISIONS

CUT TWO

ACKNOWLEDGEMENTS

The people who are mentioned in the acknowledgements of a novel are there for a reason. Be it support, encouragement or because they've begged me to be in... (just kidding).

Anyway, the list that follows is probably not exhaustive and it will probably seem familiar to people who read most of my books but here goes:

As always, I would like to thank my publisher, Darren Laws at Caffeine Nights. His continued faith in my work is both welcomed and greatly appreciated. Many thanks to everyone at Caffeine Nights.

My agent, Meg Davies, for her efforts and work.

I'd also like to thank Matt Shaw, Graeme Sayer, Michael Knight, Emma Dark and Mark Taylor. They should all know why.

A big thank you to everyone at Cineworld Milton Keynes where I seem to spend much of my spare time.

Thanks also to Claire, Dani, Leah, Belinda, Bruce, Steve, Dave, Adrian, Janick and Nicko and Rod Smallwood.

Thanks is far too inadequate a word for what I want to say to my daughter.

The most important people are, as ever, you lot. My readers. You support me, you challenge me, and you are one of the reasons I do this.

And now, I've probably been rambling for too long.

Let's go.

Shaun Hutson.

For my daughter. Always. So many words, but none

can ever express how much I love her.

"White coats define me, out of control.
I live alone inside my mind."

Anthrax

"Everything you can imagine is real."
Pablo Picasso

AUTHOR'S INTRODUCTION

Welcome to the second cut of INCISIONS. I hope you read and enjoyed CUT ONE and were so staggeringly impressed with it that you've moved onto the second volume.

As I said during the introduction to Cut One, the business of writing short stories is completely different to that employed when tackling a novel. This might seem glaringly obvious but the shorter word extent doesn't alter the way I approach a short story.

My novels tend to whip along at a hell of a pace and, hopefully, my short stories do the same. The initial idea for a story might not have the "legs" to develop into a novel. For instance there's a story in this volume called "The Poppet" which only works as a short story (at least I hope it does). There wasn't enough material to expand it into a novel. That is true of ninety percent of the tales in the two cuts of Incisions.

I grew up watching the classic compendium horror films like Tales from the Crypt, Vault of Horror and Dr Terror's House of Horrors. The stories in those films worked (well, some of them) as shorts. They would never have succeeded as full length films.

I was going to say that working on a short story requires different disciplines but then I realized that a) that sounded pretentious and b) it is not true. The same energy, ferocity and intensity present in a short story should be present in a novel. What a short story gives you is the freedom to explore ideas you might not be able to use in a novel. There are a number of stories in both cuts of Incisions that illustrate this.

For those of you worrying that I might be abandoning novels for short stories, have no fear. These two volumes were written over the course of a year but, while I was also working on full length projects. The short story ideas just hit me and needed to be written. That is the way with stories of any length. They get inside your head and there is a need to get them out.

I've found that all through my career. Some stories need to be "exorcised." I've always said that writing has saved me a fortune on therapy. For me, writing has always been a cathartic process. Sometimes for me, sometimes for my readers. I was at a horror convention once when a reader said to me "I love your books but I wouldn't want to be inside your head." It made me laugh but I know what he meant. The two cuts of Incisions have given me more chances to "remove" some of those thoughts.

What they've also done is, once again, look at what constitutes horror and what doesn't. It's an argument that has raged since millions of people bought Silence of the Lambs back in the 90's and thought they'd bought a horror book. They didn't. They bought a novel with horrific passages. Just as those who saw the film saw a film that wasn't horror but had horrific scenes. Not all the stories in Incisions are horror or what is commonly accepted as horror but, it all comes down to definitions. It always has. A spider crawling across a wall might not be horrific to many people. It only becomes horrific when that same spider crawls into someone's ear, lays eggs and we learn that the baby spiders are eating their way into the victims brain.

However, as I've said many times in interviews over the years, horror is in the eye of the beholder. It isn't always buckets of blood and erupting intestines. Not always crawling, swamp dwelling monstrosities and giant creatures rising from the sea. Sometimes it is something more simple. A disembodied voice heard somewhere it shouldn't be. Something given as a gift that turns out to be more sinister. Or, that spider crawling slowly across the wall...

There should be something for everyone in this cut. So, let's waste no more time. Dim the lights, draw the curtains (after you've made sure no one's outside looking in at you...) and start reading. You don't know what you may find. Or what may find you....

Let's go.

Shaun Hutson.

WEB

The first thing John Coyle thought when he saw his neighbour running towards him was that she looked terrified.

He had just pulled into his driveway and as he turned away from the car he saw Sarah Harris hurrying from her front garden.

"Are you okay?" John asked as she approached him.

She looked flustered and she was breathing heavily and rapidly.

"What's happened?" John continued.

"A spider," she told him. "A big one."

"Is it the same one as yesterday?"

"I don't know, I didn't ask it for ID. They all look the same to me. Big, hairy long-legged things." She shuddered involuntarily.

John smiled benevolently and the two of them set off back towards Sarah's house, pausing at the front door.

"I'm sorry about this," she said. "But you know what I'm like with spiders."

John nodded. "Don't worry about it. Everyone's scared of something, aren't they? I'm terrified of snakes."

He pushed open the front door and walked in. Sarah followed sheepishly.

"It was in the living room," she told him. "I was watching TV and it ran across the floor."

"You could have just killed it," he reminded her.

"Oh no, I couldn't do that," she told him. "I'm frightened of them but I couldn't kill them. You know that old saying '*If you want to live and thrive, let a spider run alive.*'"

John smiled and walked into the living room to look around, picking up magazines and newspapers to ensure the offending arachnid wasn't seeking cover beneath them. He checked behind plant pots and books too and found nothing. Sarah stood silently at the door watching as he moved around the room, finally shrugging.

"If it's here it's gone now," he exclaimed.

"What if it's gone upstairs?" she enquired.

"It won't have," John assured her.

Sarah sighed.

"I'm really sorry, John," she told him. "I know you must think I'm such an idiot."

He dismissed her apology again but accepted her offer of a coffee when she suggested it. They walked through into the kitchen and he sat down at the large wooden table while she boiled the kettle.

"Have you always been like this about spiders?" he enquired. "I mean, terrified of them?"

"When I was little one dropped onto my face while I was in bed," she explained. "Ever since then I just panic when I see one. It's been worse since my husband..." She let the words trail off.

"How long has it been now?"

"Nearly two years but I still miss him. Sometimes I feel as if I'm moving on but others it feels as if it was just yesterday."

"I know what you mean. I know divorce is nothing like death but I feel the same about my wife occasionally."

"Do you miss her?"

"Sometimes."

"Would you ever get back together?"

"We're different people now. I don't imagine that will ever happen."

He thanked her and sipped at the coffee she gave him.

"Have you ever thought of having some sort of therapy for your fear?" John asked. "I mean, if it's that acute maybe you should consider it."

"I'd feel stupid."

"Why? If you need help coping with your fear why worry about it?"

Sarah shrugged and sipped her own beverage.

They chatted a little longer and then John excused himself and they walked to the door together. She thanked him and waved him off, retreating back behind her front door once more. He hesitated a moment, brushing a hand across his face when he felt something touch his cheek.

It took him a moment to realise that it was a spider's web spun across part of the porch. John wiped the diaphanous threads from his skin, muttering to himself. The spider that had made the web scuttled into view briefly then dropped to the ground close by.

John crushed it beneath his shoe.

***

His office was on the fifth floor and, as he stood at one of the windows, John Coyle had a panoramic view out across the town below him. He watched as a car struggled to park in the narrow spaces below, wincing when he saw how close it came to colliding with the two vehicles on either side of it. However, that spectacle provided only a temporary diversion and, as he stepped back, he noticed something in the corner of the window.

It was a spider's web.

John sighed. The new firm of cleaners that the company was using weren't as thorough as the previous ones. He brushed the web away, muttering under his breath.

As he sat down at his desk he noticed another web

between the top and one leg of the wooden structure.

Irritated, he brushed that one away too, deciding that if this kind of thing was repeated he'd have to report it. What the hell were the cleaners doing? Why hadn't they noticed the webs? He was still considering this negligent behaviour when his office door opened.

Vishal Mattu walked in and smiled his usual practised smile.

"So," he began. "Did you see my e-mail?"

"The one about the redundancies?" John said.

"We have to lose some dead wood," Vishal told him. "That's straight from the top floor."

"They're not dead wood. They're people. People with houses, families and responsibilities," John snapped. "Stop using language you've read in some management manual."

"Better them than you, John," the other man reminded him.

"There's no way round it?"

"None. And they've got to be informed by the end of the week."

John nodded.

"It's natural selection," Vishal told him. "The ones who don't make the grade have to go."

John regarded his colleague coldly, watching as he turned and prepared to leave the office.

"Like I said," Vishal called as he walked out. "Better them than you."

John glared at his disappearing back then down at his desk again.

A small spider was scuttling across one corner of the polished wood.

John picked up a notepad and slammed it down on the arachnid.

"Natural selection," he murmured.

The rest of his day seemed to pass in one long

unending parade of meetings and e-mail answering so when the time finally came to go home he was grateful. He tidied his desk, made sure everything was switched off and made the walk to the car park where his Peugeot was waiting.

The drive home took a little longer than usual because of an accident as he left the town centre (typical that, whenever you wanted to be home quickly the fates conspired against you). However, within forty-five minutes he was pulling into his driveway, glad to be home and looking forward to slumping in front of the TV or reading more of his new book which had arrived the previous day.

As he walked to his front door he frowned slightly, catching sight of something glistening on the black-painted wooden partition. As he stepped closer he saw that it was spider web.

It was woven thickly all across the door and the brass knocker.

John frowned and brushed it away before fumbling for his front door key.

He was about to step across the threshold when he heard a voice calling his name and turned to see that it was Sarah Harris. She ran up to him, her face pale.

"What's wrong?" he wanted to know.

"I've been waiting for you to get home," she blurted. "There's another spider in my house."

John tried to hide his reaction. This was the last thing he needed right now. He smiled as warmly as he could.

"I've been waiting," she repeated.

"Isn't there someone else you could have asked for help?"

Anyone but me, basically.

She shook her head.

"This one is really big. You're the only one who understands," she told him.

John didn't feel particularly understanding but he knew how much she feared spiders and he wasn't about to ignore her pleas for help despite his own weariness. They walked to her house together, Sarah hanging back slightly as if she was reluctant to go near the building again.

"You can beat this fear you know," he told her. "If you don't it'll take over your life."

"You don't know what it's like," she said, reproachfully. "And this one is much bigger than normal."

John shuddered slightly. He wasn't frightened of spiders but the thought of confronting one particularly large specimen wasn't exactly enticing. He'd seen some as big as the palm of his hand and he wasn't too keen on repeating the experience.

"I'm not a fan of spiders myself," he went on. "When I was a kid we went on holiday to France and a spider bit my father on the hand. His whole hand swelled up like a balloon. I thought he was going to die. So I'm not exactly a fan of them myself."

Sarah listened to his story but seemed more concerned with the spider that was currently inside her house. She walked behind John as he drew nearer to her front door as if that simple action would somehow shield her from what was inside.

"Where was it?" he asked.

"Upstairs, in the bathroom," she told him.

"You wait here. I'll go and check."

He moved inside the house, checking each room in turn and finally making his way up the steps towards the first floor of the building. There was no sign of anything untoward or eight-legged in either of the bedrooms so he moved to the last of the spare rooms and then to the bathroom.

The sound of dripping water accompanied his search and he glanced behind and beneath ornaments in the small room until he was satisfied that there were no spiders.

There was however spider web in several places inside the room and, from the tackiness of the strands, it was a recent addition. As for the creature that had left it behind there was no trace. John made his way downstairs, ushered Sarah inside and explained that his latest bout of reconnaissance had once more revealed nothing.

She was grateful for this information and he left, refusing her offer of tea or coffee, wanting to relax for the rest of the evening. As he reached the bottom of her path he turned to see that she'd already closed her front door.

John made his way back home and locked his front door before getting some dinner and seating himself in a high-backed chair in the sitting room with his new book and a glass of red wine.

He read more than eighty pages before he finally drifted off to sleep, the large hardback falling from his hands with a suitably expansive thud and waking him as it hit the floor.

John yawned, recovered his senses and decided to have an early night (well, sort of early, it was just after quarter past eleven).

He was halfway up the stairs when he heard the banging on his front door.

John froze for a second, wondering who would be knocking his door at this late hour. He turned and headed slowly down the stairs, moving right up to the front door, straining his ears to see if he could detect any sounds from beyond the partition.

He was inches from it when there was more banging.

John jumped back, his heart thudding harder now.

He saw that the chain was on but he hesitated as he reached for the handle, finally opening the door a crack.

There was no one on the doorstep.

He opened it a little further and peered out into the

night, only the street lamps offering any illumination.

John was about to duck back inside the house when something loomed at him from the side of the porch. He almost shouted in surprise until he realised it was Sarah Harris.

"I didn't think you heard me," she gushed. "I was about to go around to your back door when I heard you open up."

John let out a long breath that was partly relief that it was nothing more worrying than his neighbour, then that relief gave way to irritation. What the hell was she doing banging on his door at this time of night?

"Please don't tell me it's another bloody spider?" he said, flatly.

She nodded, her eyes wide and watery with tears.

"Just kill it," he grunted. "Use a newspaper or a shoe or something but just kill the bloody thing."

"I can't," she told him.

"Sarah, it's after eleven. I was going to bed."

"Please, John. This one is very big."

"That's what you said earlier."

"But I know where they're coming from now."

He looked at her quizzically.

"They're in the attic, I'm sure they are," she went on. "They come in to get out of the cold, don't they? My boiler is in the attic. It's warm up there. No wonder they're all up there."

"Can't you call Rentokil or someone like that? They must get rid of spiders. They get rid of everything else."

"They won't come until the morning, will they? I need help now."

She looked imploringly at him and he sighed once again then nodded.

"Right, right, I'm coming, but this is the last time, do you understand?"

Sarah smiled gratefully and they set off together.

"I wouldn't have bothered you if it hadn't been such a big one," Sarah told him.

"And unless you'd figured out where they're hiding?" John chided, not attempting to hide the sarcasm in his tone.

"I think it's the same one my husband tried to get rid of," Sarah told him as they drew nearer to the house.

"Your husband?" John muttered.

"He knew how frightened I was of spiders," Sarah informed him. "That's why he went up into the attic to try and get rid of them. That's what he was doing when he fell."

John glanced quizzically at her.

"He fell from the attic ladder, the one that leads up through the trapdoor," she said. "He broke his neck."

When they reached the house, John made his way upstairs, using a long plastic hook that was kept in the airing cupboard to unfasten the attic hatch. It dropped down with a loud thump and he gazed up into the gloom beyond.

Sarah approached as he pulled down the extendable ladder and she handed him a torch.

"The light up there doesn't work," she told him. "You'll need this."

"Thanks," John sighed, putting one foot on the ladder to test its resilience. Satisfied that it was going to support his weight he began to climb.

"Be careful," Sarah called up.

John sighed and continued climbing.

He'd already determined that he would shine the torch around a few times then go back down and tell her he couldn't find any spiders. What was the point of stumbling around up here for the rest of the night? He was beginning to wonder if she was imagining the presence of the arachnids anyway. All he wanted to do now was get out of here and go home to bed.

He clambered up off the last rung of the ladder and onto the wooden floor of the attic, moving the torch around slowly, allowing the beam to play across the contents of the attic. Piles of magazines. Cardboard boxes, some empty, some still full of God alone knew what. Plastic storage boxes that were also brim full of the detritus of a life. Stuffed with memories. There were even some large speakers there, covered by dust and cobwebs. They were now little more than supports for some old brass candlesticks.

John moved deeper into the attic, using his index finger to draw a line in the thick dust that had formed on an unwanted wing-back chair.

There were even paintings up in the attic, some covered by what looked like gauze, others left unwrapped to suffer the rigours of passing time.

Two of them were thickly matted with spider webs.

Spiders. Again. Bloody spiders.

John turned back towards the trapdoor and the ladder, tiring of his mission. He peered down from the attic and saw that Sarah had left him alone. She wasn't on the landing below.

If she can't even be bothered, why should you?

John hesitated a moment then prepared to climb back down the ladder.

In the kitchen, Sarah waited for the kettle to boil. The least she could do, she thought, was offer him a drink when he finally came down.

He'd already been up there for nearly an hour. Perhaps he'd found the spiders and finally succeeded in getting rid of them.

When another thirty minutes passed Sarah began to wonder what he was doing. She made her way out of the kitchen and then up the stairs towards where the attic hatch was still hanging open.

What she saw hanging from the hatch was almost

beyond description.

Wrapped completely in silk, glistening in the cold white glow of the landing light, was the body of John Coyle.

He had been wrapped neatly from head to foot in the sticky gossamer strands, his cocooned body hanging from the hatchway, supported by more thick strands of silk.

The only thing visible were his eyes and Sarah could see those bulging madly in the sockets. He tried to scream but his mouth had been sealed shut by the tightly woven cocoon.

As she watched, the cocoon was suddenly pulled up. Tugged into the air by several swift movements until it was dragged through the hatch, disappearing into the darkness beyond.

Sarah caught a brief glimpse (and she was grateful it was only brief) of something huge crouching within the attic, something that hauled John's body up and out of sight. Something that would feed on him at its leisure. Something that had the face of her husband but the swollen, corpulent body of a huge spider.

As she backed away from the sight she murmured:

"I told you it was a big one."

THE INSTALLATION

The paved area in front of the art gallery was full of people.

Marion Heller glanced around her as she made her way across the wide-open space and she guessed that there must be more than three or four hundred individuals gathered there.

They seemed to be from all age groups and many of them were carrying banners or placards.

Marion saw some as she drew nearer the gallery's main entrance:

ART NOT PORNOGRAPHY
DEFEND GOOD TASTE
NO MORE FILTH

She shook her head, amazed that the protests were still going on. Many of these people had been outside the museum for the past week, ever since the news first broke. She couldn't help but wonder how they managed to find the time to be in this particular part of London. Were they all retired, on holiday or out of work? Marion was the first to acknowledge that opinions were a good thing but uninformed opinions could be dangerous and she felt this was a prime example.

She headed up the wide stone steps in front of the Victorian building and slipped past a handful of protesters who were walking back and forth in front of the doors trying to persuade people from entering.

This particular tactic didn't seem to be working that well and Marion saw at least four people enter the art gallery ahead of her.

She passed through the revolving door and made her

way across the foyer area of the gallery, walking up more wide steps to the first floor.

Marion passed through a heavy wooden door marked STAFF ONLY and into a corridor with offices leading off it on both sides.

She walked briskly until she came to the end of the corridor then she slowed her pace.

There were sounds coming from her office she couldn't identify immediately. As she pushed the door open she saw that the large television was on.

There were two presenters on screen; the woman, the generic blonde airhead favoured by programmes like this, was just gazing blankly ahead while the male presenter, overflowing with fake enthusiasm, did most of the talking.

It all looked familiar to Marion. It was the studio she'd left less than an hour ago.

"Were you surprised that the paintings in your gallery have attracted so much publicity?" the male presenter asked.

"People don't always understand art when it's controversial," Marion replied.

She stood watching herself on the show, a slight smile on her lips.

"Some people find it offensive," the blonde presenter trilled, checking her notes.

"Some people find the Mona Lisa offensive," Marion told her.

The first presenter came to his colleague's aid, obviously fearing that she hadn't heard of the Mona Lisa.

"But, as curator of your gallery," he began. "Aren't you under an obligation to protect people from this sort of filth?"

"It is very rude," the blonde simpered.

Marion shook her head, trying hard to hide her contempt.

"So would you call Botticelli's *'Birth of Venus'* rude?" she enquired as politely as she could. "Or Courbet's *'L'Origine du monde'* rude?"

The blonde presenter looked as if she'd just been asked to relay the theory of relativity. She swallowed hard, her cheeks reddening.

"Well, I'm sure some people think so," she said, stumbling over every word.

Marion smiled.

"I feel I have the responsibility to present the most challenging art available to the public," she went on. "And Milo Clarke falls into that category."

"Isn't it just a publicity stunt to attract attention to your gallery though?" the male presenter wanted to know.

The screen suddenly went black. Silence descended momentarily in the spacious office.

Marion looked around to see two familiar figures on the large leather sofa on the far side of the room.

"Just a publicity stunt," said Stephen Lehman dropping the television remote onto the sofa. "We were thinking exactly the same thing."

Seated beside him was Pauline Stone. Both of the gallery directors were in their fifties although Lehman looked older because of his shock of short white hair.

"You watched it then?" Marion exclaimed. "I've just come from the studio."

"We're aware of that," Pauline Stone informed her. "We're just concerned that you had to go on there to defend what is being exhibited in this gallery. You went on there to defend your choices."

"I was trying to explain to those two idiots that art is supposed to be challenging," Marion said. "I wasn't defending myself. I don't have to defend myself. I haven't done anything wrong. I don't think deciding to exhibit the newest works by Milo Clarke puts me in a position where I *need* to defend myself." Marion continued. "I thought this was the kind of thing you wanted. You said you wanted publicity for the gallery."

"Publicity, not outrage," Pauline grunted. "No one is going to give donations to the gallery if they think the only thing its exhibits are generating is controversy."

"I agree," Lehman added. "This approach might have worked in your last position but it won't work here."

"This *approach*… What is that supposed to mean?" Marion interrupted. "I was brought here to drag this gallery, kicking and screaming, into the twenty-first century. That's what I set out to do. You've already had more press coverage since I arrived than you have in the last five years."

"And for the wrong reasons," Pauline sighed.

"You knew what Milo Clarke's work was like," Marion interjected. "You *wanted* to exhibit his new installations. You trusted me to bring his work here."

"We had no idea the new work was so… obscene," Lehman explained.

"Two canvasses painted with human faeces and two with menstrual blood," Alison sighed. "No wonder people are complaining."

"And the installations are even worse," Lehman went on. "They're paedophilia. Nothing more. It's disgusting. Models of young children dressed like prostitutes and wearing make up? All that's showing is how perverted the artist is."

"You're starting to sound like the protesters outside," Marion muttered. "You're supposed to have more enlightened views when it comes to art. That particular installation is called 'Too Much Too Young.' It's an indictment of how young kids are turned into sex objects. I thought you understood that."

"All I understand is that we have protesters outside the gallery and the media are holding us up as some kind of bastion of perversion," Lehman snapped.

"Then we need to maximise the coverage we're getting," Marion retorted. "This is a big topic on social media too."

"Social media," Lehman grunted, dismissively. "A bunch of saddos with no lives who send messages to each other because they don't have any real friends."

"It's a bit more than that, Stephen," Marion sighed.

"None of that matters," Pauline said. "What *does* matter is how the gallery is perceived."

"By the public or by fundraisers?" Marion wanted to know.

"Both," Pauline told her. "You can't expect people to give money to an organisation that seems hell-bent on creating controversy."

"Most great artists have faced controversy at some state of their careers," Marion insisted.

"Even the ones who didn't use their own faeces to paint with?" snapped Lehman.

There was a long silence, finally broken by Marion.

"So, what do you want me to do?" she asked. "Cancel the exhibition? Tell the artist not to come here? He's due to arrive tomorrow for some promotional work."

"We'd better hire extra security in case someone tries to lynch him," Lehman grunted.

"Someone will have to speak to him," Pauline suggested. "Make him aware of the furore he's caused."

"I wouldn't expect him to be repentant," Marion said. "He thrives on this kind of publicity."

"Well it's too late to cancel the exhibition," Lehman said. "I fear we'll just have to go with the flow, as it were. See what happens." He looked irritably at Marion and walked towards the door of her office. "You got us into this mess," he said. "I suggest you get us out of it."

He and Pauline walked out.

Marion sucked in a deep breath, waited a moment then reached for her phone.

***

She had no idea how long she'd been sitting gazing at the laptop. Two, three hours? Her head was beginning to ache and Marion periodically reached up and tried to massage her own neck. She went from one window to the next on the laptop, reading articles about Milo Clarke, answering more e-mails, trying to contact people she needed to speak to. This had been going on ever since she arrived at her own office earlier in the day but now, as the clock ticked around to nine-thirty and night had well and truly invaded the sky, she was still at it.

"You should have just stayed at work."

The voice came from the sofa where Jake Turner was sitting gazing blankly at the TV screen.

"You've been sorting that shit out since you got home," he added, wearily.

"This 'shit' is my bloody career," she snapped.

"You knew what you were letting yourself in for when you went after Clarke. The guy's a fucking nutcase. Why are you surprised at the reaction you've got?"

"I'm not surprised, Jake," Marion said, sighing. "I'm a little perturbed at the lack of support I've had from the gallery itself." She ran a hand through her hair. "You've met Milo Clarke, what did you make of him?"

"His ego's out of control," Jake told her. "The guy thinks he's God. He wanted to check every single set-up before he'd let me photograph him. And he wanted to check every single picture I took before he'd agree to publication."

"What was he like as a person?"

"I was there to photograph him, not make friends with him." Jake grinned as she walked across and joined him on the sofa. "He knows how to push people's buttons, that's all. He loves the controversy. He thrives on publicity."

"Do you think he's talented?"

"I think he's got a talent for self-publicity. I can understand why your bosses are wary of him."

"What do you think?"

"Paintings done with menstrual blood and shit? Plaster casts of women's vaginas with used tampons hanging out of them? Underage kids dressed up like whores? I think he knows exactly what he's doing. And what I think isn't important. What do *you* think? You're the one who wanted his latest installation. What is it, anyway?"

"It's twelve piles of ash," Marion announced.

"That's it?"

"Each pile in a hermetically sealed container. Just ash. He claims it represents the impermanence of life." She sighed. "We've got that installation on one floor and the other stuff on another."

"And it opens tomorrow?"

"You're going to be there, aren't you?"

"In my official capacity," Jake chuckled.

"Good," Marion breathed. "I think I'm going to need all the help I can get."

***

Milo Clarke was a well-built man in his mid-fifties. A shock of white hair that hung down as far as his shoulders when it wasn't tied in a ponytail sat atop his head.

This particular day he was wearing an immaculately tailored charcoal grey suit with a pair of pink flip-flops.

The little toenail of each foot was painted metallic silver.

He walked into the room followed by Marion Heller, Pauline Stone and Stephen Lehman who looked on as Clarke crossed the highly polished wooden floor, looking around at the bare walls. He could see everything in his mind's eye. He could picture the canvasses that would soon cover those whitewashed walls. He could visualise every single detail of what was to be displayed in the room.

"I'm sure this room will be suitable, Mr Clarke," said Marion. "We–".

Clarke raised a hand to silence her, angry that she had the temerity to interrupt his thoughts.

He stood motionless for a moment then spun around theatrically and walked back towards the little group.

"Shall we have the exhibits brought in?" Marion asked. "They're waiting…"

"Don't call them exhibits," Clarke sighed, shaking his head. "It denigrates their worth."

"What would you like me to call them?" she replied, doing her best to keep her temper.

"They don't have a name," Clarke snapped. "Names are labels. Labels signify possession. No one possesses these creations."

Marion nodded slightly. She was already tiring of Clarke's pretentiousness. He'd been at the gallery for more than two hours and he hadn't stopped issuing demands, complaining about everything from the coffee to the weather, occasionally just sitting for minutes at a time silently staring at his phone.

She'd had enough.

"I'll oversee the installation personally," Clarke said. "I don't trust anyone else to prepare it adequately."

"Very well, Mr Clarke," Stephen Lehman intoned. "You know best."

"Yes I do," Clarke agreed.

He turned his back on them again as they walked out of the room and into the corridor beyond.

"My God, what an insufferable man," said Pauline Stone.

"You won't be complaining when your profits go through the roof," Marion reminded her.

"If they do," Lehman noted. "There are more protesters outside today. I'm not sure any of the public will be able to get inside to see any of the exhibits."

"The media have got to see it first," Marion reminded him. "Once it's been viewed then Clarke will give his press conference."

"God knows what they'll make of it," Pauline Stone grunted.

"Well, they've got two hours to have a good look and get their questions ready and then the conference starts," Marion said, ducking into a room to the right of the corridor.

The room set aside for the press conference was a lecture theatre. A long table had already been set up in there, microphones arranged at strategic intervals along it. Many of the newspapers and TV stations that were going to be present had already set up ready for the conference. The floor of the room was covered with cables and leads, the entire place seemingly filled with lights, ready to be shone on Milo Clarke.

Marion took one last look around the room then followed her colleagues.

They ate a modest lunch in the office of Stephen Lehman then, two hours later, returned to the lecture theatre which was now packed with people from all branches of the media. Marion was sure there were more than had been initially invited.

She watched as Lehman and Pauline Stone took their places at the long table then she finally faced the assembled throng, her heart thudding a little faster against her ribs.

"Thank you everyone," she began, trying to hush the babble of conversation that filled the air. "As you know, Mr Clarke doesn't do press conferences so I and my colleagues will be answering any questions you may have."

"I'm not surprised he doesn't give press conferences," shouted a voice from near the back of the room and the exhortation was met by some approving cheers.

"I'm assuming everyone has had a chance to look at the installations by now?" Marion enquired.

"Is Clarke too frightened to face questions?" a journalist near the front asked.

"He's a busy man," Marion said. "He just doesn't like to analyse his work too closely. He says it detracts from its initial impact."

"He's sick," another called.

"His work does provoke extreme opinions," Marion countered, looking around the room for other questions and hoping that not all the enquiries and comments would focus on Clarke's extreme style.

Another journalist raised a hand and Marion pointed to him.

"Is it true that Clarke was recently arrested for having sex with an underage girl?" the man asked. "While he was in the Far East, I believe."

"I'm here to answer questions about his work, not his private life," said Marion.

"But his private life sometimes spills over into his work," the journalist continued. "I think the two are linked. It's relevant."

"Any artist reflects elements of their life in their work," Stephen Lehman offered.

"Is it true that this gallery accepted Clarke's new installations purely to create publicity?" a woman near the back asked.

"Not at all," Marion told her. "We wanted the installation here because of its challenging nature and because we knew that people would respond to it."

"Even if that response was anger or disgust?" the

woman persisted.

"Everyone views art in a different way," Marion told her. "The important thing, in Mr Clarke's opinion, is that art should provoke some kind of reaction, irrespective of what that reaction might be. He feels that indifference is the worst enemy an artist can have. That's why his work is so confrontational."

There was more irritated murmuring inside the room.

"Clarke should be in here answering these questions himself," someone shouted.

"There will be a Q&A with Mr Clarke on our gallery website," Pauline Stone said, trying to make herself heard above the growing din.

"Is it true that he physically threatened a number of journalists recently who criticised his work?" a short-haired woman from the BBC wanted to know. "Four of them disappeared shortly afterwards."

"I don't know anything about that," Marion protested. "Besides, it was never proved."

"He was responsible for their disappearances," the journalist continued. "One of those missing is a close friend of mine."

The words hung in the air for a moment then Marion raised her hands.

"If there are no more questions about Mr Clarke's work then I'm going to close this press conference," she said.

"The man is dangerous," the journalist called, more insistently now and other voices began to join his.

Marion moved her hands once again in a gesture designed to show that the conference had been terminated. She motioned to Lehman and Pauline Stone to get to their feet which they did, following her out of the room, the shouts and calls still ringing in their ears.

***

Milo Clarke sat back and smiled, his eyes still fixed on the laptop screen.

He was watching footage of the press conference, happy with the reaction that he and his work had once again provoked.

"I could have done with your help in there," Marion said, taking a sip of her coffee.

"They're fools," Clarke said. "Ignorant, uneducated fools."

"They have a right to their opinions," Marion told him.

"Ignorant fools," Clarke went on, waving a hand in the air.

"If you spoke to them, they might understand your work. You could explain–".

"Creativity isn't about explaining things," Clarke interrupted. "It's about presenting work and waiting for the reactions it engenders."

"You can't expect favourable reactions when you're so hostile…"

"Do you think I care what they think about my work?" he snapped, again cutting across her. "Do you think I care what anyone says about it? I don't create my installations for *their* approval. It do it because I have things to say. Things I have to share."

Marion thought of saying something else but realised that her words would be futile. Instead, she topped up Clarke's coffee cup. She turned when she heard the knock on the office door.

When she opened it she thought the man standing there looked vaguely familiar.

"I want to speak to Milo Clarke," he snapped. "My name is Mark Burton. I was at the press conference earlier. I'm a journalist."

"Mr Clarke is about to leave," said Marion, attempting to bar the newcomer's way when he attempted to push past her.

"I want to speak to him," Burton insisted.

As Burton blundered into the office, Milo Clarke got to his feet.

"I want to know what happened to my friend," Burton said, pointing an accusatory finger at the artist. "She was a journalist. She questioned you about your work. You were physically and verbally abusive to her."

"I don't know what you're talking about," Clarke said, wearily. "But if you don't leave I'll call the police."

"Do it please, Mr Clarke," Burton snapped. "I'd like the police involved. They might get to the bottom of what happened to my friend."

The older man drew in a breath then smiled.

"Go on then," he said. "Ask me your questions."

Marion looked perplexed but Clarke merely shook his head.

Burton reached into his pocket and pulled out his phone. He quickly scrolled through the photos and pushed the device towards Clarke.

"That's her," Burton said, indicating the photograph. "Her name is Claire Tyler."

"And I'm supposed to remember her?" Clarke sneered. "She's hardly exceptional, is she?"

"And these people too," Burton went on, revealing more photographs. "You threatened all four of them with violence because of things they'd said about your work. They've been missing for weeks."

"And you're trying to blame me? That's slander."

"Are you denying you threatened them?"

"They made their comments. I made mine."

"You threatened to kill them and then they disappeared."

"I think it's time you went, Mr Burton," Marion insisted, trying to usher him back towards the office door.

"Yes, or you might end up like your colleagues," Clarke said, smirking.

"You haven't heard the last of this," Burton snapped, allowing himself to be pushed over the threshold.

Marion shut the door behind him and leaned against it, her gaze now fixed on Clarke.

"Have you met the people he talked about?" she said.

"I might have, I don't remember."

Clarke turned and looked out of the office window. From this vantage point he could see Burton as he crossed the wide paved area at the front of the gallery.

"People insult me and my work," Clarke murmured. "They expect me to just accept their lies."

"And what do you do to the people who criticise you, Mr Clarke?" Marion asked.

There was no answer.

***

"Knowing what Clarke's like he probably engineered the whole thing for publicity," Jake Turner said.

"This is the girl that disappeared," Marion said, pointing at the screen of her laptop.

Turner got to his feet and ambled across to the desk where she sat, leaning over her shoulder to glance at the image.

"This is the girl that disappeared," Marion told him. "This is the one that Burton was getting so worked up about this afternoon."

"He's probably in on it too, it's probably just some huge scam cooked up by Clarke."

"I know he's a media whore but threatening people?" Marion shook her head. "Telling them he'd kill them?"

"You said he was passionate about his work," Turner said, smiling. "He's just trying to build up his profile."

"But what if he was responsible for the

disappearances?"

"If every artist who'd ever been criticised killed their critics then every writer, film maker, painter and sculptor in the world would be in prison."

Marion looked again at the picture of the missing journalist.

"I don't know," she murmured. "With Clarke, you just get the feeling that when he says he's going to do something, he actually will."

Turner shook his head and turned away.

Marion got to her feet, pulling her jacket from the back of the seat.

"Where are you going?" Turner asked, watching as Marion stepped into her trainers and snatched up her car keys.

"I've got to check something at the gallery," she told him.

"At this time of night?" he muttered, glancing at his watch.

Marion was already halfway out of the door.

She hurried out to her car, clambered behind the wheel and drove off, the sound echoing through the still late-night streets.

The drive to the gallery took her less than forty minutes on streets normally choked with traffic.

Marion parked her car and hurried across the open area in front of the imposing building, hurrying up the steps where a homeless man was sitting wrapped in a blanket.

He glanced hopefully at her as she passed but she merely swept past him, slowing her pace slightly only when she approached a thick black wooden door to the left of the main entrance. She took a key from her pocket and used it to unlock the door, quickly slipping inside and disabling the alarm by using the keypad close to the entrance.

Once inside, Marion used the narrow corridor she'd

emerged into to make her way up to the first floor.

She slapped on lights as she went, heading for the area of the gallery that housed Milo Clarke's installations.

Her footsteps echoed around her as she walked, amplified by the bare floors.

She reached the room she wanted and moved slowly inside, switching on lights as she did. The banks of fluorescents in the ceiling sputtered into life, casting a cold white glow over the contents of the room.

Marion walked slowly towards the newest of the installations, her eyes fixed on the hermetically sealed containers that formed the artwork. They were on a tall, black marble pedestal and, as Marion drew nearer, she frowned, convinced that the display looked different to the way it looked the last time she viewed it.

There had been four of the containers before but now there were five. She crossed to the closest and gently lifted it from its position, unscrewing the lid.

When it came loose she saw the contents.

Thick, grey ash.

"Trying to discover my secrets?"

The voice lanced through the air and startled her so badly she almost dropped the container.

Milo Clarke was standing near the doorway.

"You're not supposed to touch the exhibits," he said, quietly.

"It's larger than it was before," Marion said. "There were four containers. Now there are five."

"It grows, like life."

"What's in the cylinders?" she wanted to know.

"Life," Clarke grinned. "Or what was *once* life." He took a step towards her. "The four journalists who disappeared."

Marion looked down at the ash.

"Oh my God," she gasped. "You killed them?"

"And burned them," he added. "Transformed them

into something far more useful than they were in life."

"But there are five containers here. Is Mark Burton in the newest one?"

"He wouldn't mind his own business. He paid the price." He moved closer. "Just as you must."

The lights suddenly went out. The entire room was plunged into impenetrable blackness.

Marion gasped.

When the lights came back on Clarke was only three or four feet from her. He was holding a length of gleaming wire in his hand. As Marion watched he swung it gently by one of the two wooden grips at either end. She could see that it was cheese wire.

"I added that little touch earlier," he said, pointing to the ceiling. "Light or dark. You find what you need in one of them."

"You'll never get away with this," Marion told him, her voice catching.

"We'll see," Clarke murmured, stepping closer, the cheese wire now stretched taut before him. "After all, it's all in the name of Art, isn't it?"

The lights went out again.

SOMETHING TO BELIEVE IN

The air smelled of blossom.

A scent of spring that was carried on the gentle breeze.

As Bill Palmer stepped out of the cab of the lorry he took a deep breath and savoured the beautiful aroma. Days like this made you feel happy to be alive, Palmer thought, smiling.

He glanced at the slogan stencilled on the side of the truck:

MOVE AND STORE, WE DO MORE.

He'd come up with that himself eighteen years ago when he first launched the company. Business had been good ever since that first day. Things had changed since then, of course. The world was a different place and the business had changed accordingly. The only thing that had been on the side of the truck apart from the slogan had been the phone number years ago, but now the number sat alongside social media details. It wasn't something that interested Palmer himself but his twenty-four-year-old daughter took care of that side of things. His twenty-two-year-old son managed the financial side of matters. It truly was a family business and Palmer felt an extra swell of pride when he thought about that.

He looked up and down the street. A tree-lined avenue with large, older properties. It was an affluent area. Most of the gardens were well kept, either by their residents or by gardeners. Palmer looked now at some particularly large and impressive rose bushes that formed part of the barrier between the pavement and the garden of the house he was to visit.

The scent was intoxicating and he stood close to the

blooms, enjoying the aroma.

"Will we be able to shift everything on our own?"

The voice interrupted his little vigil and Palmer turned to see the source of the sound.

Jack Ross was standing there with his hands dug in his pockets, gazing at the house before them.

"If we can't I'll get a couple of other guys in," Palmer informed him. "The lady who lived here had been here for more than sixty years apparently."

"Oh fuck, the house will be stuffed to the limit with shit then," Ross murmured.

"There will be a lot of personal belongings in this dwelling if that's what you mean," Palmer said, smiling.

Ross merely sighed.

"It's really quiet around here," he added.

"The lady who died was in her nineties," Palmer told him. "She probably appreciated that. As you get older you learn to appreciate a bit of peace and quiet."

"Is that your excuse then, Bill?" Ross chuckled.

They made their way slowly up the path towards the front door, high hedges on both sides shielding them from prying eyes.

They'd reached the door when another voice made them both turn.

"Hello," said the young woman standing at the end of the path. "I saw you pull up. You're the guys to clear the house, right?"

"Are you a relative?" Palmer asked.

"Oh God, no," Caroline Bishop told him. "Just a neighbour."

"How well did you know her?" Palmer asked.

"Well, just as well as neighbours know each other I suppose," Caroline said. "She was a nice lady. A bit weird sometimes but... I used to do her shopping for her at the end when she couldn't get out of the house."

"What do you mean, weird?" Ross wanted to know.

"She kept notebooks," Caroline went on. "Anything that went on around here, up and down the street, she wrote it down. She spent most of her days sat at her window looking out." She raised her eyebrows. "Who called you to clear the house? She didn't have any family."

"Her solicitor," Palmer explained.

"You're going to have your hands full," Caroline told them, smiling. "Would you like a cup of tea? I was just making one."

"That's very kind," Palmer said. "Yes please."

Caroline turned and disappeared into the house next door, her footsteps dying away.

Palmer slid the key into the lock and pushed.

The door would barely open because of the piles of mail and newspapers inside the hallway.

Palmer pushed harder and the door finally swung back to reveal a long hallway beyond. It too was crammed full. Boxes. Files. Pieces of furniture. It was difficult to walk down the hallway because of the tables on either side.

"Oh Jesus," Ross murmured.

Palmer walked on, heading towards the nearest of three white-painted doors.

He pushed it open to reveal the kitchen beyond.

There were more boxes in the room. Some piled on the floor, others on the large kitchen table and even the worktops. Palmer looked around with a resigned expression on his face wondering where best to start.

"Do you think there's anything valuable here?" Ross enquired, pulling at a box lid.

"In here?" Palmer mused, also running his gaze over the contents of the room. "Probably not. As for the rest of the house…"

"Old people sometimes have loads of valuable shit hidden, don't they?" Ross said. "Maybe her mattress is stuffed with twenty-pound notes."

"I wouldn't hold your breath," Palmer told him.

They both turned as they heard movement out in the hall and, a moment later, Caroline appeared holding two mugs of tea which she set down on the kitchen table. The two men thanked her and sipped at the newly arrived beverages.

"She lived alone?" Palmer said.

"One of the older neighbours said she used to live with a guy a few years back," Caroline told them. "Long before I moved in next door. But he moved out or died. She was alone for the last few years of her life."

"Didn't you ever say anything to her about her hoarding?" Palmer enquired.

"It was none of my business," Caroline exclaimed.

"Well, we'd better get on," Palmer said.

"I'll be back later with another cup of tea," Caroline told him. "I think you might need it."

And she was gone.

"You start here," Palmer said. "I'm going to have a look upstairs."

Ross nodded, watching as his employer headed out of the room. He could hear his footfalls on the stairs as he climbed.

Palmer made his way up the narrow staircase, stepping over boxes here and there until he finally reached the landing. He poked his head through the first couple of doors and was somewhat relieved to see that they weren't as overflowing with rubbish as the rooms downstairs. Perhaps, he reasoned, the old woman had found it more difficult to get up and down the stairs towards the end, so had simply stashed everything in the downstairs rooms.

His initial relief was somewhat dented when he looked into the last bedroom.

The boxes were piled so high they were almost touching the ceiling.

How the hell had she managed to put them up there?

What was in them? Palmer walked in, shaking his head and reaching for the lid of the nearest box.

It was full of notebooks. Yellowed, cracked and battered, bleached it seemed by the passage of time. He flipped open the first of them and saw that every single line was covered by Violet Monroe's neat handwriting. The notebook seemed to be in chronological order, written like a diary. There were entries about the weather, the food she'd eaten, what had happened in the street that day. Every seemingly pointless and trivial detail was entered within.

Palmer turned the pages and finally found one that bore just three words:

I MISS HIM.

A couple of pages further on there was another page with just a few words on it:

I WOULD GIVE ANYTHING TO HAVE HIM BACK.

There were more blank pages, and then:

I CANNOT GO ON WITHOUT HIM.

He felt suddenly overcome with sadness. This poor woman had obviously spent her last few years coping with the pain of loss like so many did. Palmer even managed to ignore the fusty smell of the pages as he continued to flick through the notebook.

THERE IS NO POINT WITHOUT HIM.

Palmer swallowed hard, wondering why the words were affecting him so deeply. He wasn't usually a man to show his emotions easily, let alone be touched by the feelings of others, but this was something new for him.

SHOW ME WHAT I MUST DO.

He frowned.

The next few pages were blank. And then:

I WILL DO WHATEVER IT TAKES.

He put the notebook back and pulled another from one of the boxes. It was laid out the same way. Page upon page of trivial details about her everyday life, even what she had watched on the television or listened to on the radio and then, every few pages, words scrawled in capitals in the centre of the page.

I WANT HIM BACK.

NO MATTER WHAT THE COST.

Palmer shook his head. Every thought she ever had spilled out onto paper, he mused. He even felt a little ashamed for intruding on these thoughts but, nonetheless, he sought another of the notebooks and flicked through the yellowed pages, sitting on the edge of the single bed as he read.

Time seemed to have lost meaning for him as he scoured the notebooks, reaching for a new one as soon as he finished one. Those he had already read now began to pile up on the bed beside him.

When he heard footsteps outside the room he barely looked up.

Jack Ross walked in and saw him seated there surrounded by the notebooks.

"You just been reading those all day?" Ross wanted to know.

"I just glanced at a couple of them," Palmer informed him.

"Glanced? It's nearly five o'clock. You've been in here for over six hours."

Palmer swallowed hard and glanced at his watch, at first not believing that the time could have flown past so quickly.

"I'm sorry," he said, shaking his head. "It only seemed like a few minutes. I... I'm sorry."

He exhaled deeply, his eyes suddenly feeling heavy. He felt as if he hadn't slept for days.

"Anything interesting in there?" Ross wanted to know.

"Not much to be honest," Palmer confessed. "It's just really sad. She must have been so lonely. No one should have to feel like that." He put down the notebook he was holding, leaving it open on the bed then the two of them made their way out of the house and back to the waiting truck.

As they clambered in, neither of them noticed that they were being watched.

From the window of her sitting room, Caroline Bishop watched them go.

When she was sure the lorry had driven off she turned and walked across the room to a small cabinet, sliding open the top drawer. From inside she took a bunch of keys, selecting one of the larger ones. It looked like a back door key. Bigger and more unwieldy than the thinner ones on the ring.

Caroline looked at it for a moment, her hands shaking.

***

The room inside the hospital was small.

It seemed to be crammed with equipment. So much so that there was barely enough room to fit the single bed in the centre of it.

As William Palmer entered the room he heard the persistent rhythmic beeping of the oscilloscope and it raised the hairs on the back of his neck as it always did.

He crossed to the single bed and sat down on the plastic chair beside it.

In the bed itself, Julie Palmer was breathing slowly with the help of a ventilator. She'd been in a coma for the last five months and Palmer had visited every single day, sitting for hours at a time holding her hand, talking to her and praying to a god he didn't believe in to bring her out of this appalling state.

Even now he laid the small bouquet of flowers he'd brought with him on the foot of the bed and held Julie's hand tightly, kissing it gently.

"Hello," he said, still holding her hand. "I brought you some flowers." As he spoke he got to his feet, removed the dead blooms from a vase and replaced them with the new carnations he'd brought. When he'd finished he brushed some hair from his wife's forehead and then sat down again.

He was there for another hour before he spoke again.

"I know you can hear me," he whispered. "I know you're going to come back to me."

He didn't even bother fighting back the tears. He never did. They ran down his cheeks in warm rivulets, some dripping onto the sheets.

Only when the door opened did he wipe them away.

The nurse who walked in smiled warmly at him and then continued with her duties. She moved from machine to machine, checking what she needed to check, noting it down on the sheet she carried.

"Has there been any change?" Palmer wanted to know.

"No, Mr Palmer," she said, flatly.

"Will there be?"

"You'd have to speak to one of the doctors about that," she told him.

Palmer nodded.

"Why don't you go and get yourself a coffee," the nurse advised. "Have a bit of a break? She knows you're here."

"Do you think so?" he asked, wiping tears away with his fingers.

"I've worked in this unit for six years," the nurse continued. "I've seen people come out of comas that have lasted for years. It's always possible she will."

"It's hard to keep believing sometimes," Palmer admitted.

"That's only natural, Mr Palmer," she said.

"If only there was something I could do to help her," Palmer offered, his gaze fixed on his wife.

"You can pray," the nurse told him and she was gone.

"I've tried that," he said, his words dying inside the quiet room.

"I don't think anyone is listening."

***

The heat was almost oppressive.

Even inside the small bedroom the air was heavy and almost unbearably warm.

Palmer could hear sounds of movement below him as Jack Ross carried more and more of the detritus inside the house outside to the waiting lorry and then trailed back in again. Once or twice the younger man stopped for a cigarette, standing at the end of the short path while he smoked it. On one occasion he stood there chatting with Caroline Bishop who had emerged from her house to join him.

However, none of that activity had caused Palmer to stir from his own vigil inside the bedroom. He had read through seven or eight of the notebooks left by Violet Monroe and he was now thumbing through another.

Each one he finished he carefully replaced in the box he'd taken it from, trying to retain some kind of chronology with the scribbled tomes, to ensure that each one was read in the correct order.

I WILL GET HIM BACK.

I WILL DO WHAT I HAVE TO DO.

NOTHING WILL STOP ME.

The sentences stood out among the aimless ramblings. As if they'd been written in another hand. A more forceful and driven script that almost burned from the pages.

Only when he heard a knock on the door of the bedroom did Palmer put the notebook down.

"Are we having lunch?" Jack Ross asked, glancing

around the room. "It's one o'clock."

"Yeah, come on, I'll buy you lunch," Palmer said, getting to his feet.

They walked out of the house together and climbed into the truck. Palmer drove about half a mile until they came to a cafe called The Cherry Tree. It was what might have been called a "greasy spoon" a few years ago.

When they walked in there were people sitting at most of the plastic-topped tables but Palmer found an empty one near the door and motioned for Ross to join him.

They sat and were served quickly by the single waitress who was taking care of all the customers.

When the food arrived, Ross eagerly devoured his sausage, egg and chips.

"When you said you were paying for lunch I thought you meant something posher than this," he said, smiling.

"It's posher than you're used to," Palmer reminded him.

"I need some food to keep up my strength," Ross went on. "There's so much rubbish in that house."

"I know, it's sad. A whole life just put in boxes and driven away," Palmer mused.

"What's so interesting about those notebooks?" Ross enquired, taking a swig of his tea. "You're spending more and more time reading them."

"Most of it is just trivial stuff. The things she saw out of her window, but she keeps talking about a man. Some guy who lived with her. He must have died because she talks about not being able to go on without him. Then there's stuff about how much she wants him back. There's even talk about meeting someone who could help her."

"Who could have helped her if the guy was dead?"

"A psychic maybe. Lots of people turn to clairvoyants when they lose someone close."

"It's bullshit though, isn't it? People can't talk to the

dead."

Palmer raised his eyebrows.

"Grief does funny things to people," he murmured.

***

When the doctor entered the room, Palmer stood up. It was almost an instinctual reaction. An acknowledgement of the newcomer's expertise and importance.

David Turner motioned for him to sit again and patted him warmly on the shoulder.

"She looks as if she's about to wake up," Palmer mused.

"If only that were true, Mr Palmer," the doctor told him.

"Is there really no chance?"

"I wish I could offer you some hope, Mr Palmer but... there's no reason to believe your wife will ever recover."

Palmer swallowed, the words hitting him hard.

"How long do I leave her... like... like this?" he said, motioning towards his wife. "When do you have to switch her off?"

"That's your decision to a degree, Mr Palmer," the doctor informed him.

"But she's not suffering, is she?"

"And she's not improving either, Mr Palmer. You're the one who's suffering, every time you come here. Every time you see her."

"If there's just one chance," Palmer said. "One chance in ten million that she'd wake up, I'd wait."

He squeezed his wife's hand.

"I just wish I could change places with her," he said, a single tear trickling down his cheek.

He sat there for another hour before making his way home. By the time he got there both his children were in bed. Palmer made himself a drink and slumped on the sofa in his sitting room.

There were two boxes on there that he'd taken from Violet Monroe's house earlier in the day.

He began reading through them.

It was another two hours before he finished. He looked at his watch and saw that the time had crawled around to 3.11 am. Palmer realised it was time for him to go to bed but, despite the fact his eyelids felt as if they'd been weighted, he reached for another of the notebooks and began looking through it.

Three hours later he was still sitting there. Outside, the dawn was beginning to claw its way across the sky.

Palmer hurried upstairs, showered and then changed before making his way out to the waiting lorry.

He made his way through the deserted streets with ease, finally arriving at Violet Monroe's house. Using the key he'd been given by her solicitor he let himself in and headed straight upstairs to her bedroom, to the other notebooks.

That was where Jack Ross found him three hours later.

"I thought you were picking me up this morning?" Ross said. "I had to get a taxi here."

"Sorry," Palmer said, without looking up. "Something came up."

"Something in those bloody notebooks?" Ross grunted, turning away and making his way down the stairs.

Palmer continued reading.

It was another half hour before he finally got to his feet. Carrying one of the notebooks he made his way out of the house.

"Where are you going?" Ross called, seeing him leave. "Shall I carry on here?"

Palmer didn't answer.

Ross watched as he headed on down the street, finally turning into the driveway of a larger house about two hundred yards further down the leafy thoroughfare.

He walked up to the front door and rang the doorbell, waiting for an answer. When it didn't come he rang again. Still silence. Palmer moved to the side of the house where there was a metal gate and a path leading around the rear of the place.

He was about to open it when the front door opened.

"Can I help you?" the woman standing there called.

Palmer walked back to face her.

"I'm sorry to bother you," he said. "I wondered if I could have a word with you. About one of your neighbours? Mrs Monroe."

The woman looked warily at him.

"She died recently," the woman said.

"I know," Palmer replied. "I'm clearing her house at the moment."

"How did you know I was her friend?"

"These," said Palmer, holding up one of the notebooks that he'd pulled from his back pocket. "Your name is mentioned quite a few times in some of these notebooks. "I wondered if you could fill some gaps for me."

The woman's brow furrowed a little more.

"She lived with a man, didn't she?" Palmer went on. "She mentions him in the notebooks. She talks about his death. How badly it affected her and what she was going to do to bring him back."

"She got confused towards the end," the woman said.

"She says you were going to help her."

The woman suddenly stepped back from the door and tried to push it closed but Palmer managed to get a foot between the wooden partition and the frame.

"Please," he said. "I need to know what you were going to do. I have to help my wife and I want to know what I can learn from these notebooks and what you and Mrs Monroe did."

"She was old," the woman snapped. "She was

confused. You shouldn't take any notice of what you read in those books."

Again she tried to shut the door but Palmer left his foot there to prevent it.

"My wife is dying," he snapped. "I need to know. I need to help her."

"If you want to help your wife, stay away from those bloody notebooks," the woman shouted and, this time, she managed to slam the front door.

Palmer stood there silently for a moment then he turned and walked away, glancing back towards the house when he reached the end of the path.

He could see the woman watching him from one of her windows. Palmer stood there for a moment longer then   walked   off.

***

I'M AFRAID TO MEET HIM BUT I KNOW I MUST. HE'S THE ONLY ONE WHO CAN HELP ME.

Palmer looked at the words written in the notebook and then wrote the same words on a piece of paper.

He blinked hard, barely able to keep his eyes open. He had been sitting on the sofa reading the notebooks for the last three hours and it was well after midnight, he knew that without even checking his watch.

He was still sitting there when the sitting room door opened.

His daughter entered the room slowly, almost cautiously.

"Dad, you're still up," she said softly. "What's wrong?"

"Just reading," he told her, smiling. "Are you all right?"

"I came down to get a drink of water," she explained. "I saw the light under the door."

Rhiann Palmer sat down opposite her father and glanced at the pile of notebooks beside him.

"You're obsessed with those," she said, pointing to them. "Every hour of the day I look you're reading them. What the hell is so important about them?"

"I think there might be something in here to help Mum," he told her.

"Even the doctors can't help Mum," Rhiann said. "How are some old notebooks going to help?"

"The woman who wrote these, she lost someone close to her."

"Mum isn't dead," Rhiann said, cutting across him.

"I know but just hear me out." He pulled the laptop closer to him and beckoned Rhiann to join him. There were several photos on the screen of a tall, dark-haired man in his early fifties.

"His name is Neil Sanderson," Palmer explained. "He's a medium."

"Dad…" Rhiann sighed.

"Listen, I know it sounds ridiculous but I think he can help us. I think he can help your mum."

Rhiann got to her feet.

"I don't want to hear this, Dad," she said. "Mum needs medical help. Not some bullshit artist."

"I'm going to speak to him," Palmer insisted. "He helped Violet Monroe, he can help us too."

"How did he help her?" Rhiann hissed. "If he helped her why isn't her husband alive now?"

Palmer didn't speak. Not even when Rhiann stormed out and slammed the door behind her.

***

The sun was blazing in the sky but the breeze that was blowing was chilly and Palmer shuddered involuntarily as he waited for the door of the house to be opened.

He was about to knock again when Helen James appeared at the door. She looked warily at him and was about to close the door again when Palmer raised a hand to stop her.

"Why are you here again?" Helen asked. "I told you when you came yesterday that I didn't want to talk to you."

"I know, I know," Palmer told her. "Just one quick question and I'll leave you in peace."

Helen hesitated a moment then nodded gently.

Palmer reached into his pocket and pulled out a picture he'd printed.

"Do you know this man?" he asked, allowing Helen to inspect the image.

Helen nodded.

"His name's Neil Sanderson."

"His name is mentioned in Violet's notebooks, just like yours."

"I recommended him to her after her husband died. She needed help. She couldn't cope. I thought he might be able to ease the pain."

"So did she go to see him?"

"Yes she did but he gave her false hope."

"What did he tell her?"

Helen began to push the door shut again.

"Please," Palmer pleaded. "I have to know what he said to her."

Helen slammed the door.

Palmer stood there helplessly for a moment then wheeled away. He headed back up the road towards Violet Monroe's house. He was thirty or forty yards away from the pathway when he saw Jack Ross signalling furiously to him.

Palmer broke into a run, covering the ground quickly.

"Where the hell were you?" Ross asked.

"What's wrong?" Palmer wanted to know.

"I found something. Come on."

The younger man led the way through the house into

the kitchen where he gestured towards the rear wall.

Palmer looked surprised as he gazed at what Ross was showing him.

"I found it when I moved some boxes away," the younger man said.

There was a door set into the rear wall.

It was wooden and had, at one time, been painted white but most of the paint was peeling off like leprous flesh. Beneath it, the wood looked rotten, the parts of it that weren't covered in mould.

"Where do you think it leads?" Ross murmured. "I bet wherever it is, it's full of rubbish like the rest of the house."

"Let's find out," Palmer said, trying the handle.

He turned it, surprised when it twisted in his grip. The rusted metal creaked ominously and, for a moment, Palmer wondered if it was going to come off in his hand. He turned it again but the door didn't budge. Palmer pressed his shoulder against it but it still wouldn't budge. Ross helped, throwing his own weight against the thick wooden partition.

It cracked open about an inch, the frame of the door splintering in a couple of places.

"It must have expanded because of the damp," Palmer grunted, throwing his shoulder once again into the thick wooden door.

It gave a few more inches and, as it did, the smell poured out like water from a broken bottle.

"Jesus," Ross gasped, enveloped by the sudden invisible clouds of rank air.

Damp, mildew, decay and neglect. It seemed almost palpable it was so strong and powerful.

The two men kept on battering at the door until it finally swung back on its rusted hinges, slamming into the wall behind.

They both peered into the gloom beyond, towards the

top of a flight of stone steps that led down into even more impenetrable blackness. The walls on either side, no more than three feet apart, were bare brick, glistening and dripping in places with damp. There was an earthy smell mixed with the scent of decay, as if the floor of the subterranean room were pure earth and nothing more.

Palmer took a step across the threshold.

"There's a torch in the truck," he said to Ross and the younger man hurried off to retrieve it.

Palmer moved slowly and cautiously down the first of the stone steps, careful not to slip on them. He put out a hand to steady himself, wincing when he felt how cold and wet the walls on either side were. Another two or three steps down and he could barely see a hand in front of him. He waited, hearing Ross approaching again from above him. The younger man switched on the torch and shone it into the stairwell, advancing to join his companion.

Palmer took the torch from him and aimed it ahead, allowing the broad beam to cut through the blackness and guide them. He shone it downwards as they reached the bottom of the steps, the beam picking out a wide stone and earth floor for the cellar. He stopped and shone it around at the walls.

The underground room was large, possibly running under the whole house.

Corners of the cellar were still in darkness despite the torch beam. Palmer played the light over the nearest wall.

"What the fuck is this?" Ross murmured.

Every single inch of the brick walls was covered with words. All sizes. Some tiny. Some massive. Millions and millions of words, some of them not even separated. Palmer moved closer, not recognising the scribbled symbols. They weren't English, that much he did know. Latin? Some other language?

Ross lifted his phone and aimed it at the nearest wall, the dark space momentarily lit by the bright flash.

"It's Aramaic," he said, flatly. "According to Google Translate."

"Can you decipher any of the words?" Palmer enquired, still looking around.

Ross focussed on some of the words nearby and then consulted his phone once more.

"It says 'their lives are mine to offer,'" he explained. "Whatever the fuck that means."

"What about the rest of it?" Palmer murmured.

Again Ross aimed the phone at the millions of letters.

"It's the same sentence written over and over again," he said, softly.

Palmer backed across the cellar, turning sharply when he collided with something.

There was a large wooden table in the centre of the room, the surface scored by many deep incisions and gashes. A dark brown fluid covered much of the surface and some of it flaked off as he rubbed it with his fingertips.

"'*Through their deaths will come life when the words are spoken*'" Ross intoned. "That's what it says here." He pointed to another part of the wall.

Palmer felt the hairs rise on the back of his neck. He suddenly wanted to be out of this underground room, away from what he saw before him.

Ross looked around and tried to concentrate on another part of the wall, raising his phone once again to capture the mysterious words.

"'*Faith will restore them*,'" he murmured.

Palmer looked around at the other walls now. All similarly covered with letters and symbols.

"Do you think that old woman did all this?" Ross asked.

Palmer had no answer for him. He was already heading

back towards the stairs that would carry him up out of the subterranean room.

***

There had been talk for a long time that The Adelphi Theatre was going to close down.

It was used as a cinema for five days a week but, for the other two, it hosted live stage shows.

The posters outside the theatre now were promoting just such an event.

William Palmer stood looking up at the facade of the Adelphi for a moment then walked across the street towards the building. There didn't seem to be much activity inside the foyer and Palmer feared he had missed the show. He could see staff members standing around chatting but not much else. Moving to the street at one side of the theatre he saw four or five figures gathered around one of the side entrances.

Palmer made his way towards the small group, surprised when one of the women there turned to face him, smiling warmly.

"Hello," she said, happily. "Have you seen him before?"

Palmer looked puzzled then the woman gestured to the poster on the wall beside them. It showed Neil Sanderson standing there in a dinner jacket smiling happily.

"I think he's wonderful," the woman went on. "I've had private consultations with him too. Very reasonable. When my Tiddles died I needed someone to speak to... to..."

"Tiddles?" Palmer asked, puzzled.

"My cat," the lady went on. "When she died I couldn't bear it but he spoke to her. He told me she was happy where she is now."

"Neil Sanderson spoke to your dead cat?" Palmer said, trying to hide his incredulity.

"He spoke to my husband as well after he died," the lady continued.

"What did he say?" Palmer enquired.

"Mr Sanderson said that my husband was happy and that he was watching over me. It made me feel much better."

"It was the same when my mother died," a younger woman told him. "He was marvellous. He told me things about her that he couldn't possibly have known. People say he's a fake but they don't understand him."

The other people standing nearby nodded.

A man in his fifties stepped forward.

"He told me so much about my wife," he said. "He's a wonderful man. So gifted. Who do you want him to contact for you?"

"I just want to talk to him," Palmer explained.

"He'll certainly help you," one of the women added.

Even as they spoke, Palmer saw that the stage door was opening and, moments later, Neil Sanderson emerged. He was an unremarkable-looking man in his late forties who was distinguishable only by his long ponytail. He looked a little shy and, when he saw the people gathered around the stage door, he visibly paled.

"Mr Sanderson," Palmer said, taking a couple of steps towards him. "I need to speak to you."

"I can't speak now, old chap," Sanderson said. "I've got to get home."

"It won't take a minute," Palmer assured him. "I want to know if you remember this woman."

He held up his phone and showed Sanderson the photograph of Violent Monroe that was on display there.

The other man shook his head, pausing to pose with one of the women for a selfie. He signed some autographs too, happily scribbling his name on whatever was pushed towards him.

"What about these words?" Palmer went on, scrolling to a photo of the words he'd found written on the walls of Violet Monroe's cellar. "You gave her these words. What do they mean?"

Again Sanderson looked at the phone then towards a car that had just pulled up at the kerbside.

"You don't need those words yet," he said, looking Palmer directly in the eye. "Your wife is still alive."

Palmer swallowed hard, momentarily freezing where he stood. He watched as Sanderson hurried towards the waiting car, climbed into the passenger seat and was driven away.

Palmer spun around and raced back to his own car, the sheer stupidity of what he was attempting to do never even entering his head. He pressed down hard on the accelerator and guided the car out onto the road, driving much too fast but desperate to catch up with the car that had picked up Sanderson.

It was a dark blue Astra and, Palmer reasoned, with so little traffic on the streets at this later hour, he should at least have a chance of spotting it. He turned a corner, muttering to himself, driving across a zebra crossing despite the fact there was a pedestrian on it.

He looked frantically ahead but could see nothing.

There was a roundabout approaching and Palmer was wondering which turning to take when he spotted the Astra up ahead.

He coaxed more speed from his own car, hurtling across the roundabout in pursuit of the Astra.

When he was within a hundred yards of it, he slowed down, content to follow the tail-lights now.

The Astra drove for another ten or fifteen minutes then turned into a tree-lined avenue. Palmer watched it intently, seeing it pull up outside a large property that was almost hidden from the road by high privet hedges. He drove past and parked a hundred yards or so up the road, using his mirrors to see Sanderson climb out of the car.

The older man walked briskly from there to the driveway of the house, disappearing from view behind the hedges. Palmer swung himself out of his car and hurried back down the road towards the property, walking up the drive towards the front door.

He reached it and knocked hard using the large brass knocker.

A moment later and the door was opened. Neil Sanderson gazed out at him, looking a little puzzled.

"Mr Sanderson, I'm sorry to bother you," Palmer began. "But I really must speak to you."

"You were at the theatre earlier," Sanderson intoned.

"Yes, I was," Palmer confessed. "You have to speak to me. Please."

"About the words or about your wife?"

"How did you know about my wife?"

"What I have is a gift to some but a curse to others, Mr Palmer," Sanderson sighed. "I see things I want to see but sometimes I see things I don't care to see."

"Is that what you told Violet Monroe?" Palmer snapped. "What did you tell her?" He fumbled for his phone and pushed it towards Sanderson, showing him again the picture of Violet Monroe's cellar wall. "She wrote those words because of you. Because of something you told her. What was it? What made her do that?"

"She came to me for help and I gave it to her."

"Those words are Aramaic for Christ's sake. How could giving her words in an antique language be a help to her?"

"They're an incantation," Sanderson told him, his voice low. "They only work in conjunction with other factors. They only work if you believe."

"Believe what?" Palmer snapped.

"That life can be restored to those who are lost."

"You're crazy."

"Every religion in history has relied on faith, Mr Palmer."

"So if I speak those words, my wife will be cured? Just like Violet Monroe's husband?"

Sanderson didn't speak.

"Is that what happened?" Palmer continued. "You told her how to restore him to life. That's what the words are for."

"The words only work if you believe. They're dangerous. There's a price to pay."

"You expect me to believe that reciting those words will bring the dead back to life."

"You don't believe. The words are worthless to you."

"Violet Monroe believed, didn't she?"

"Yes, she did but she knew there was a price to pay." He began to close the door. "It's a question of love, Mr Palmer. How strong is yours?"

"It's impossible," Palmer rasped.

"It is for you because you don't believe," Sanderson told him.

"What price is there to pay?" Palmer demanded.

"Would you change places with your wife?" Sanderson asked. "Would you replace her? Would you let her have *your* life? That was the price Violet Monroe understood but she was prepared to pay it."

"I have to die for my wife to live?" Palmer murmured.

"If you believe, Mr Palmer," Sanderson said, closing the door. "If you believe."

He shut the door.

Palmer stood there for a long moment then he turned and wheeled away, stalking off into the night.

He barely slept that night and the following day seemed to drag interminably. He apologised to Jack Ross and left early, driving straight to the hospital.

He spent an hour with his wife and then made his way

to David Turner's office. The doctor seemed quieter than usual and their conversation was a little strained. Even when Turner told him that his wife had developed a blood clot deep inside her brain his voice never changed intonation.

"But why now?" Palmer said. "After all this time?"

"I have no idea, Mr Palmer," Turner told him, wearily.

"And there's nothing you can do?"

"It's inoperable."

Palmer sat back on his chair slightly, trying to take in the information.

"Are you saying there's no chance?" he murmured.

"I'm saying that the time might have come to consider terminating the care she's receiving."

"You mean switch her off?"

Turner raised his eyebrows.

"Who would do that?" Palmer wanted to know. "Who would physically turn the machines off?"

"A senior doctor usually," Turner sighed.

"Can I do it?" Palmer asked. "She is my wife, after all."

"That's highly irregular, Mr Palmer. I... I... really don't think..."

"Who has more right than me to do it?" Palmer snapped.

"I'd need to speak to someone," the doctor murmured.

"Well, you speak to who you need to speak to and I'll go and see my wife," Palmer said, getting to his feet.

He walked out of the office and made his way back to the room where his wife was lying immobile in her bed. The ever-present blip of the oscilloscope added the usual soundtrack. Palmer sat down, holding his wife's hand tightly.

He gazed at her face, struggling to control his emotions now.

"Come back to me," he said, tears beginning to course down his cheeks. "Please."

After a moment or two he reached into his pocket for his phone, scrolling through to the photos of Violet Monroe's cellar wall. He looked at the words scribbled there then began to slowly and evenly recite them.

Over and over again.

The same words spoken in the same quivering tone. Repeated endlessly.

***

Doctor David Turner walked purposefully through the hospital, his face set in hard lines.

As he reached the door to Julie Palmer's room he slowed his pace a little. He sucked in a deep breath as he opened the door.

"Mr Palmer..." he began but the words froze in his throat.

William Palmer was propped up in the hospital bed. Connected to tubes and machines. His face was blank. His eyes slightly open but unblinking.

Turner stopped, momentarily overcome by the shock of what he saw.

Palmer in the bed. No sign of his wife.

Only his phone lying discarded on the top of the blanket covering him.

Turner crossed to the occupant of the bed and felt for a pulse.

Nothing.

He pulled open the gown that Palmer wore, massaging the area around the heart. There was nothing there either. The steady beeping of the oscilloscope had become one, long, unbroken note.

Turner pressed harder and more urgently on Palmer's chest.

The single note of the oscilloscope seemed to be deafening inside the room now.

***

The sunset was beautiful.

Outside, beyond the confines of the hospital the world was lit by a sumptuous golden light. It was magnificent. It promised much.

She could feel the warmth even from inside the building and, as she stepped out into that glorious sunset, she extended both arms and stood there motionless for a moment, ignoring the looks that passers-by gave her.

What did she care now?

Julie Palmer strode towards the burnished sunset with a broad smile on her face.

DADDY'S HOME

The rain was coming down with such force, Frank Robson was genuinely beginning to wonder if it would break the windscreen.

It wasn't just *hitting* the car, it was slamming into the vehicle with such ferocity it seemed as if each droplet had been fired from a weapon.

Robson already had the wipers on double speed but could still barely see more than ten feet ahead of him as he drove. More than once he slowed down to a crawl in his efforts to negotiate the darkened and storm-blasted road.

There were numerous fallen branches scattered across the tarmac, lumps of wood that had fallen or been snapped from the trees that overhung the road. The road was narrow and flanked on both sides by trees that spread their branches out across the thoroughfare to form a canopy in places. Piles of wet leaves had already formed at the roadside, now scattered again by the strong wind. The shallow ditches that also ran along the side of the road were already filled with water and overflowing and Robson wondered how long it would be before they spilled their loads over the black tarmac. If that happened then the country road would become impassable. He wanted to make sure he was off it before that eventuality.

Beside him in the passenger seat his wife, Hailey, was also glancing worriedly out at the elements but also at her phone.

"Who are you trying to call?" Robson wanted to know.

"I'm not," Hailey told him. "I'm trying to send the

babysitter a message to tell her we'll be late but I can't get a signal."

"The satnav's fucked too," Robson told her, pointing at the screen above the dashboard.

"Where are we? Why the hell did you come this way?"

"Do you want me to answer those questions in order?" Robson grunted. "First, we're about two miles from Pear Tree Farm and second, I thought it would be quicker. Any other questions?"

"Pear Tree Farm? Oh God."

"Hailey, what happened there happened nearly nine months ago," he sighed.

"It still happened," she retorted. "A whole family butchered."

"I'm driving *past* it, not asking you to go in and clean the place," Robson snorted.

Hailey glanced at him and shook her head.

"They were disembowelled you know," she informed him. "Things were carved into their skin. Satanic things."

"That's crap. The papers just printed that to make it seem more interesting. I don't know why you even read stuff like that."

"Because it's interesting. If there's some maniac wandering around I like to know about it. I don't bury my head in the sand like you do."

"I just don't want to know about things like that."

"Why? Scared?"

He was about to answer her when there was a loud thud from the front of the car.

"Jesus," Robson hissed, gripping the wheel more tightly as he hit the brakes. The car skidded to a halt.

"What did you hit?" Hailey gasped, peering out into the rain-lashed darkness.

"I didn't see anything," Robson told her.

"Have a look."

"Get out in this weather? Do me a favour. It was

probably just a rabbit or something."

"That was a big bang, Frank, it must have been bigger than a rabbit."

"Maybe it was a deer. You know those little ones that live in the woods around here."

"That's horrible," Hailey said, looking genuinely distressed.

"Yeah, I ran over Bambi," Robson grunted. "Now, shall we move on instead of sitting here trying to figure out what I hit?"

He jammed the car into gear and drove on.

"What if it *was* a person?" Hailey demanded.

"Who the hell is going to be walking about out here in this weather?" Robson wanted to know. "It was a deer or a badger or something like that."

He slowed down again slightly as the rain seemed to intensify for a moment, visibility dissolving into nothing for a few seconds but then Robson leaned forward slightly, peering out into the darkness.

"What is it?" Hailey asked, seeing that he was squinting at something.

"I thought I saw something in the road," he told her.

"Another animal?"

"No. It was too big to be an animal. It looked more like a person."

"You just said no one would be out here walking about in this."

"I saw something, I know I did." He leaned closer to the windscreen and then suddenly jammed on the brakes again.

Hailey turned sharply in her seat.

"Now what?" she snapped.

"Look," Robson said, jabbing an index finger in the direction of the roadside.

They both strained their eyes to see in the gloom and the pouring rain but even in such appalling conditions it was easy to make out the shape of a car that had pulled off the road and was sitting about ten yards away, close to the high hedge that separated the road from the fields beyond.

"They might need help," Robson said.

"Just drive on," Hailey urged.

"Oh, come on, we can't just leave them here. They might have broken down. I'll go and check."

He was already out of the car and running towards the other vehicle, watched by Hailey.

She saw him approach the other car and move around it, looking in through the windows. A moment later he pulled open one of the rear doors and motioned to her. Hailey hesitated, not wanting to get out in the pouring rain but Robson's frantic gestures towards her finally goaded her into scrambling out and running across to him.

He said nothing but merely pointed towards the back seat. As Hailey looked in she saw the baby lying there.

It was about ten months old. Wrapped snugly in a blanket and gurgling quite happily.

"If the driver went for help he left the baby here," Robson offered.

"Who the hell leaves a little baby on its own like that?" Hailey muttered. She reached for the child and lifted it up, heading back towards their own car.

"What are you doing?" Robson wanted to know.

"We can't leave him here on his own," Hailey said, climbing back into the passenger seat.

Robson followed, wiping rain from his face. He glanced at the baby and then at Hailey who was holding the child tightly to her.

"What if the parents come back?" he asked. "If they find the baby gone they'll be frantic."

"They shouldn't have left him alone in the first place," Hailey countered. With her free hand she fumbled for her phone. "I'm going to call the police." She exhaled wearily as she saw that there was still no signal. "Just keep driving until we get a signal."

Robson hesitated for a moment then pulled away, guiding the vehicle slowly down the rain-blasted road.

They hadn't travelled more than five hundred yards when he slowed down again and, this time, Hailey could see why.

The man was standing in the middle of the road, both his arms upraised.

The headlights of the car picked him out in the gloom and he waved his arms frantically, taking a few steps towards the speeding vehicle.

Robson eased down on the brake and watched as the man moved towards them.

He was in his late thirties, his face pale and rain-drenched but there was a slight smile on his lips.

"Can you help me?" he said, advancing towards Robson's side of the car. "I was on my motorbike and I came off. I need to get home."

"Where do you live?" Robson enquired.

"Just down here," the man told him, gesturing off down the dark road. "If you could drop me at the end of the road that would be great."

"Where's your bike? You said you fell off," Robson said.

"It skidded under a hedge," the man explained.

Robson looked him up and down. He seemed uninjured. His clothes weren't damaged in any way. He certainly didn't look as if he'd just fallen off a speeding motorbike. Robson hesitated a moment then nodded, indicating the rear door.

The man scrambled in gratefully, wiping rain from his face.

"It's not far," he said, sitting back. "In fact, it's just down there." He leaned forward again, pointing towards a narrow dirt track that led off from the main road. A large wooden gate that stood open, separated the track from the road.

"Have you got a landline phone in your house?" Robson asked. "We need to make a call but can't get a signal."

"No problem," the man said, cheerfully. "Come in and use my phone." He leaned forward again, this time his gaze focussing on the baby which had drifted off to sleep in Hailey's arms. "How old is he?" the man wanted to know.

"Nearly a year," Hailey told him.

"He's beautiful," the man said, softly. "He must be content to sleep through this lot." He smiled.

The car bumped over some ruts in the dirt track, overgrown bushes scraping against the side of the vehicle as Robson guided it along the narrow route. The darkness was almost impenetrable now and even the car headlights seemed to have trouble cutting through the gloom. Robson glanced to his left and right. At the overgrown foliage and the low hanging trees that snatched at the car with skeletal branches. He could hear those bony twigs scratching on the roof of the car as he drove.

"There," the man in the back seat said suddenly, pointing towards the outline of a house up ahead.

It was in total darkness. Not a light on anywhere and such was the state of disrepair leading up to the building that Robson thought the abode looked as if it hadn't been inhabited for years. He brought the car slowly to a halt, looking out at the house.

"You can use my phone if you want to," the man said, climbing out of the back seat.

Robson nodded and prepared to follow him but Hailey grabbed his arm as if to restrain him.

"Let's just go," she said, nervously. "I don't like the

look of this place."

"It's a bit run down, I'll give you that," Robson chuckled. "But let me go in and call the police and then we can get moving."

Hailey retained her grip on his arm for a moment longer then nodded and allowed him to slip out of the car. She watched as he hurried up the short, overgrown path to the front door where the man was standing waiting. They both disappeared inside and Hailey returned her attention to the sleeping baby. She was amazed at how deeply and soundly the child had been sleeping since they first found it. Hailey touched its cheek with one finger and was almost relieved when it stirred slightly. She was still considering what kind of parents abandon a baby in the back of a car when she saw movement ahead of her.

Someone was emerging from the house again.

She could see that it was the man and as he drew nearer, the baby woke and began to cry softly. Hailey rocked it, glancing up at the man who was smiling down at her.

"Where's my husband?" she wanted to know.

"Still inside, still on the phone," the man said, his eyes never leaving the baby. It was still crying softly.

"He wants his daddy," the man said.

Hailey felt the hairs on the back of her neck rise.

"He knows he's home," the man went on, his soft voice making Hailey's flesh crawl.

"What are you talking about?" she gaped.

"This is my house now," the man breathed. "It has been since those other people called me nine months ago."

"Who are you?" Hailey wanted to know, her heart beating harder.

"The people who lived here before knew me. That's why they summoned me. But they were fools. They thought they could control me. That's why I had to teach them a lesson. Perhaps you heard what happened to them."

Hailey was shaking gently now.

"They were murdered," she said, quietly. "Mutilated."

The man laughed. "They deserved it," he purred, his lips turning up at the corners into a grin. And now, as he leaned closer, Hailey saw his eyes clearly for the first time.

They were like swollen grapes jammed into the sockets but they were yellow with a black slit running vertically across the iris like those of a cat.

"Give me my son," he rasped, holding his hands out for the baby. "Can't you see the family resemblance?" the man grunted. "Pull back the blanket. Look at his legs." He smiled, watching as Hailey did as he instructed.

The child's legs were covered in thick black hair from thighs to feet and where the feet should have been there were two heavy lumps of bone that resembled hooves.

Hailey screamed.

The baby turned its head and looked at her, its own yellow eyes now gleaming in the darkness.

The car doors suddenly swung open as if pulled by invisible hands.

"They said the people who lived here were killed by Satanists," the man said, grinning. "Not Satanists. Satan." His laugh seemed to fill the air, ringing in Hailey's ears.

Then he was upon her.

WHO'S THERE?

That bloody woman.

That was the first thought in his head as he walked out of his daughter's bedroom.

Normally he felt elated and upbeat when he'd finished reading Charlie a story before tucking her up in bed for the night, but tonight, the only thing that kept going around in Michael Hennessey's mind was that one sentence.

That bloody woman.

He meant his mother-in-law. June. Why couldn't she keep her thoughts and ideas to herself? Especially when it came to death and religion. Michael certainly didn't want to have to explain concepts of death, heaven, God and anything else spiritual to his daughter just because June had been banging on about it.

Charlie was four for Christ's sake. And she'd had enough to cope with over the last year or so as they all had.

The death of a sibling was unbearable for the child left. The death of a child was intolerable for a parent, and Michael and his wife knew that only too well. Their six-month-old son, Alfie, had died of meningitis eighteen months ago. He hadn't passed on or been taken or any other useless euphemism people liked to use. He'd died. God hadn't taken him into his arms, he wasn't sleeping in heaven or in the arms of the Lord. Alfie had died.

Michael wandered into the sitting room where his wife was laying on the sofa.

"Is Charlie okay?" Paula asked.

"She's fine, considering."

"Considering what?"

"Considering the shit she's been hearing from your mum. Telling her about God and heaven and how Alfie was taken up there by God to be with the angels."

"That's my mum's way of coping with Alfie's death."

"Maybe it is but it's not *our* way. It's not the way we wanted for Charlie, is it?"

He sat down next to his wife, resting one hand on her thigh, stroking gently.

"It just leads to more questions we didn't want to answer," Michael told her. "Do you really want her to grow up thinking there's an invisible man who lives in the sky who has a list of ten things she shouldn't do because if she does *any* of those things she'll burn in hell for the rest of eternity? I'd like her to grow up with a more... reasoned outlook."

Paula smiled.

"We'll just raise her as an atheist then, shall we?" she murmured. "When it happened, when Alfie died, I thought that God must hate us."

Michael raised his eyebrows. "Hate him back," he hissed. "It works for me."

He got to his feet and crossed to the wall, switching on the small device plugged into a socket there. Michael adjusted the volume on the baby monitor and then sat down again, flicking TV channels until he found something worth watching.

There was suddenly a harsh crackle of static from the direction of the monitor.

The lights on it began glowing brightly and the unmistakeable sound of voices filtered into the room.

"Is that Charlie's monitor?" Michael said, looking around. "It sounds as if there's someone in the room with her."

"Somebody else nearby must have the same monitor," Paula explained. "They sometimes pick up signals."

She moved closer to the monitor, trying to decipher the words that they heard. Most were drowned by the savage static but others were clearly audible.

"*You're going to die.*"

The voice that roared the words was low and guttural.

Paula and Michael both looked intently at the monitor as if that simple act might enable them to see who had spoken the words.

"*You're all going to die,*" the voice bellowed again.

"Go and check Charlie's monitor," Paula said, her face pale.

Michael hurried off to do that simple task, hoping that the sounds weren't filling his daughter's room too.

Paula moved nearer to the monitor, crouching beside it but all she heard this time were the odd crackles of static and some movement from Charlie's room. Michael returned a moment later and shrugged, explaining that their daughter was fast asleep.

There were no more sounds that night and by the time Paula dropped Charlie at the nursery the following morning she'd almost forgotten about the incident. Walking beside her, Louise Porter and Beth Farmer had also just entrusted their offspring to the care of the nursery until four that afternoon. The three women walked back up the gentle slope leading from the nursery, back towards where their cars were parked. It was a chilly morning but the sun was forcing its way out from behind the clouds and it looked as though the day would be a bright one.

The three women chatted happily as they walked and finally Paula interjected.

"What kind of baby monitor have you guys got?" she wanted to know.

The other women looked quizzical and then Paula explained what had happened the previous night.

"Someone nearby must have the same make," Louise

offered.

"You'd better be careful," Beth chuckled. "If you can hear *them*, they might be able to hear *you*. You and Mike had better keep it down when things get passionate."

They all laughed.

"Seriously though," Beth went on. "Ask around and see who's got the same one as you."

"There are only two or three couples near us that have got a young child," Paula announced. "It shouldn't be too hard to track them down."

"What kind of noises were you hearing then?" Louise enquired. "You said they were weird."

"It was horrible," Paula said, shuddering slightly at the recollection. "Someone was shouting about people dying. They said 'you're all going to die.'"

"And it couldn't have been a radio or TV you overheard?" Beth enquired.

"No. It was definitely someone shouting," Paula told her. "Someone angry. Someone really loud. I'm just glad Charlie didn't hear it."

The women reached the top of the gentle crest, said their goodbyes and clambered into their cars. The drive back took Paula less than twenty minutes even including a brief stop for some milk at a small supermarket close to her home. As she parked she noticed a familiar figure pushing a pram along the road and she hurried out of her car to catch up with the other woman.

"Julie," Paula called but the other woman didn't turn around.

Only when Paula caught up with her did Julie Howard turn to face her.

She smiled wanly, most of her face covered by large-framed dark glasses.

"I thought you didn't hear me calling," Paula said.

"I wanted to get home before Jack woke up," Julie explained, motioning to the sleeping baby in the pram.

She was already turning the pram, ready to walk away.

"Are you okay?" Paula asked.

Julie merely nodded and re-adjusted her dark glasses slightly on her aquiline nose.

"I've got to go," she said, flatly.

As she put a hand to her face, Paula could see that the other woman was shaking and that there were tears trickling down her pale cheeks. As she took off her dark glasses to complete the job more thoroughly, Paula gasped.

Beneath the dark lenses, both of Julie's eyes were black and bruised, the puffy flesh around them swollen and dark.

"Oh God," Paula murmured. "How did you do that?"

"It was an accident," Julie muttered.

"Did your husband do it? You can't let him do that to you, Julie, you–"

"I said it was an accident," Julie snapped, turning away. "I've got to go."

"If you need to talk, let me know," Paula insisted.

Julie was already striding off down the street pushing the pram before her. Paula watched her go and then turned away, walking back towards her own house.

She spent the afternoon inspecting the baby monitor in Charlie's room and the one in the sitting room, even unscrewing the faceplates at one point and inspecting the inner workings despite the fact she hadn't got a clue what she was looking for. There were no wires burned out or damaged and Paula was satisfied with her inspection until that evening.

As she and Michael sat in the room relaxing static began to well loudly from the monitor, followed by low breathing.

"That's just Charlie breathing," Michael murmured, listening to the rhythmic contented sound.

There was more loud static.

"It was doing that this afternoon," Paula explained. "And I heard voices again. Like the one we heard last night."

"It must be picking up a signal from another monitor nearby."

"The only couples around here with a small child apart from us are Gemma and Phil, and Julie and her husband."

"What's his name?"

"I don't know. I'm not sure I want to know." When Michael looked quizzical, she described their meeting earlier in the day. Particularly Julie's black eyes. "He must have done it. How else would she have got two black eyes like that?"

"He always seems like a decent enough guy when I've spoken to him," Mike offered.

"Wife beaters usually come across as charming I'm sure," Paula grunted.

"You can't prove he did it. You'd better keep this to yourself. If you're wrong and word gets out..."

"What? You think he might hit me too?" she said, irritably. "Big brave man, isn't he?"

Mike was about to speak again when they heard a voice lance from the monitor.

"Shut your mouth," it snarled. "I won't tell you again. Shut your mouth or I'll kill you."

They both jerked their heads around in the direction of the sound, focussing on the harsh words.

"Please don't hurt us," a woman's voice implored and Paula raised her eyebrows.

"That's Julie's voice," she breathed. "I know it is."

"I'll kill you *and* your child," the male voice snarled.

"No, please," the woman wailed again and then there was a massive static blast and silence.

"That was Julie, I know it was," Paula insisted.

"Oh, come on, that's a bit of a coincidence, isn't it?

You see her this morning and she's got a black eye and now we hear her on that." He jabbed a finger in the direction of the monitor. "You can't know for sure, Paula."

"Do you think I'm making it up?" she said, challengingly.

"No but we can't know for sure what's going on. We've got know way of even knowing that was her voice we heard just now. It could be anyone around here."

"No one else has child monitors except the people I mentioned before."

"Then maybe it's a signal from another device, like a radio or a phone or something."

Paula shook her head.

"So we get new monitors," Mike offered. "I'll buy new ones tomorrow."

"So we don't have to hear that a woman is being terrorised?"

"We don't know that."

"He was threatening to kill her, Mike. Her and her child. Do you just want to ignore that? I'm not sure I do."

They locked stares for a moment then Mike turned away.

"I'm going to check on Charlie," he murmured, disappearing out of the room.

Paula nodded, her gaze drawn once more to the monitor.

***

The following morning was cold but bright and Paula glanced at the glistening spider webs on the hedges as she made her way down the street.

Her breath clouded in the air before her as she walked but she seemed not to notice the chill in the air. She glanced down into her handbag and saw the baby monitor nestled there.

As she turned onto the path that led up to Julie

Howard's front door she swallowed hard.

Wondering how to do this?

She walked up to the door and rang the bell.

If she's got the same monitor then chances are it was her voice you heard last night.

Paula shifted from one foot to the other as she waited for the door to be answered.

When it wasn't she crossed to the window and peered in. There was no sign of anyone so she headed off along the path that led around the side of the house. She passed through the gate that led into the back garden, making her way up to the back door which she also knocked.

No answer.

Paula hesitated a moment then made her way back around to the front door where she knocked once again.

Finally tiring of the lack of response she turned to walk away. She was halfway down the path when the front door opened.

"Can I help you?"

She heard the man's voice and turned to see a tall, brown-haired man standing at the threshold.

"I was looking for Julie," Paula said. "I'm a friend of hers. My name's Paula Hennessey."

"I'm her husband," he announced. "I'm David."

So you're the bastard who's been hitting her, are you?

Paula smiled her best fake smile.

"Julie's not here right now," he said. "But you're welcome to come in and wait. She won't be long."

Paula shook her head.

"I'll come back," she told him.

"Anything I can help with?"

Paula hesitated. "Well, I don't know," she said. "I... it's silly really. We've been having some trouble with our baby monitor. Picking up strange noises and voices on it. I know that similar kinds sometimes do that and I

104

wondered if you had one like ours."

"We have, as a matter of fact," he said, smiling. "What kind of noises have you heard?"

"Strange ones," Paula told him, vaguely. "Listen, I'll come back when Julie's here."

"She won't be long. She's taken our son to her parents for a couple of days. She thought he might settle there. He hasn't been sleeping very well and neither have we."

"Julie told me. Lack of sleep can make you bad tempered, can't it?"

It can make you hit your wife.

"You say you heard strange noises," he continued.

Paula nodded.

"We had that in our last house," he went on. "That was why we had to move out. It got too much. Didn't Julie tell you?"

"No."

"I'm not surprised. She was probably worried you'd think she was crazy."

"What happened then?"

He pushed the front door open wider.

"You might want to come in for a coffee while I tell you," he said, quietly. "It's a long story."

Paula hesitated then finally accepted his invitation. He led her through into the kitchen and they chatted amiably as he made them coffee. She asked him about his work and discovered he was a copywriter who occasionally worked from home (this was one of those days). Once the preliminary niceties had been concluded he began to describe their last house and what had gone on there.

Paula cradled her coffee mug in both hands as she listened to him and only when he'd finished did she finally sit back in her seat, exhaling deeply.

"Why didn't you get help?" she wanted to know.

"From who?" he asked. "Who'd have believed us? Whatever it was it... it drove us out of the house. The only way to get away from it was to move."

"And all that started when you used the Ouija board?"

"We were stupid, I know, but we were drunk. At the time it was just a bit of fun. If only we'd known."

Paula was about to speak when she heard the front door opening. A moment later, Julie Howard walked in. She was still wearing the large dark glasses she's had on the previous day but, as she entered the kitchen she took them off. Paula could see that some of the bruising around her eyes had begun to yellow and discolour at the extremities. She sat down at the table, squeezing David's hand as he set down a mug of coffee before her.

Paula glanced at the hand.

Is that all part of the act?

"You thought I did that, didn't you?" David said, gently touching Julie's face but looking at Paula. "You wouldn't be the first." He sat down next to Julie. "I told Paula what happened? Why we moved here? What happened in the last house."

"You should have said something," Paula told Julie.

"It's not the sort of thing you tell someone you've just met," Julie murmured.

"But why did it hurt you?" Paula enquired. "Whatever it is?"

David got to his feet and began unbuttoning his shirt. He finally pulled it open to reveal that his chest was a patchwork of bruises and bright red lacerations.

"Oh God," Paula murmured. She was sure that some of the marks were bites.

"I was trying to protect Julie and my son," he said, still displaying the damage to his torso. "It didn't like that." He smiled, a note of bitterness in his tone.

"You've got to get help," Paula told them.

"You need to be careful too," David informed her.

"What do you mean?" Paula asked.

"If you've heard this… whatever it is, through the

monitor, then, it might know you're listening," Julie told her. "It might come after you."

"And keep a close eye on your daughter," David said.

"It doesn't care who it hurts," Julie added.

***

Mike Hennessey had tried three times to call his wife but, each time, the call had gone straight to voicemail and, despite his pleas for her to ring him back, there had been no reply.

Now, as he drove home at the end of another day, he reached for his phone once again and dialled her number.

He was delighted when it connected this time. He said her name into the device but there was no answer. Only a loud burst of static.

Like that they'd heard through the monitor.

Mike sighed and pressed the phone to his ear again but the hissing and crackling that came from it this time was so loud he was forced to pull his hand away.

He glanced at the phone as if it were a venomous reptile.

His musings were interrupted by the loud blaring of a car hooter.

The driver gestured angrily at him as he drove past and Mike raised a hand by way of apology. There was a public phone up ahead and he pulled the car over beside it, wondering if the fault might be with his own phone.

He dialled the number he wanted and waited, trying to ignore the smell of urine that filled the air inside the box.

Again it connected and he said Paula's name urgently but there was no answer except more of the hissing and words that he thought he could make out. Words spoken with such vehemence that he began to shake.

"You're going to die. All of you."

Then he heard a scream that he knew was from Paula.

He slammed the phone back onto the cradle and ran back to his car, scrambling behind the wheel and pulling out into traffic. Again another car almost collided with him but this time Mike ignored the angry driver, intent only on getting home as fast as he could. He guided the car swiftly along the streets, mounting the pavement twice in his haste to avoid parked cars.

He finally brought the car to a halt outside his house, dragged himself from behind the wheel and ran towards the front door.

The house was silent as he entered.

He called Paula's name but got no reply so he moved into the sitting room then the kitchen. Both empty.

There were dirty plates and bowls in the sink and on the table, evidence that she'd eaten dinner and also fed Charlie. A small cuddly teddy bear was also propped on the table. It watched him with blank, glassy eyes.

As he made his way upstairs he found another stuffed toy on the stairs.

Again he called Paula's name and again he got no reply.

As he reached the landing he slowed his pace slightly, moving towards Charlie's room. He entered quietly, surprised to find his daughter sleeping soundly. Mike crossed to her, looking down at her resting form, watching as her chest rose and fell.

From somewhere else in the room he heard whispered words. Low, guttural sounds that raised the hairs on the back of his neck. He looked towards the monitor but the lights on it were off.

Then he saw that one of the doors of the wardrobe on the far side of the room was partially open. When he realised that there was a red spatter on the white wood he hurried towards it, his eyes widening in terror as he realised the red mark was blood.

It was partly congealed, indicating that it had been there for some time, and Mike pulled the door open.

Paula was inside, slumped to one side, several large and deep gashes on her face and neck.

Mike gasped and pulled her from the wardrobe, some of her blood smearing his clothes.

He spoke her name but she didn't open her eyes. He was so intent on waking her that he didn't notice Charlie sit bolt upright in her bed.

Her head turned slowly to look at him and then, unseen by Mike, she slipped out of bed, dragging something from beneath her pillow, her hand closing around it.

Had he turned he would have seen that it was a claw hammer, the prongs already stained crimson.

She advanced towards him, the hammer now raised high above her head.

***

Julie and David Howard heard the hissing sound coming from their baby monitor and Julie looked towards it then nodded gently. Several loud screams filled the room, erupting from the monitor. They thought they heard low growls too, and the thud as a hammer struck bone four or five times.

David got to his feet and crossed to the monitor, turning down the volume.

"We did warn them," he said, quietly.

"It's left us now, that's all that matters," Julie echoed.

David nodded again.

"It's not our problem any more," he breathed.

He switched off the monitor.

THE POPPET

"I don't care what she's done. I can't stand her."

Claire Bennett exhaled angrily and glanced up at the darkening sky.

Clouds were gathering in huge, lowering banks, sometimes blotting out the moon but threatening more of the rain that had fallen earlier.

"She's only lived in the village for four months and she's trying to take over," Claire went on, turning the steering wheel and guiding the Land Rover down a narrower country road.

On either side, high bushes grew up to six feet in height, shutting out views of the dark fields beyond.

"She's only trying to help, Claire," Polly Bishop remarked, a little concerned that Claire's anger seemed to be causing her to drive faster. "She worked in London at a big PR company, she knows how to handle these things. It's not like she's asked for any money to help us out. She—"

"I don't care if she worked in London," Claire blurted. "I *lived* in London for years before I moved here. And we don't *need* her help. She's turning our beliefs into a laughing stock. She doesn't understand. Bloody young girls. I mean, what is she? Thirty-five, thirty-six? What does she know?"

"You're not jealous because she's younger, are you?" Polly offered.

"Absolutely not," Claire said. "I'm happy to be my age. I'd rather be fifty-three. I don't want to be young again. I don't want to be like... her."

"She just thought that advertising the ceremony would

attract more people and that we might be able to make some money from it," said Polly, a little cautiously.

"We don't have the ceremony to make money from it, Polly. We're not pagans because of the monetary reward. It's a belief for us, isn't it? Not a bloody cash cow."

She turned the wheel again, the road narrowing even more before it finally broke up and turned into little more than a dirt track.

Ahead of them they could see the dull glow of several fires, the sickly yellowish-orange light broken up by the trees around them. As they moved further up the dirt track the trees grew more thickly on either side and also ahead of them, although there was an open space where a number of vehicles were already parked.

"I mean, look at that," Claire spluttered, motioning towards the cars. "This is supposed to be just for us. There'll be all sorts of people here tonight just gawking at us as if we're animals in a zoo. And it's all down to bloody Zoe Carson."

"I just think you should give her time to settle in," Polly offered. "I mean, she's new here. She doesn't know anyone yet but—"

"Exactly," Claire snapped. "She's new here. And yet she walks in as if she's lived here all her bloody life. Trying to take over. Trying to be in charge. I don't like her type. Why can't she just keep her bloody ideas to herself?"

"But she's a pagan like us, Claire. We all share the same ideals and values."

"She's no pagan," Claire snorted. "What does she know about our way of life? The closest she's ever come to paganism is watching *The Wicker Man* on TV."

Polly glanced out of the side window, watching as Claire brought the Land Rover to a halt about twenty yards from some of the other parked cars. Both women clambered out of the stationary vehicle, reaching onto the back seat to retrieve wellington boots which they slipped on, exchanging them for their usual footwear. That done they trudged off towards an open wooden gate that led them through into a field.

On a slight rise off to their right there was a thick outcrop of trees and, beyond these, several fires were blazing, their flames rising into the night sky. The two women walked across the field, occasionally sinking into the mud. In the worst places it almost dragged the boots from their feet.

"Is Frank coming tonight?" Polly asked.

"No. Frank thinks this is all a bit of a joke," Claire exclaimed. "But he doesn't complain when I get home because I'm usually horny after the festival and he knows I'm going to shag him." She chuckled.

"Oh Claire, you're naughty," Polly said, smiling and shaking her head.

"Well, paganism is about sex, isn't it? That's one of the reasons I was attracted to it. Just because Frank isn't a pagan doesn't mean he can't benefit too, does it?"

Both women laughed again, the sound drifting across the darkened field.

As they began to climb the gentle slope that led up towards the trees they became aware of more and more people gathered on the edges of the wood. There must be more than a hundred of them standing there gazing at the three leaping bonfires that had been set up.

When they drew nearer they were suddenly greeted by a familiar voice.

"Oh God, here we go," Claire sighed as Zoe Carson approached, arms outstretched.

"Hello," she trilled.

"Hello, Zoe," Claire replied, fixing on her best fake smile. She embraced Zoe as warmly as she could. "I'm pleased we put up those flyers about the festival. It looks as if more people than usual are here."

"Well, I think my social media campaign might have a little more to do with it," Zoe announced, hugging Polly. "I bet you never had as many here when you used to just rely on word of mouth around the village, did you?"

Claire didn't answer but merely trekked on, further up the slope towards the three bonfires.

Their light illuminated a large area between them.

A pattern had been made on the cold earth. Lines that twisted and turned into the shape of a labyrinth. At one end a man was standing and he waved enthusiastically in Claire's direction when he saw her.

"John was saying he thinks it's been a better turn out too," Zoe informed her, waving to the man. "People have been walking the labyrinth for the last thirty minutes. It seems to be going really well."

"It always did," Claire grunted, still trying to retain her forced smile.

She watched as several other people edged forward from the watching group, each of them approaching the man who was standing beside a small table. He took something from each newcomer and laid it on the table.

"Are they paying?" Claire said, a note of disgust in her voice. "People don't pay to walk the labyrinth."

"I thought we could use the money to buy some paint for the meeting place," Zoe offered.

Claire sighed again.

"You've thought of everything, haven't you?" she breathed.

"Well, it's best to be prepared, isn't it?" Zoe told her.

"You know we'll have to come back in the daylight to tidy the site up?" Claire said. "Or have you prepared for *that* too?"

"You tell me what time you want to be here in the morning and I'll help you," Zoe said, waving happily to some other women who were moving towards them.

Claire walked along beside her, careful not to step into

any of the particularly deep puddles that pockmarked the ground. Most were filled with rancid water by now.

"So what made you move to the West Country from London then?" she asked.

"I just got fed up with city life," Zoe told her. "After my husband died I wanted a more relaxed way of life."

"You were lucky you could buy a place here," Polly told her.

"Well, I bought it with the insurance I got from my husband's death," Zoe informed her. "I wouldn't really call that lucky, would you?"

"How did he die?" Claire wanted to know.

"Heart attack. I found him in bed with his lover."

Claire frowned.

"I'm sorry," she breathed.

"I'm not," Zoe snapped. "They both had it coming."

She walked on, outpacing the other two women over the uneven ground, greeting the others who had approached them. She hugged each one warmly as Claire watched.

"I told you she was trying to take over," Claire murmured.

"I didn't know that about her husband," Polly offered, glancing at the other woman.

Claire didn't answer.

"It's sad, isn't it?" Polly went on.

Claire nodded almost imperceptibly and walked on.

"You know what it's like," Polly persisted.

"Frank had a mild stroke," Claire reminded her. "Not a bloody heart attack. It's hardly in the same league, is it?"

Polly shook her head.

"Caught him in bed with his lover, eh?" Claire murmured, her eyes fixed on Zoe.

***

It was past one a.m. by the time Claire got home.

She parked the Land Rover outside the house and hurried in out of the drizzly rain, noticing that the light in the sitting room was on.

As she entered she pulled off her wellingtons and left them in the hallway. She could hear the television blurting out from the sitting room and she walked in to see her husband fast asleep on the sofa, his mouth open, the TV remote still gripped in one hand.

Claire crossed to him, took the device from him and lowered the volume on the TV.

She glanced into the fireplace and saw that there were just embers there now, smoke rising from the barely glowing remains of the coals. She wondered about starting another but then decided it wasn't worth it. It was almost bedtime.

"I thought you would have gone to bed," she told him as he woke, yawning and rubbing his eyes.

"I wanted to make sure you got back safely," he told her as she disappeared into the kitchen and filled the kettle.

"You let the fire go out," she reminded him. "It's bloody freezing."

"I fell asleep," he told her.

"I noticed," she called.

"How did your meeting go?" Frank enquired.

"It went well," she called. "Lots of people there."

"Including that woman you don't like?" Frank called.

"Yes," Claire grunted. "Including her."

"What's she done to make you dislike her so much?" he wanted to know.

"She's a busybody. Always sticking her nose in where it isn't wanted."

"Takes one to know one."

She heard him laughing from the other room and she shook her head dismissively.

"Oh, shut up, Frank," Claire sighed. "You don't know what it's like. I've been running things for the last three years and then she turns up and starts trying to change everything."

"She's only trying to help."

"She's trying to take over. I know her type."

Claire made the tea and carried a mug through into the sitting room.

"Where's mine?" Frank asked.

"I thought you were going to bed now I'm home," she said, seating herself at the far end of the sofa and reaching for her phone.

"I thought we might have... a little fun," Frank said, lecherously. "You're usually well up for it when you come home from one of your shindigs."

"They're not shindigs, Frank. They're festivals and no, tonight I'm *not* up for it. There's something I've got to do."

"Please yourself," he said, getting to his feet. "Don't sit up all night."

Claire nodded and watched as he wandered out of the room and then she returned her attention to her phone, finding Facebook on the device. She hurriedly found Zoe Carson's profile.

She went straight to the photos section and scanned the pictures there. Zoe and some of her friends. Zoe outside a pub. Zoe at the seaside.

Claire raised her eyebrows and sighed.

Zoe at a wedding. Zoe in her garden.

Claire clicked on the first picture and enlarged it.

It showed Zoe standing at her back door, hanging baskets on either side of her, both full of colourful flowers in full bloom. There were more pictures showing a large pond and Zoe inspecting one of the frogs that had obviously made the pond its home. Another of Zoe surrounded by flowers. Again Claire enlarged the picture.

She recognised the blooms.

Foxglove. Also known as digitalis.

More pictures. More flowers. Claire recognised those too. The purple and blue bell-shaped blooms.

Aconite.

Highly toxic. One gram of it could cause paralysis of the respiratory centre or cardiac arrest.

Heart attack. Just what killed Zoe's husband and his lover. Coincidence? Was she crediting Zoe with more cunning and expertise than she deserved or had she happened upon a kindred spirit?

Claire knew aconite was lethally effective. It's what she'd been putting in Frank's food for the last three months.

She didn't want anything as spectacular or sudden as a heart attack. The doses she was giving her husband were enough to cause a series of small strokes. The cumulative effect would be enough. There was no residual build-up of aconite in the bloodstream. It was all absorbed without a problem. No evidence. Another few months and it would all be over.

Claire smiled and looked at the pictures again.

She was still thinking that when her phone buzzed to signal an incoming message.

There was only one person it could be at this time of night. She opened the message immediately when she saw the ID on it.

JOHN WILSON.

She smiled and shuffled on the sofa, her bare feet drawn up beneath her. A sudden thrill running through her as she read the message:

I WANT YOU.

She sighed, wistfully.

I WANT YOU TOO she replied, her hands shaking slightly as she sent the message.

I WISH WE'D HAD MORE TIME TONIGHT.

She smiled as she read the next message.

I WISH WE'D HAD TIME TOGETHER.

Claire nodded to herself and replied:

SO DO I.

"Claire."

She heard the call from upstairs and sighed irritably.

"Are you coming to bed?" Frank called.

"Yes," she shouted back, angrily.

She sent one more quick message, her face now set in hard lines.

GOT TO GO. SEE YOU TOMORROW.

She got to her feet, took one last look at the screen of the laptop, then slammed it shut.

***

The morning was cold.

Frost clung to the hedges and grass and a thick mist also drifted across the landscape, obscuring much of it as Claire drove.

It was earlier than she normally liked to be up, let alone out and driving around, but the field where the previous night's ceremony had been held had to be cleared. That was one of the provisions of her and her group being allowed to gather there by the farmer that owned the land. He didn't mind them using the field for their own purposes but he did insist on it being pristine again when they'd finished.

Claire didn't mind tidying up. It was just a matter of picking up the odd bits of dropped litter and raking over the area where the labyrinth had been drawn. Nothing major.

It was a small price to pay for the freedom to use the area whenever she and her friends wanted it.

She turned a corner, slowing down slightly when she saw that the mist was even thicker as she reached the outskirts of the village.

She flicked her lights on to full beam but that did little to help and merely reflected back off the curtain of fog. Claire allowed the Land Rover to crawl along at less than fifteen miles an hour. There wasn't much else on the road at this time of the morning, fortunately. She glanced at the dashboard clock and saw that it was just past 6 a.m. She'd thought about calling Polly and asking for her help but there was no need for that. What she had to do wouldn't take more than an hour.

Squinting through the thick fog she drove on.

Along the dirt track leading to the field she thought that the fog was clearing a little and she eased into a higher gear, finally bringing the vehicle to a halt close to the wooden gate that led into the field.

Claire swung herself out of the Land Rover, retrieved a couple of black plastic bags from the back seat and a rake from the boot, and set off across the open space, the cold mist closing around her like a chilled hand.

She almost stumbled twice as she made her way towards the labyrinth and the remains of the bonfires that had lit the hillside the previous night. The fog around her feet swirled like a layer of disturbed dust, tendrils of it seeming to reach up as if to ensnare her.

She squinted through the hazy curtain, frowning slightly.

There was a dark shape on the higher ground ahead of her.

Barely discernible in the mist but nevertheless just visible as a shadowy outline.

Claire slowed her pace.

The fog was clearing slightly on the higher ground and she moved more slowly towards the area where the figure was.

As Claire began to move up the gentle slope a light breeze blew most of the thickest fog away.

The figure turned to face her.

"Hello, you," John Wilson said, happily.

Claire smiled broadly and hurried across to him. They embraced warmly and she found herself looking into his eyes, trying to resist the urge to kiss him. Finally, that urge overcame her. She pressed her lips to his and held them there, feeling his tongue begin to glide urgently against hers. When they finally broke the kiss John smiled broadly.

"I thought you'd be here early," he said. "I thought you might want some help tidying up."

"Have you been here long?" she wanted to know.

"Literally just got here," he informed her. "I parked on the other side of the wood, that's why you didn't see my car."

Claire looked around at the hillside and nodded.

"There's not much to tidy up anyway," she noted. "You get the rubbish, I'll rake over the labyrinth." She handed him the plastic bags.

"Okay," John agreed. "Then we could go and get some breakfast at the pub if you like."

"There are other things I'd rather be doing with you," she purred. "But breakfast will do for now."

As she turned away he slapped her backside playfully.

Claire grinned.

As John moved higher up the slope, pushing some litter into one of the black bags, Claire began raking over the furrows cut into the earth, transforming the lines of the labyrinth back into bare earth again.

She had done most of it when she noticed something at the heart of the carefully etched area.

Claire moved closer, her brow furrowing slightly. She knelt down, now close enough to the object to see it clearly.

"Oh, God," she murmured.

The object before her was about twelve inches long,

made of clay. It was roughly fashioned but was still unmistakeable in its construction.

"Claire."

The sound of her own name wasn't enough to make her take her attention away from what she was gazing at. Only when John Wilson joined her in looking did she finally manage regain a measure of control.

"I just found it," she breathed, her gaze fixed on the object.

"What is it?" he wanted to know.

"It's a poppet," Claire told him, her voice cracking slightly.

"What the hell is that?" John demanded.

"A pagan magic doll," she murmured.

"Like a voodoo doll?" John asked.

He looked more closely at the object and he saw that it was in the shape of a doll. The arms and legs had been carved from a solid piece of heavy clay, features hewn roughly into the face of the figure. Some pieces of hair in the form of black wool and cotton had even been attached to the head in an effort to make it look more realistic, and it was wrapped in more pieces of thin wool, designed to make it look as if it were wearing clothes.

"Some kid must have dropped it last night," John offered, aware of how pale Claire had become as she continued to gaze at the effigy.

"No," she said. "That's no kid's doll. I told you, it's a poppet. Someone put that there deliberately. Someone who knows what they're doing. Someone who knows that it would be found." She swallowed hard. "It's an effigy, designed to bring harm, even death, to the one it's modelled on," Claire snapped.

"But who's it modelled on?"

Claire could only shake her head.

"We won't know that until we know who put it there," she said.

"So you're trying to tell me that this thing was placed here with the intention of causing some kind of harm to someone in our circle?"

"Yes."

"But who the hell would want to do that? And why?"

Again Claire had no answer.

She got to her feet slowly, her gaze still fixed on the poppet. John watched as she took a step backward, never looking away from the small effigy.

"We'll have to tell the others," John suggested. "If that thing is what you say it is then someone might be in danger." They both looked more intently at the crudely fashioned model.

"Who the hell is it supposed to be?" John murmured. "I mean, it's not very accurate as an effigy, is it?" He chuckled.

Claire didn't share his amusement.

"It doesn't matter what it *looks* like," she said. "It's what it means. What it signifies. Intent is All." She let out a long breath. "We can't let this go. We can't just ignore it."

"But Claire…"

"John, this is serious," she snapped.

"But I don't understand who would want to cause someone in the circle harm," John murmured. "What are they hoping to gain?"

"Control," Claire said flatly.

"Of what?" John enquired.

"The circle," Claire told him. "Or someone in it."

***

The meeting of the circle usually took place every three months. At it there would be discussions about forthcoming events, mainly local but sometimes involving travel to other sites. The entire circle usually made the relatively short journey to Stonehenge to celebrate the winter and summer solstice but, for the most part, those involved confined their actions to the local stone circle that stood just outside the village.

Claire now stood on the small stage of the village hall looking around at those gathered before her. She had sent messages via social media the day before to summon the members of the circle.

There were about thirty of them. Most were people she'd known since she and Frank first moved here from London. She liked them. They were like an extended family for her. They made her feel loved.

There was one exception.

Zoe Carson was sitting on the front row looking immaculate as usual. Claire kept glancing at her as she addressed the gathering. Was that a smile on the younger woman's face? A smirk? She barely took her eyes from Claire.

Or did she?

Claire cleared her throat, wondering if Zoe was *actually* staring at her or if her own imagination was starting to run wild. She looked at John Wilson and then at Polly Bishop, both of whom smiled reassuringly at her.

"I apologise again for calling this meeting at such short notice," she said. "But there is something that has to be discussed." As she spoke she dug her hand into the Waitrose bag that lay on the lectern in front of her.

Those in the small audience leaned forward expectantly.

"I found *this* when I was clearing the labyrinth," Claire said, holding up the poppet accusingly. It was now wrapped in silk. A precaution.

There were murmurs in the room, some of bewilderment, some of concern.

Claire looked directly at Zoe.

"If someone thinks they're being funny then I'd like to tell them they're not," she said, sternly. "This is not a joke. This is serious."

"It's only a little doll," Trisha Follet said, smiling.

Claire didn't share her amusement.

"Trisha," she began, sighing. "I realise you're new to paganism but please try to understand that, for those of us who take this way of life seriously, *this* is much more than that." Again she waved the doll in front of her. "Whoever left it in the labyrinth was trying to make a point."

"What kind of point?" Trisha wanted to know.

"This doll is intended to do harm," Claire went on, her gaze resting briefly on Zoe Carson. "As I said, I have no idea what kind of person would do such a thing but I think we have to find out and nip this kind of behaviour in the bud."

"Who do *you* think left it, Claire?" Zoe asked.

"I have no idea," Claire said, shaking her head. "Just as I have no idea who the harm is intended to."

"Why would anyone do it?" Polly Bishop wanted to know. "We're all friends in this circle. Who would want to hurt anyone here?"

"I agree, Polly, but how well can you know *anyone?*" Claire exclaimed. "Who knows what goes through a person's mind? We don't know what the person who left this poppet is after, do we?"

Again her gaze drifted towards Zoe.

"I just want to say that if whoever left it is prepared to own up and apologise then I think we should forget about it," Claire said. "But if not..." She allowed the words to trail off.

"I think you're making a lot of fuss over nothing," Trisha Follet offered.

"Well, then let's hope that *you're* not the one who is the subject of this... hatred," Claire snapped, glaring at the other woman.

"Claire's right," Zoe Carson said, standing up. "This is

bad but I think we should just get rid of the poppet and forget this ever happened."

There were rumbles of approval from inside the room.

"And let someone in the circle carry on thinking negative thoughts about one of the other members?" Claire snapped. "We can't do that. This poppet is a sign that someone inside the circle has a real problem." She held the doll in the air again, brandishing it as if it were an unexploded bomb. "This is evil."

There was such conviction in Claire's voice this time that no one in the room spoke for a minute or so. The silence was finally broken by Polly.

"Who is it meant to be?" she asked, pointing at the poppet. "I know it doesn't matter if the features or build aren't accurate but we have to know who the magic is directed at."

"Well, it's got dark hair so the intended victim must have dark hair," Trisha Follet offered.

"Half of the people in the circle have dark hair," Claire observed.

"So does that mean the other half are suspects?" Trisha asked, chuckling.

Some of the others laughed too, much to Claire's annoyance. She shot angry glances around the room, waiting until the stillness descended once more.

"I know *I* didn't put it in the labyrinth," she said. "I suggest that whoever did has a good think about what they've done and owns up."

With that, she pushed the poppet back into the Waitrose bag and walked away from the lectern.

John saw her heading towards the exit and hurried to intercept her.

"Do you fancy getting a drink before you go home?" he asked.

Claire smiled.

"I'd love to," she said. "But I should get back to Frank.

If I'm out too long he gets anxious."

John nodded. "I'll message you later," he breathed.

"You'd better," Claire said, squeezing his arm.

***

She was halfway home when her front tyre burst.

Fortunately she was on a deserted road, driving slowly when it happened so there was no danger and she managed to bring the vehicle to a halt on the grass verge without any problem.

She walked around to the front of the Land Rover and looked down at the tyre. It was completely flat. Claire kicked it then prepared to retrieve the spare. Before she did she called Frank on her mobile, told him what had happened and assured him that she shouldn't be more than another hour or so.

She'd changed tyres before so it wasn't a problem and, when she'd finally finished, she stood back looking down at the new addition, satisfied with her own handiwork.

What had caused the blow out? Had she driven over something sharp? She looked closely at the original tyre but could see no rents or gashes in the rubber. She'd been lucky she wasn't doing more than thirty at the time though. If she'd been doing a decent speed she might have been in trouble.

Bad luck?

Or something else?

She glanced at the passenger seat of the Land Rover where the poppet still lay inside the Waitrose bag.

Could it have been that?

Claire dismissed the thought, slid behind the wheel and started the engine.

It was approaching dusk now and the sky was darkening considerably, large banks of grey cloud scudding across the heavens. Claire switched on her headlights, glancing once or twice in the direction of the poppet.

She rounded a corner and put her foot down slightly, aware that Frank would be wondering where she was despite the fact that she'd already warned him.

On this part of the drive home, tall hedges flanked the road on both sides, cutting out more light and forming the perimeters of fields. Claire drove on, shivering involuntarily. It seemed much colder inside the Land Rover now. She fiddled with the heater as she drove but noticed that it was already on maximum. Again she shivered, looking once more towards the poppet.

When she looked at the road again she something dark on the tarmac just ahead.

Claire almost screamed and twisted the wheel violently to one side to avoid whatever was standing in the road.

There was a shriek of rubber on tarmac then the Land Rover ploughed into the grass verge, mud and water spraying up in all directions, but she grappled with the wheel and kept control of the vehicle, slamming her foot on the brake to bring it to a juddering halt.

Her heart hammered against her ribs and she raised one shaking hand to her face, stumbling out of the Land Rover, her eyes scanning the road behind her, trying to see what she had come so close to hitting.

It looked like a badger but it was bigger.

The dark shape ambled across the road then disappeared through a gap in the hedge.

Claire fought to control her breathing then finally climbed back into the Land Rover again. She waited a moment, her hand shaking as she re-started the engine.

She had gone no more than fifty yards when she reached across onto the passenger seat, grabbed the poppet and hurled it out of the open window.

The little doll disappeared into one of the ditches at the roadside and Claire drove on, her face set in hard lines.

It was another twenty minutes before she got home.

She parked the car and sat silently behind the wheel for a moment before heading for the front door, wondering why the house was in darkness. Frank usually put on the lights when the first hint of evening coloured the sky and now it was almost dark. Yet there were no signs of illumination in the sitting room as she pushed her key into the lock and entered.

"Frank," she called.

"In here," he said and she wandered into the sitting room, switching on lamps in the process.

"Why are you in the dark?" she murmured. "Too lazy to put the lights on?"

"I had to answer the phone," he told her. "The chimney sweep rang. He said can he come tomorrow instead of next week? He said he's busy."

"Oh, God," Claire sighed.

"It was you who wanted an open fire," Frank reminded her, watching as she knelt in front of the grate, using a poker to tap at the chimney opening. "What are you doing anyway?"

"Just seeing how badly its caked up," she told him, pushing higher with the poker.

"That's his job, not yours," Frank reminded her.

Claire ignored her husband and continued jabbing upwards into the black maw of the chimney. She moved back quickly when something fell from it.

It landed with a thump and Claire looked at it, a chill racing up and down her spine.

Laying on the coal and pieces of wood was the poppet.

Claire reached for it, gripping it in one shaking hand. There was soot on the little doll, some of the dark material smeared on the features and the woollen garments it wore. Some of the strands of hair were singed.

131

"I wonder how that got there," Frank said, smiling.

Claire looked at him then back at the poppet.

Frank took it from her, turning it over in his hand.

"Do you know what it is?" she said, her voice barely more than a whisper.

"Of course I know," he told her. "You think just because I don't come along to your bloody meetings that I don't know what you're up to?"

She looked blankly at him.

"You think I don't understand?" he went on. "I know what you've been doing. I know about the stuff you've been putting in my food. I know you're trying to kill me."

As he spoke he pressed the poppet tightly between his palms.

Claire gasped for breath. It felt as if someone were tightening a vice around her chest and upper body.

Frank pressed his hands more tightly together.

White lights danced before Claire's eyes now. She could barely suck in a breath. Pain was starting to spread throughout her torso. Pain that was intensifying, spreading into her neck and skull.

Frank snapped off the head of the poppet.

Claire felt sudden searing pain between her shoulders, then nothing. She slumped backwards and lay motionless on the carpet.

Frank knelt beside her, pressing two fingers to her neck, feeling for a pulse. There was nothing.

He smiled more broadly.

"It only works if you believe, doesn't it?" he murmured, grinning down at the dead body of his wife.

He stood there for a moment longer then reached for his phone, tapping the digits he needed.

"It's done," he said, quietly, his gaze still fixed on Claire's immobile body.

"I'll be there in ten minutes," Zoe Carson told him on the other end of the line.

"It's okay," Frank told her. "No rush. I'd better call the police and ambulance and report this."

"See you soon, Frank," Zoe breathed. "Love you."

"Love you too," he murmured and terminated the call.

Then he placed the poppet gently on the coal and wood in the fireplace and lit it, watching as the flames began to leap higher.

Frank Bennett smiled.

THE HIT

Frank Hacket hated hospitals.

He hated the smell of disinfectant and he hated the fact that they reminded him of his own mortality. For many he realised they were places of hope, salvation and belief but Hacket saw them as places of pain, suffering and death. Once you went in, your chances of coming out again were slim as far as he was concerned.

He'd seen that happen with both his parents when he was younger and, more recently, he'd seen it happen with his wife. Just four years earlier she had died after spending three weeks in intensive care, the victim of a drunken driver and an accident that should never have happened. Apart from the smells and all the painful memories that hospitals brought back, Hacket hated the places mainly because he couldn't smoke inside them and, right now, he needed a cigarette.

He walked to the lift that would carry him to the tenth floor, glancing to his right and left, noticing that there were patients and visitors seated in the cafe off to his right. They were sipping cups of tea and coffee, exchanging cordial and banal words.

Hacket continued on to the lift, hitting the call button and waiting for it to arrive. When it did he was relieved to find there was no one in it. He had no desire to be caught in some meaningless conversation with a patient or visitor while he rode to the tenth floor.

He moved to the back of the car, turned his gaze upwards towards the floor indicator panel and watched as each successive floor was reached and then passed. When the number ten was finally illuminated, Hacket stepped out of the lift and turned to his left, heading along a corridor that ended with a large picture window.

On either side of the corridor there were doors, all of them firmly closed.

There was a vending machine about halfway up the corridor and Hacket paused for a moment, wondering whether or not to get himself a coffee, but he checked his watch, saw that he was running a little later than he'd have liked and decided against it. Punctuality was a big thing in Frank Hacket's life. He hated being late. He hated it when other people were late. To him it smacked of laziness or unprofessionalism and he couldn't abide either of those traits in himself or others.

As he passed the first of the doors, a nurse emerged from the room beyond pushing a small trolley. Hacket stepped aside to let her through and she nodded and smiled by way of acknowledgement. As she tried to turn the trolley she bumped it against the wall and a small roll of surgical tape fell to the floor. Hacket hastily retrieved it and handed it to her. She thanked him and headed off in the other direction, the sound of the trolley wheels squeaking softly until she disappeared into one of the other rooms, closing the door behind her. Hacket continued up the corridor until he reached the last of the closed doors.

He walked in without knocking and found himself in what looked like a waiting area. There were several brown plastic chairs arranged around a low table that was strewn with magazines and plastic cups from the vending machine. On one side of this table sat a man in a grey suit, busy with a newspaper crossword, his brow furrowed in concentration. He got to his feet and smiled as Hacket walked in, extending one huge hand in the newcomer's direction.

He was a big man, so broad across the shoulders and chest it looked as if the material of his suit was in danger of splitting due to the amount of muscle and sinew it had to contain. The pen he was holding looked like a matchstick held between his thick fingers.

"Hello, Frank," he beamed.

"How you doing, Wally?" Hacket asked, gripping the other man's hand as firmly as he could while worrying that his own might be crushed to powder by the vice-like grip.

"Can't complain," the big man said. "What about you? Busy?"

"Always busy, Wally."

The big man chuckled.

Hacket nodded towards the door behind the huge figure.

"How is he?" he wanted to know.

"Not good," the big man told him, his features softening. "He's been asking for you."

Hacket nodded and moved towards the other door as the big man slapped him across the shoulder affectionately with a blow that would have sent lesser men sprawling.

"Has anyone else been in?" Hacket asked.

"He only wants to see you," the other man explained.

Hacket hesitated a moment longer then opened the door and slipped through as quickly and quietly as he could.

The first sound that met his ears when he walked into the next room was the steady blip of an oscilloscope.

The machine was set up next to the single bed that was in the middle of the room. In that bed there was a figure, propped up on pillows with eyes closed and head bowed. On either side of the bed there were drips. Hacket could see clear fluid making its way from plastic bags into the veins of the motionless recipient in the bed.

The man who lay there was in his mid-fifties but looked twenty years older. His skin was like parchment

139

and the veins on the backs of his hands appeared black against the milky whiteness of his skin.

Hacket stood looking at him, his eyes drawn to the man's chest that was rising and falling almost imperceptibly. The curtains at the large picture window were drawn to prevent the sun from shining directly into the patient's eyes. Motes of dust turned lazily in the single ray that had managed to penetrate. Hacket walked slowly towards the bed, his gaze on the occupant.

The man in the bed didn't stir and Hacket wondered if he was asleep. He looked at the bedside cabinets on either side of the patient. Both had vases of flowers on them, and arrayed around those were cards mostly bearing the legend GET WELL SOON.

Hacket admired the sentiment but doubted the possibility.

He wondered how long he'd have to wait until the patient woke up. He wasn't pressed for time but he didn't relish the prospect of having to hang around in the hospital for any longer than he had to.

There were two plastic chairs beside the bed and Hacket was about to settle himself on one of these when the man in the bed raised his head.

"I thought it was the nurse come back to take more blood," the man said, quietly. "I thought she'd leave if she saw I was asleep. They're good like that."

"Morning, George," Hacket said. "I would ask how you are but I can see."

"I won't be running any marathons in the next few days, let's put it that way," the other man said. "Have a seat." He motioned to one of the plastic chairs and Hacket seated himself.

George Vaughn lifted a hand to scratch one cheek and Hacket saw the drip attached to it, that clear plastic vein running into him like so many others, each resembling some kind of benevolent circuit cable. The blip of the oscilloscope continued with its weary tone.

"I won't waste your time, Frank," Vaughn said, trying to take a deep breath but not quite managing it because of the pain it caused him. "I haven't got much time left to waste."

"Is it that bad?" Hacket wanted to know.

"What does it look like? It's spread to the other lung and they say it could spread to my brain before the end of next week. I've got less than a month if I'm lucky."

"I'm sorry, George."

"Some might say it's poetic justice I suppose. What with the line of work I've been in. Karma and all that. That is what they call it, isn't it?"

"Something like that."

Vaughn coughed, clutching at his chest with one gnarled hand.

Hacket got to his feet and reached for the nearby jug of water. He poured some into a beaker and handed it to Vaughn who finally managed to take a sip when the coughing fit subsided.

"Fucking cancer," he grunted through clenched teeth.

Hacket took the beaker from him and seated himself again.

"Do you want me to get someone?" he asked. "A nurse or something?"

"They can't do anything for me anyway," Vaughn said. "They just keep pumping me full of fucking morphine but even that's not working as well as it used to." He sighed. "Listen, Frank, I've got a job for you."

"I'd have thought you'd got more important things on your mind, George."

"This is important," Vaughn snapped. "It's a special job. Five million if you do it before the end of next week."

"Five million? Who's the target? The Queen?"

Vaughn motioned to the top drawer of the nearest bed

141

side cabinet.

"All the information's in there," he said.

Hacket opened the draw and took out a small manilla file that he proceeded to flip open.

There were a number of photographs inside. Mostly of a large country house and the driveway that led up to it. Others showed the vast overgrown lawn that guarded the approaches to the house. Most of the pictures had been taken in bright sunlight that only served to illustrate even more starkly how badly cared for the house and its grounds really were. Hacket raised his eyebrows as he considered each one, turning several over to discover there was an address written on them in black ink.

"So the target is here?" he asked, raising one of the pictures.

"He was last seen there two days ago," Vaughn told him. "He moves around a lot but he always comes back to that place."

"There's no name or description of the guy I'm supposed to hit."

"You've got the address where he lives. He lives alone. No family. No security. What more do you want? His fucking inside leg measurement?"

"No security? In a gaff like that?"

"He lives there alone."

"Are you sure your intelligence is right? I don't want to go walking in there and find out he's got half the fucking SAS guarding him."

"He's alone there," Vaughn said, coughing. "Now, can you do the job or not?"

"Have I ever turned one down before?"

"No."

"Ever fucked one up?"

"No."

Hacket pushed the photographs back into the envelope.

"So what's he done to you, George?" he asked. "What's he done that's pissed you off so much you'd order a hit from your deathbed?"

"You never normally ask," Vaughn reminded him.

"You never normally pay me this much. I'm just checking there isn't more to this guy than you've told me."

"Just kill him. I pay for the job, Frank. Getting it done is your problem. How you do it is up to you. If you don't trust me you can have half the money now and the other half on completion."

"I trust you, George. I'll pick up all the money when the job's done."

Vaughn nodded.

"Just get it done before the end of next week," he said. He coughed again and the oscilloscope speeded up slightly before settling back into its usual rhythm.

Hacket waited a moment longer then got to his feet. He held up the manilla envelope again then pushed it into the inside pocket of his jacket and turned to leave.

"One thing, Frank," Vaughn said, almost as an afterthought.

Hacket hesitated.

"As soon as the job's done I want you to come back here and tell me," Vaughn went on. "And I want you to bring me something."

"Go on."

"I want the index finger from his right hand," Vaughn said, flatly.

"For what you're paying me, you can have the whole fucking arm," Hacket smiled.

"Just the finger," Vaughn insisted. "The right index finger."

Hacket nodded then turned towards the door once again, slipping out of the room. As he closed the door behind him he heard Vaughn coughing again.

The huge man in the grey suit looked up from his crossword puzzle as Hacket entered the room again.

"Did you get it sorted?" he wanted to know.

Hacket nodded.

"See you around, Wally," he said, one hand on the handle of the door beyond.

"Frank, what do you reckon this is?" the big man said, waving his crossword in the air. "'If you get rid of someone, you give them this.' Six letters, first letter is B."

"Bullet," Hacket said, smiling. And he was gone.

He stepped out into the corridor beyond, walked to the lift and rode it to the ground floor, relieved that no one had joined him during the short journey.

As soon as he reached the car park of the hospital he reached for his cigarettes, lighting one up and puffing on it gratefully. He watched as an ambulance, blue lights spinning, swept into view then he wandered back to his car. The drive home took him thirty minutes.

***

The house in the photographs was called Westfield Grange.

It didn't take Hacket long to discover that, just as it didn't take him long to work out that it was about three hours' drive from him. It was approachable through leafy countryside and several small villages that seemed to vie with each other for which was the most picturesque.

Hacket stopped in the nearest one to Westfield Grange for some lunch, sitting at the end of the bar in a pub called The Three Horseshoes. He managed to get through his shepherd's pie and vegetables without being disturbed. Only as he was enjoying his dessert and another glass of non-alcoholic lager did the balding man behind the bar amble over to him.

"How was your food?" the man wanted to know, busily

polishing glasses and then replacing them beneath and behind the bar.

"Very nice," Hacket told him. "My compliments to the cook."

"I'll tell the wife, she'll be glad to hear that," the man chuckled.

"Do you own this place?" Hacket enquired.

"We run it. We bought the lease about twelve years ago."

"So you must know what goes on around here. In the village and that."

"You can't really avoid it."

"Everybody knows everybody else's business in a village, right?" Hacket said, smiling.

The barman also smiled and nodded in agreement.

"How much do you know about the owner of Westfield Grange?" Hacket enquired.

"He's not as friendly as the last owner," the balding man announced. "The last owner used to have an annual barbecue in the grounds of the house every springtime but no one's even seen this owner."

"Perhaps he just likes to keep himself to himself," Hacket offered.

"The lady who used to clean there was sacked not long after he moved in. Hardly anyone visits the place. He got rid of his gardeners, too. The place is a real mess now."

Hacket could certainly have attested to the overgrown nature of the grounds and gardens after seeing photographs of the Grange, but he merely nodded sagely and let the balding man go on.

"So he never comes in here for a pint then?" Hacket said, smiling.

"Never."

"Do you know if he's got any family?"

"If he has no one's ever seen them."

Again Hacket nodded almost imperceptibly.

"How do you know about the Grange?" the balding man wanted to know.

"I'm a bit of an amateur historian," Hacket lied. "I like buildings from that period."

The other man nodded enthusiastically and Hacket was happy that he'd fallen for the lie so readily. Hacket finished his drink, paid his bill and wandered out to his car.

The drive to Westfield Grange took him another thirty minutes.

He drove past the high stone wall and wrought iron gates that guarded the driveway and grounds of the building then he drove back, pulling his car off the road into a small copse of trees that effectively hid the vehicle from anyone who was passing.

He sat behind the wheel and smoked a cigarette, then he clambered out of the car and walked to the boot where he selected the tools he would need for the job. Usually he preferred doing his work from a distance and he favoured a Parker-Hale M85 7.62mm sniper rifle but this time closer contact was necessary so he settled for a 9mm Taurus PT-92, checking the ten-round magazine before slipping it into the shoulder holster he wore.

The five-inch bowie-knife he slid into the sheath on his belt.

Suitably equipped, Hacket climbed back behind the wheel of the car and reversed onto the road. He drove along the narrow track to the gates of Westfield Grange and then, leaving the engine running, swung himself out of the vehicle and approached the entryway looking around for surveillance cameras, careful to keep his face hidden from any that might be mounted on the high walls around the grounds. There was an intercom on the right-hand pillar and Hacket pressed the buzzer there.

No one answered but, to Hacket's delight, the gates swung open.

He stroked his chin lightly.

This was too fucking easy.

He reached almost subconsciously inside his jacket and touched his fingers to the butt of the Taurus, as if to remind himself that he could pull the automatic any time he needed to. His heart began to beat a little faster. As he drove down the long driveway he glanced into the rearview mirror and saw the iron gates close behind him.

Was he being watched even now? Surely whoever owned this place couldn't be as lax with security as he appeared to be. This was crazy. Hacket wondered again if he was being set up but, he reasoned, why would Vaughn want to do that to him? He shook his head as if to dispel any such paranoid thoughts, finally bringing the car to a halt in front of the short flight of stone steps that led up to the front door of the Grange.

His feet made crunching noises on the gravel of the driveway as he made his way to the main entrance. He waited there for a second, eyes constantly alert for any movement but there was none. Hacket banged the door three times, using the large ornate knocker set in the centre of the wooden partition. Having done that he ducked back along the side of the building, hurrying past the ivy-covered brickwork and finally pausing beside a window.

He used the bowie-knife to slide the sash window open a few inches, completing the task by sliding his fingers into the gap and easing the window up until it allowed him to slip inside.

Hacket eased himself soundlessly over the sill, finding himself inside a large and thankfully empty room.

Once again he was struck by the lack of security, wondering how anyone with such obvious wealth could live like this without any apparent concern for this kind of eventuality. Admittedly not everyone faced the prospect of being shot by a hitman, Hacket mused, but there was always the danger of burglars. The owner of this place didn't appear to have considered any of those eventualities and, again, Hacket wondered what that person could have done to George Vaughn to merit this kind of treatment.

He moved towards the door of the room, placed his hand lightly on the handle and turned it.

The door was unlocked.

Hacket opened it slightly, peering out into the large hallway beyond. A broad corridor snaked away to his right and left and, as he eased himself out into it, he saw that there were indeed CCTV cameras set high up on the walls but they didn't seem to be working. The wide lenses didn't move as he did, the red lights on them didn't blink. Hacket decided that even if they were working they didn't appear to be triggered by motion. Nevertheless, he was also certain by now that whoever inhabited this house was aware of his presence. He slid the Taurus from his shoulder holster and slipped off the safety catch.

Directly in front of him was a large dining room, to his right a corridor that led down to another set of double doors. Hacket chose that particular route, moving quickly and quietly until he reached the doors where he stood listening, trying to catch any sounds coming from beyond.

There was nothing but silence and, again, Hacket wondered if the target was merely sitting on the other side of the doors waiting for him. He gripped the pistol more tightly and pushed the doors, both of which swung open.

Hacket ducked back slightly then peered into the room and saw that it too was empty.

There was a staircase rising from the centre of this room and Hacket moved towards it, climbing it swiftly but quietly, the automatic held before him, ready in case anyone appeared before him. The staircase bent to the left and then the right before finally opening out onto a landing.

Hacket paused again, seeing two doors before him.

The silence remained oppressive but, he realised, it was also doing nothing to mask his approach.

He moved as quietly as he could towards the first of the doors, closing his hand gently around the handle.

The door opened easily and Hacket stepped inside.

The room was completely devoid of furniture and lit only by overhead fluorescent lights that made him shield his eyes, so bright was the cold whiteness pouring from these overhead strips.

The only thing in the room was a child's cradle.

It stood right in the centre of the small room and, as Hacket moved cautiously towards it, he wrinkled his nose. There was a strange antiseptic smell in the air, something he hadn't noticed anywhere else in the house.

More than a little unsettled now, Hacket backed out of the room, closing the door behind him.

He turned towards the next door and opened that too.

It also opened onto another blindingly white room but this one was occupied.

There was one single high-backed chair in the centre of the room and, in that chair sat a man.

He had his head bowed. His chin was touching his chest as if he was asleep. Hacket couldn't see his face, only that he was dressed in an immaculately pressed charcoal grey suit. If he'd heard Hacket enter the room he certainly showed no signs of acknowledging it.

As Hacket stood there in that doorway he detected that antiseptic smell he'd noticed in the previous room. That smell he hated so much. That stink of hospitals and sick beds. Of wards and examination rooms.

"Is this your house?" Hacket asked.

The man raised his head, looked at Hacket

unconcernedly and nodded slowly.

He was in his mid-fifties. An unremarkable looking man with brown hair that was greying at the temples and deep lines across his forehead that looked as if someone had dragged a fork across his flesh there.

"Are you on your own here?" Hacket went on.

The man nodded again, his gaze now fixed on the barrel of the automatic.

"No one else lives here?" Hacket persisted.

The man shook his head.

"Then you're the one I'm looking for," Hacket told him.

"I knew you'd come," the man said, a slight smile on his thin lips. "I knew it would be you."

"How?"

"I just knew."

Again the man smiled.

"You have no idea what you're doing," he intoned.

"I'm doing my job," Hacket told him.

"So was I," the man said, his smile fading.

The man held his gaze now and Hacket looked back at him, his own features impassive.

Hacket shot him three times.

He stood there for a moment looking down at the body then he holstered the Taurus and reached instead for the bowie-knife. There was one more task to complete before he left.

***

As the lift bumped to a halt at the tenth floor, Frank Hacket ran a hand through his hair then stepped out into the corridor beyond.

He walked along to the room he sought and entered, hearing talking and even laughter coming from the room beyond that. Hacket crossed to that other door and stood beside it for a moment, listening to the sounds from the other side of the wooden partition. Finally, he knocked once and walked in.

George Vaughn was sitting in a chair next to the bed.

Wally Grant was standing beside him, smiling benevolently at his employer. He also nodded happily in Hacket's direction as he entered but Hacket barely saw the gesture. He was more concerned with Vaughn. Transfixed by him.

Gone was the deathly pallor. His eyes were no longer sunken into their sockets like punctured balloons, instead they looked bright and alert, fixing Hacket in a welcoming gaze as he walked in. Vaughn even got up out of his chair and took a couple of steps towards the newcomer, extending his right hand as an added gesture of welcome. Hacket felt the strength in the grip. A strength he could not have imagined being present the last time he saw the stricken older man.

There was a small plaster on the back of Vaughn's hand. A final reminder of the drips that had been attached to him the last time Hacket had visited.

"Leave us alone for a minute, Wally," Vaughn said and the big man nodded and retreated from the room, patting Hacket appreciatively on the shoulder as he passed.

Vaughn waited until the big man had left the room then perched on the edge of the bed.

"So, miracles do happen?" Hacket said, smiling. "You look great."

Vaughn smiled.

"I feel great," he exclaimed.

"What happened?" Hacket persisted.

"You did what I paid you for, that's what happened."

"I'm not with you."

"The hit. You carried it out."

"Who was he, George?"

"You didn't guess?"

Hacket shook his head.

"Did you bring me what I asked for?" Vaughn went on.

Hacket reached into his inside pocket and pulled out a small wooden box about the size of a mobile phone. He handed it to Vaughn who opened it and inspected the contents.

There was a slim index finger inside the box. It had been severed at the third knuckle and the blood had long since congealed on the raw end.

"I don't get it, George," Hacket confessed, watching as Vaughn ran appraising eyes over the digit.

"I was dying, Frank," Vaughn told him. "You could see that. Doctors couldn't help me. Drugs couldn't help me. *You* saved me." He looked at Hacket and smiled.

"How? By killing the guy in that house? I still don't get it."

"He would have come for me, Frank. Next week. Next month. But one day he would have walked in here, he would have touched me with this finger," Vaughn held up the small box and its grisly contents. "And he would have taken me. Now do you get it?"

"You're trying to tell me I killed death?" Hacket smiled.

"The Grim Reaper himself."

"Bullshit."

"You don't believe me? Just because he wasn't sitting there in a black cloak holding a fucking great scythe?"

"George, come on."

"Look at me," Vaughn insisted. "You saw me before. How do you explain this? How do you think I got better? I was dying the last time you were here. I was waiting for death. But now I don't have to wait any more. You got rid of him."

"So I'm the man who killed death?"

"Spot on. They should build statues to you." Vaughn smiled.

"So what now?" Hacket persisted. "No more famines in Africa? No more refugees drowning in boats? No more casualties in wars?"

"I don't know and I don't give a fuck. I hired you to protect me. No one else."

"George, this is ridiculous."

"Is it?" Vaughn snapped. "Look at me. How do you explain what's happened to me?"

"I can't but how come it was so easy? Why has no one tried it before?"

"Fuck knows but you did it. You did what you were hired to do." He pulled open the drawer of the bedside table and pulled out an envelope which he handed to Hacket. "And now you're getting paid. Take it. You earned it."

Hacket took the envelope and slipped it into his inside pocket.

"Not going to check it?" Vaughn asked.

"I trust you, George," Hacket told him. "If I killed death I'm not going to think twice about blowing *your* fucking head off, am I?" He smiled, hesitated a moment longer then turned and walked out of the room.

He walked slowly. As if the newly acquired knowledge Vaughn had imparted to him had somehow slowed him down. As he walked through the hospital he glanced at patients wondering if some of them would now survive because of what he'd done.

And yet he knew how ridiculous that supposition was. How the fuck could anyone kill death? How could anyone stop the approach of their own end? How could a man snuff out an entity capable of annihilating entire civilisations? It made no sense.

He was still considering that when he walked out of the hospital's main entrance.

He lit up a cigarette, told himself again that he was losing his mind and walked on.

The speeding ambulance that had come hurtling around a corner was doing seventy when it hit him.

Hacket was catapulted a good fifteen feet into the air by the impact.

He hit the ground again with a sickening thud and lay there gazing at the sky, wondering why he felt no pain. It puzzled him even more when he realised that both his legs, several ribs, one shoulder, his pelvis and two fingers were shattered. Hacket concluded that he must be in shock, that was preventing him from being consumed by the agony that would normally have enveloped him.

His right femur was smashed. The jagged end of bone was protruding from his thigh, dark matter oozing from the centre of the bone. As Hacket looked at it he realised it was marrow. The thought made him nauseous, but only a little less than the fact that he had also sustained a massive gash to his lower abdomen that had caused several lengths of intestine to bulge from the bloody rent. Hacket tried to push the slippery coils of gut back into his abdomen, his fingers slipping on the reeking pieces of viscera. His intestines looked like the tentacles of a crimson octopus.

As a nurse and paramedic ran towards him, Hacket turned in their direction.

His head was almost at a right angle, practically touching his shoulder because of his broken spine and gashed neck. The blood that was spurting into the air from one of his severed carotid arteries didn't bother him either.

Hacket got to his feet, the nurse and paramedic now gazing blankly at him. He took a couple of faltering steps, glancing down at his own smashed body, his right leg dragging along uselessly as he shuffled across the tarmac leaving a thick trail of blood on the ground behind. Each time he drew breath he could hear the air hissing in his punctured lung.

"The man who killed death," Hacket murmured, a twisted smile spreading across his lips.

And he began to laugh. As he did, his head, which was still hanging at an impossible angle, began to move backwards and forwards, the shattered vertebrae grinding together.

When he felt the vibration from his mobile phone he reached for it without thinking.

On the other end of the line was George Vaughn.

"I saw what happened to you, Frank," he said. "I was watching from my window."

"What the fuck is going on?" Hacket slurred, blood bubbling over his lips.

"I told you. You killed him. You killed death," Vaughn chuckled. "If you hadn't, you'd be in the morgue now. Enjoy it."

"But I'm crippled," Hacket roared. "I look like a fucking freak."

"At least you're still alive, Frank."

"How can I live like this?"

"It's better than dying, Frank. *Anything* is better than dying."

Vaughn hung up.

Hacket dropped the phone, allowing it to slip from his shattered fingers.

He stood in the hospital car park and screamed.

COLD CALL

It was a shit job.

A soul-destroying, brain cell-killing, cunt of a job.

But it was a job.

That's what Jack Farley kept telling himself. It was, at least, a wage every month. Granted, that wage was less than half of minimum wage but it was better than signing on, wasn't it? Or was it? Jack sat back from his desk slightly, frowning. In the last two or three days he'd come to wonder if traipsing into this office every day *was* better than signing on. There was more dignity in signing on than there was trying to sell loft insulation to vulnerable pensioners over the phone, Jack thought. There was nothing dignified or even morally redeemable in working here at Warmer Homes.

He'd been an employee for the last three months. That fact alone made him one of the longer serving members of staff. Most didn't last more than a week or two. Many that passed through its doors didn't even last a day. During his time at the company, Jack had seen a number of people turn up for their first day or two only to think better of it and not turn up again. A combination of the appalling pay, the dreadful working conditions and the dickheads who ran the company was enough to test anyone's patience.

The titular "boss" was a guy called Leon. A mouthy twat in his early forties who seemed to have learned his employer/employee skills at Dachau. He came across more like a drug dealer than a businessman, drove a car that made him look suspiciously like a pimp and treated his staff with the contempt and lack of respect usually displayed by people who've acquired some dodgy money from nefarious deals but had garnered none of the class that should go with a man responsible for the livelihoods of others.

He had his own office but would periodically walk into the main part of the call centre two or three times a day shouting and threatening staff, reminding them how grateful they should be to have a job in the shithole he ran (situated in four rented offices inside a third-rate hotel).

If it wasn't him it was his head "surveyor." A balding, perma-tanned salesman called Dave who seemed to speak exclusively in clichés gleaned from bumper stickers. His most recent stroke of genius to boost productivity was to give everyone limitless cans of Red Bull to drink in the hope that the increased energy would somehow promote more sales. It didn't, but there was no convincing Dave that he was wrong. Staff could, he assured them regularly, earn more money than people working in "the city." Jack had barely been able to suppress a contemptuous laugh the first time the idiot had come out with that particular gem. He was fairly sure that cold callers in a telesales centre didn't earn more than stockbrokers, but what did he know?

Apart from Jack, who was approaching his thirty-fifth birthday, most of the staff were young girls in their late teens or early twenties. Leon seemed to like that kind of employee mainly because none of them had been in other jobs before and had no idea what a good boss actually was. He also found it easier to dominate and intimidate young girls which, Jack thought, spoke volumes about the prick. There was also Hamza of course, the idiot who sat on the far side of the room. The man who liked the sound of his own voice more than anyone Jack had ever met. He was convinced Hamza breathed through his arse because the prick never shut his mouth long enough to take a breath. If Jack had cared enough he would have hated him.

The daily task of running the office was split between a couple of office managers. Whether they bought into Leon's bumper sticker philosophy (Jack had actually heard him say "there's no I in team.") no one knew but one of them had busied herself recently with decorating the office with excruciating slogans such as "don't count the days, make the days count" and "you got this." Jack found it laughable. Just as he found it contemptible that he and other employees were expected to work in swelteringly hot conditions (the office had no air con, just three fans and was like an oven in the summer and a fridge in winter), their breaks often removed or suspended until the requisite number of old people had been called.

He sat now gazing blankly at his screen. Any second a name and address would flash up before him and Jack would repeat the same script he spewed out more than one hundred and eighty times a day.

"Hello," he began as the name appeared. "Is that Mr Jenkins?"

"Who wants to know?" said the voice on the other end of the line.

"My name is Eric," Jack said, trying to sound as chirpy as possible (Leon insisted on positivity during calls). "I was just wondering if you remembered when the insulation was put in your loft."

"Why don't you piss off," the voice on the end of the line said, wearily. "I've had about ten calls on this subject this week."

"Well, sir, it might not have been from our office," Jack pressed.

"Oh, just get a proper job will you," the voice rasped.

There was a click as the phone was hung up.

Jack sighed, sat back from his desk slightly and hit one

of the keys on his laptop. It brought up a visual that consisted of reasons for the termination of the call. These included 'not interested' (the most common reply), 'renting or council' (you couldn't sell loft insulation to tenants) 'too old' (you also couldn't sell it to anyone over eighty-five) and 'TPS' (this was the Telephone Preference Service that some people used). It was supposed to shield them from nuisance calls but Warmer Homes seemed to have found a way around it.

Jack took the next call. It was just dead air. The next was just a voice that said "yes" and then hung up. He waited for the next, glancing around the office at his companions.

Most of them were in their late teens or early twenties. Desperate for work, unable to hold down a job requiring more intelligence or discipline or trying to accumulate enough cash to pay for either their next tattoo, piercing or night out on the booze. There wasn't much in the way of ambition in the office or its denizens. Jack sometimes felt ashamed that he was a part of it. But what the hell. Work was work, wasn't it? Even if it made cleaning toilets look like brain surgery.

He took a sip of his drink then glanced at the screen again as the next call was connected.

"Hello, is that Mr Phillips?" Jack said, cheerily.

There was no reply. He logged it as 'dead air.'

The next call came almost immediately.

"Hello, am I speaking to Mr or Mrs Bennett?" Jack enquired.

"Yes," the voice told him, hesitantly. "Who is this?"

"My name's Eric," he said. "I just wondered if you remembered when the insulation was put in your loft. Was it five years ago or is it newly installed?"

"It's more than five years," the woman on the end of the line told him.

Jack sat forward in his seat. "Ah, well, if it's old

insulation then it might contain too much fibreglass," Jack went on, warming to his subject. "But we've got surveyors in the area doing complimentary checks, just to make sure everything is up to standard and installed correctly, and if you're under eighty-five and a homeowner you're eligible for one of these free checks. I don't know if you come into that category at all, Mrs Bennett."

There was silence on the other end of the line.

"Mrs Bennet," Jack persisted. "Do you come into that category? If you do, you–"

"I'm eighty-six," the woman told him.

"Ah," Jack sighed.

That was the only problem with harassing vulnerable pensioners, he thought, many of them didn't actually qualify for a surveyor's check because of their age. Jack raised his eyebrows. *Surveyors*. They were actually con artists and cheap salesmen who only used the pretext of the inspection to get inside the old people's houses so they could pressure them into buying loft insulation.

"I'm afraid we can't offer you the check then," Jack sighed. "Thanks for your time."

He terminated the call and shook his head irritably, entering the call as 'too old.'

The next call came immediately.

"Hello, is that Mr Collins?" Jack asked, stifling a yawn. Silence.

"Hello," Jack persisted.

He was about to terminate the call and log it as 'no answer' when a low voice at the other end of the line murmured:

"Help me."

Jack frowned, rolled his eyes and spoke.

"Hello, is that Mr Collins?" he enquired.

"Please help me," the voice repeated. "Please."

There was a sudden, deafening scream then a sound

that Jack could only describe as inhuman. The line went dead.

"Jesus," he gasped, his heart thudding hard against his ribs. He pulled off his headset and glared at it as if the monstrous sound had been contained in the padding that went over his ears. As he pushed them away his hand was shaking slightly.

"You okay?"

The voice came from beside him.

Jack looked around blankly.

Megan Frost was looking directly at him, smiling. She was younger than Jack and waiting for the results of her exams to see whether she could pursue her hopes of going to university. To say she was more intelligent than the rest of the denizens of the call centre would have been an understatement.

Jack continued to gaze at her then nodded slowly.

"I heard something," he said, pointing at his headset.

"What was it?" Megan wanted to know.

"I don't know," Jack told her.

"Something wrong?"

The new voice belonged to Carl Thompson. He was the office manager. A likeable enough guy in his thirties.

Jack explained what he'd heard through the headset.

"Call them back," Carl advised. "See if the same thing happens again."

Jack hesitated then nodded. "I don't suppose you want to do it?" he said to Carl.

Carl smiled. He took Jack's headset from him and slipped it on, then he hit the 'dial now' button on the screen. And waited.

Jack watched him but, finally, Carl merely shook his head.

"No answer," he said, handing the headset back to Jack. "Right everyone," Carl called, addressing the whole office. "Let's really smash this out. Come on, people we've got ten more leads to get. Let's do this before break time."

Jack gazed at his screen for a moment longer then hit the button that would connect him with another call.

"Hello, is that Mr Porter?" he said, his mind elsewhere.

"What?" the voice snapped.

"Is that Mr Porter?" Jack repeated.

"Oh, get lost," the voice hissed and slammed the phone down. Jack shook his head and prepared to take the next call.

"Hello, is that Mr Peterson?" he said, clearing his throat. "Hello. Hello."

The address showing on his screen made Jack frown. It was a local one. The dialler that had been calling numbers for them all day had been focussed on some part of Wales. This number was showing as a location less than ten miles away. Jack sat forward slightly.

"Hello," he said.

The sound that filled his ears was enough to freeze the blood in his veins.

"Jesus," Jack snapped, swallowing hard.

There was a scream either of fear or pain, Jack couldn't decide. Then what sounded like deep, guttural breathing.

"Help me," a voice shrieked.

Silence.

Jack grabbed for his notepad and scribbled down the address that was showing on his screen. He had barely finished transcribing it when it vanished from the monitor. He let out a deep breath and stroked his chin thoughtfully, his hand shaking slightly.

It was less than an hour until his shift finished and Jack glanced distractedly at his watch and the clock at the bottom of the computer screen repeatedly as the time passed. When the time came he got to his feet and hurried out of the office, heading down to his car. He glanced at the piece of paper where he'd scribbled the location of the last call and drove off.

It took him less than twenty minutes to reach the location.

Jack sat back in his seat, his eyes scanning the area before him.

It was a field. Flanked on both sides by trees, protected by a rotting wooden fence. What had once been a road or dirt track cut through the overgrown grass and weeds but, in most places, it had been obscured by the creeping vegetation. Recent rain had left several deep, dark puddles in the walkway. At the end of it, partially obscured by trees and bushes, Jack could see the outline of brick walls, now broken and crumbling.

How the hell could a call have come from this location?

Jack climbed out of his car and walked to the wooden fence that formed a perimeter around the field and its contents. The wood was covered in green mould in places. In others it was broken and barely serviceable as a barrier. He swung himself over part of it and set off up the partially hidden dirt track towards the ruins of the building.

He was about a hundred yards from it when his phone rang.

He glanced at it and recognised the number. Smiling he pressed it to his ear.

"Hello, you," he said, smiling, stepping over a puddle.

"Where are you?" Claire Renton asked. "I'm doing a roast tonight."

Jack smiled.

"I won't be long," he told his fiancée. "Do you want me to pick anything up?"

"No. Just don't be too long, I don't want the dinner to spoil," she told him.

As he walked he chatted happily to Claire until she told him she could smell burning and had to rush off. Jack was still smiling when he slid his phone back into his pocket.

He was close to the ruined building now and he could see that much of the roof had collapsed. Bare beams, rotten with age and damp, were exposed like huge wooden ribs poking from a barely hidden corpse. There was still some glass in a few of the windows but most had been shattered during the years of neglect. There were stones, empty bottles, squashed cans and some tree branches scattered across the floor of the dilapidated building.

Jack walked slowly around it then finally turned and headed back towards his car.

High above him, the banks of thick cloud promised more rain and the evening was approaching fast. He felt the need to be away from this place before it was dark. He didn't know why but it suddenly seemed imperative.

The hair on the back of his neck rose inexplicably. He increased his pace, breaking into a run, anxious to be away from this place even though he had no idea why.

He heard movement behind him and spun around.

Close to the ruined building the high grass was waving and it wasn't just the wind disturbing it, Jack was sure of that. He stood motionless for a moment longer, eyes scanning the overgrown area before him.

Sure enough, a dark shape moved into view, escaping the confines of the high grass and edging onto the dirt track.

It was a rabbit.

Jack sighed, smiled and watched as it hopped unhurriedly across the pathway and into the high grass on the other side.

He set off back to his car, looking up at the sky accusingly as the first spots of rain began to fall.

It poured for most of the night and was still drizzling when Jack set off for work the next day. He parked in the usual place (he was one of the few in the office who actually drove).

The morning passed with the usual brain-numbing banality. Calls were made and taken, Jack noting addresses with a little more intent than normal. He had lunch, read some of his book then returned to his desk for an afternoon of predictable tedium.

When the address from the previous day, the address he knew was an overgrown field and ruined building, popped up on his screen, Jack sat forward on his chair.

"Hello," he said, his voice catching a little.

There was no answer. No sound on the other end of the line.

"Hello," Jack repeated.

Still nothing. The line went dead. It rang again almost immediately and he looked at his screen, checking the location.

"Hello," he said, again noting that the screen was not displaying a name.

There was a low rasping sound, almost a growl. Then a scream.

The breath caught in his throat.

The address showing on the screen looked familiar.

There was another scream then a sound that reminded him of whimpering. It was rapidly drowned out by another animalistic roar.

Jack was about to say something when the office door was flung open.

Leon blundered in, looking around contemptuously at his staff, his brow furrowing more deeply than usual. He crossed to Jack's desk and looked down at him. Jack shot his boss a quick glance thinking, as he had done on other occasions, that the other man resembled a gorilla that someone had shaved and then clothed.

"What are you doing?" Leon grunted. "You better get some leads. You've only got two leads all day. That's not good enough. You need to get more."

Jack sucked in a breath, his eyes still on the screen and the location it was showing.

"Are you listening?" Leon persisted. "I said you better get more leads."

"I'm on a call," Jack told him, not taking his eyes off the screen and motioning to his headset with one index finger.

"Well, you better get a lead out of it," his boss continued. "I'm not paying people to just sit here all day. If you need help, ask. Ask the people around you. You're a team, a family. Ask for help."

Resisting the temptation to tell his boss to fuck off, Jack winced again when another loud scream drummed in his ears.

He pointed to the screen.

Leon peered myopically at it.

"This call is coming from inside this building," Jack told him. "Look at the address that's on the display."

"That's impossible," Leon grunted, sneeringly.

"Look at it," Jack snapped, tapping the screen with his index finger.

Leon leaned closer and saw that the address showing on the screen was indeed the same address as that of the call centre.

"I heard someone scream," Jack told him.

"No way," Leon said. "You need to concentrate on your work more. That's not good enough. You need to get leads and—"

"Listen," Jack hissed, cutting across him, pulling off his headset and pushing it towards his boss who snatched it from him and slid it onto his ears, barely able to fit the device over his large head.

"That's impossible," Leon grunted. "The only people in the hotel are on the same floor as us."

"What about the rooms upstairs?" Jack asked.

"There's no one in those offices," he was told. He

reacted as he heard something loud through the earpieces.

"You heard it too, didn't you?" Jack snapped.

Leon tugged off the headset and dropped it on Jack's desk.

"I'm going to find out what this is about," he said and sloped off towards the office door, pausing briefly to say something unintelligible to the office manager who was gazing at his own screen.

When Jack put his headset back on he could hear that horribly familiar breathing once again, seeping through the earpieces like smoke through a grate.

Carl sidled over to join him, glancing at the screen.

"What's happening?" he wanted to know. "Leon said he's going upstairs to check out the empty offices. He said he'll be back in about ten minutes."

Jack explained about the noises. The screams. The breathing. And the location of them being right here in the hotel.

"That's impossible," Carl told him. "The dialler is set for South Wales. It wouldn't call a number here."

Jack merely shrugged.

"Maybe you'd better go and help Leon look then," he exclaimed. "See what he finds."

Carl shrugged and then merely retreated to his seat at the head of the room. Ten minutes passed. Then more. It was over an hour before Carl again got to his feet, wandering around the room with his hands dug deep in his pockets. When he finally reached Jack's part of the room, Jack raised a hand to attract his attention.

"Is Leon back yet?" Jack asked.

Carl shook his head.

"Perhaps he found something up there," Jack said, smiling.

Carl glanced at his watch but didn't speak. He retreated to his chair once more but this time he took to rocking gently back and forth in it. Another thirty minutes passed before he walked back to where Jack was sitting.

"I'm going to look for him," Carl said. "Want to come with me?"

"I couldn't give a fuck if he ever comes back, to be honest," Jack exclaimed.

"He's not answering his phone either," Carl went on.

Jack merely raised his eyebrows.

"You don't like Leon, do you?" Carl said, smiling.

"I think he's a cunt," Jack breathed. "I know he's a mate of yours but that's how I feel."

"He can be a bit much at times," Carl confessed.

"A bit much? Where did he learn his employer/employee skills? In a concentration camp?"

Carl looked a little vague but motioned again for Jack to join him and the two of them headed out of the office and down the short corridor that led away from it.

It opened out into a large seated area and then contracted once again into a corridor as a set of double doors were negotiated. In this next corridor was a lift and a doorway leading to some fire stairs. The two men decided to take the lift up to the next floor and they both stepped in when it arrived.

"He can't have got lost," Jack observed. "I know he's a dumb fuck but even Leon couldn't get lost just going up to the next floor."

Carl said nothing but stepped out ahead of Jack when the lift bumped to a halt at the next level. They both stood beside the doors as they slid shut, glancing around at the area they'd entered.

"I've never been up here before," Jack said, looking around.

The area was dimly lit, the walls decorated in dark blue and purple making the whole hub of corridors seem gloomy. Wall lights appeared to be operating at less than full power because the glow they were giving off was more sickly yellow than bright white.

"Who works up here?" Jack wanted to know as they headed towards a set of fire doors.

"No one," Carl told him. "It used to be used for guests when the hotel was busy but I don't think anybody's been up here for over a year."

"I can see why," Jack murmured.

As he reached out to touch the door he recoiled slightly. The metal felt sticky. Jack rubbed his hands together, preferring not to know what had caused the tackiness on the door.

Through the open doors lay another corridor. This one was almost in darkness.

Only two or three wall lights burned, creating little puddles of illumination around them doing little to light the narrow walkway. There were doors on both sides of the corridor and, as he touched the nearest of them, Jack again felt that stickiness. He drew a finger through it and inspected the tip of the digit. Whatever it was, it was clear but it created thin membranous strands when Jack pressed another finger to it then pulled them gently apart.

This time Jack wiped his hands on his handkerchief, disgusted by the feel of the material.

Carl pushed the door nearest to him but it was locked. So was the next one. And the one after that.

They moved further along the corridor, testing each door, one of them on each side of the narrow walkway.

It was the very last door that finally opened slightly when Carl turned the handle.

He hesitated for a moment then stepped across the threshold, slapping on the lights in the process. Jack watched him for a moment then joined him inside the room.

It was empty.

Nothing but the bed and sparse pieces of furniture

that featured in each of the hotel's rooms.

"Why do they still keep stuff in the rooms?" Jack murmured, looking around. Everything in the bedroom was covered by a thin patina of dust. He trailed one finger through the layer on the top of the nearby chest of drawers.

"Maybe they'll reopen one day," Carl suggested, also looking around. "I stayed here once. I got pissed one night and booked a room." He laughed but the sound was hollow and humourless. Jack merely raised an eyebrow by way of acknowledgement.

"Are there more rooms up here?" he asked.

"Not bedrooms," Carl informed him. "Conference rooms."

They retreated out of the bedroom and back into the corridor.

"This is crazy," Jack murmured. "If he was up here he'd have heard us. He'd have been here by now."

"So where the fuck did he go?"

Jack shrugged.

"You go back to work," Carl said, finally. "I'll keep looking for him."

Jack nodded and turned back in the direction of the lifts. He was quite happy to let Carl continue with the search. Whether he found Leon or not was of no interest at all to Jack. He headed back down to the call centre and took his seat once again, ignoring the puzzled looks of his companions.

An hour later Carl hadn't returned either.

Jack felt unaccountably anxious. He wondered if this was all some ridiculous joke but then remembered that Leon didn't have a sense of humour. Jack found himself glancing towards the door every time it opened.

He was still wondering what was happening when his next call was connected.

There was a crackle of static then a deeper, more liquid

sound, like someone sucking in breath through a mouthful of phlegm.

"Hello," Jack murmured, noticing there was nothing displayed on his screen.

Silence.

"Hello," he said again a little more loudly.

At the other end of the line he hard guttural breathing. Then what sounded like whimpering. Jack tapped his headset.

"Hello," he said a little more forcefully.

"Jack, help me."

He recognised the voice immediately and his whole body felt as if it had been injected with ice water.

The voice on the other end of the line was Claire Renton.

"Jack, please," she sobbed. "Help me."

"Claire?" he gasped. "Claire."

There was a loud roar from the other end of the line then he heard Claire again.

"Please help me," she said, her voice choked with tears. "Come now." There was a growing note of hysteria in her tone now. "Now." The last word was screamed. "I'm at home. I'm—"

The line went dead.

Jack tore off his headset and ran for the door, his face set in hard lines, his heart thudding madly against his ribs.

He ran from the room, down the corridors to the stairs and out into the car park where he clambered into his car and guided it out onto the road, pressing down hard on the accelerator. It shouldn't take him long to get to Claire's. What he would find when he got there he tried not to imagine. When he tried to swallow his throat was dry.

He drove fast. He drove recklessly. More than once he considered trying to ring her but decided against it. The most important thing was getting to the house.

He turned the wheel sharply as he reached the turning he sought, narrowly avoiding a woman who was crossing. She shouted something angrily at him but Jack didn't hear it. He sped down the street, finally hitting the brake hard to bring the car to a halt, leaping out from behind the wheel.

Jack ran up to the front door and banged several times on it.

When there was no answer he rushed across to the metal gate that separated the front garden from the narrow path that led to the rear of the house. Tugging it open, Jack ran through, trying to glance through the nearest window.

He could see only darkness inside the house and realised that the curtains there were drawn.

He fumbled for his phone and called Claire's number, waiting anxiously.

When there was no answer he banged furiously on the back door. Only silence greeted his efforts.

He heard movement to his right and turned to see the old man who lived next door peering over the hedge quizzically.

"Can I help you?" he asked.

"I'm Claire's boyfriend," Jack blurted.

"I know who you are," the older man interrupted.

"I need to see her," Jack went on. "She's not answering her phone and I can't make her hear."

"She went out earlier," the older man told him. "Just before you got here."

"Where?"

"How do I know?"

"Was she on her own?"

The old man merely shrugged.

"You saw her go out," Jack snapped. "You must have seen if she was on her own or not."

Again the older man only shook his head, looking Jack

up and down appraisingly.

Jack spun around and headed back to his car, slipping behind the wheel. He started the engine but reached for his phone, finding Claire's number. He switched to speaker phone and drove off, listening to the dial tone then the constant ringing.

He didn't know where the hell he was going. He didn't know where *she* might have gone. Her best friend lived on the next estate, he decided to try there first.

On the passenger seat, the phone continued to ring.

Jack drove on.

As he rounded a corner onto a road with deserted properties on either side the phone was finally answered.

"Claire?" he gasped.

"Hello," the voice at the other end said.

"Claire?" Jack murmured but he knew that the voice belonged to a man. It sounded familiar.

"Hello, can I help you?" the voice said.

The voice that sounded identical to his own.

Jack swallowed hard.

"Is that Mr Farley?" the voice asked.

Jack sucked in a breath.

"Is that Jack Farley?" the voice went on. *His* voice.

"Who are you?" Jack demanded.

"I want to speak to Jack Farley," the voice went on.

"Where's Claire?" Jack snapped.

"I don't know. I wanted to speak to Jack," the voice insisted.

"I'm Jack," he shouted.

"So am I," the voice told him, chuckling.

Jack looked down at the phone, ready to say something else. Ready to vent his rage and frustration.

That simple glance was enough to take his attention away from the road for a split second. Long enough for him to miss the cat dashing in front of him.

Jack twisted the wheel savagely, the car going out of

control. He had time to shout something unintelligible before he sped towards the brick wall. The car slammed into it, demolished part of it and flipped onto its side. The impact was enough to send the steering column slamming back into Jack's chest, crushing his sternum. Blood burst into his mouth and poured over his lips, his head snapping forward to connect hard with the dashboard. The impact knocked him unconscious, which was just as well because as the car exploded he didn't feel the flames licking around him.

Neither did he hear the voice on the melting phone:

"Jack Farley? I want to speak to Jack Farley."

And then, there was only silence.

THE NEW NEIGHBOURS

The SOLD sign stood outside the house proudly.

Orange and black with the name of the estate agent in the middle of it, it reminded Danielle Ridley of some kind of beacon. A reminder to everyone in the neighbourhood that they were going to have new faces among them.

She felt a little bit guilty about peering through her net curtains at the house across the street like some ageing busybody. Dani wasn't ageing (she was in her early thirties) and she certainly didn't consider herself as a busybody. She was just curious.

Curious. Nosey. It amounted to the same thing, it just depended on your point of view.

"And you still haven't seen them?"

She turned in the direction of the voice that came from behind her.

Gina Bates put down her tea and joined Dani at the window. She was a couple of years younger but the two women could have passed for sisters such was the similarity.

"They always arrive about midnight, they stay for an hour or two then they go," Dani said, peering at the house opposite. "I couldn't see them because the street lights were out."

"Tell me about it," Gina sighed. "I've e-mailed the council about that. They're always out. There's going to be an accident."

"I mean, who views a house in the middle of the night?" Dani mused.

"Perhaps they both work?" Gina offered.

"They probably do if they can afford a place like that, but why only come in the dead of night?"

"Maybe they're vampires," Gina chuckled. "Or they just like their privacy. Perhaps they're celebrities or something like that and they don't want anyone to know they're moving in." She sounded quite excited at the prospect. "Did you see them leave?"

"I told you, I couldn't see anything because it was dark but they've been coming backwards and forwards to the house for weeks now and no one's seen them or spoken to them because they always come at night." Dani finally moved away from the window and seated herself next to her friend on the large sofa. "No one saw the previous owners move out either. How do you move house without a removal van?"

"Even Julie hasn't seen anything and she lives right next door," Gina murmured. "I told Paul but he just said I was a nosey cow and I should mind my own business." She chuckled.

"Marcus would have been the same with me," Dani said and her expression darkened. She suddenly looked very sad, as if even the mention of her dead husband had caused a wave of gloom to descend upon her. She lowered her gaze slightly and Gina wasn't slow to pick up the mood change. She slipped an arm around her friend's shoulder.

"Are you okay?" she murmured.

Dani nodded. "Sometimes it just hits me harder that he's dead," she said, softly. "It's been nearly two years, I suppose I should be over it by now."

"Don't be silly," Gina told her. "No one expects you to just forget about him or what happened. It's going to take time. You always knew that."

The two of them sat in silence for a moment, sipping tea, then Gina spoke again.

"Maybe when the people across the street move in it'll

give you something else to think about," she said.

Dani smiled.

"I hope so," she said.

The day passed slowly as it always seemed to now. After Gina left Dani worked for five hours straight up in her 'home office'. It was only a bedroom with a desk and some filing cabinets in it but it made her feel more officious and it seemed to focus her on the task of designing. She'd been a freelance designer for about six years now and work, fortunately for her, came in regularly enough to keep her occupied. She'd been particularly grateful for that fact in the months following her husband's death. The mortgage had been paid off by the various policies he'd had but Dani had found she'd needed to lose herself in something and the work had been a welcome respite from her grief. It hadn't removed it but it had masked it. The more time she spent with her mind occupied the better.

Now, as she finished the last of the red wine, she glanced blankly at the TV screen and then at her watch. Almost midnight. It was time for bed, she decided.

She moved around the room switching off lights and appliances. Only as she neared the bay window did she catch sight of movement out on the street. Or, more to the point, *across* the street. Her own sitting room was in darkness so Dani knew that she could watch without fear of being seen. She squinted through the gloom, fixing her gaze on the two shapes that moved from a car towards the front door of the house across the street.

The new neighbours. Back again, she thought.

As she watched she saw two more shapes scramble from the car, much smaller and unmistakeably children from their size and stature. They could, Dani guessed, be no more than four or five, maybe even younger. She watched as they scurried across to the front door then disappeared inside. The door closed.

Dani reached for her phone, found the number she sought and tapped out a message. It read:

NEW NEIGHBOURS HERE AGAIN.

Dani waited a moment, hoping the reply would be instantaneous but then remembered that the recipient might be asleep in bed. She glanced at the house opposite once more finally hearing the electronic ping as a message arrived.

NO ONE HERE.

Dani looked at the message that had come back from Julie Craig in puzzlement. She hurriedly sent another:

I CAN SEE THEM.

Julie returned another message moments later:

WHAT ARE YOU TALKING ABOUT?

Dani sent another text that read:

LOOK OUT OF YOUR WINDOW!

But Julie's only reply was:

NO ONE THERE.

Dani frowned, her gaze now fixed on the house opposite. She was still standing there fifty minutes later when the car she had seen pull up drove away.

***

The cafe was relatively quiet.

Staff bustled around cleaning tables and re-filling shelves and counters, but apart from that Dani and Gina were the only customers apart from an elderly couple who were sitting at a window table with their weekly shopping around them.

Dani sipped her coffee, her brow furrowed.

"I don't know what her problem is," she grunted.

"You know Julie," Gina offered. "She sometimes puts her mouth in gear before her brain's engaged."

"She almost accused me of being alcoholic," Dani snapped.

"What exactly did she say?" Gina enquired.

"I called her this morning to talk about what happened last night, you know, the people across the street arriving to look at the house and she practically accused me of being drunk when I texted her last night."

"Because she hadn't seen them arrive?"

"She couldn't have missed them, Gina. They had their kids with them. Julie must have seen something."

"What else did she say?"

"She said she understood I'd had a few problems and that I should stay off the booze. That was when I hung up. Bitch."

"You were drinking a lot."

"I know but I don't drink that much now. She didn't have to accuse me."

"Do you want me to have a word with her?"

"And make her think I came running to you like some helpless little kid? No thanks."

The two women sat in silence for a moment then Gina reached forward and gently touched one of Dani's earrings with her index finger. "They're lovely," she observed.

"Marcus bought them for me," Dani told her. "For our first wedding anniversary." She sipped more of her coffee then put the mug down a little too heavily causing the older couple in the window to look around. "Julie can say what she likes. I don't care. She was right, though. I did have problems with drink after Marcus died."

"How big a problem?"

"A bottle of wine a night. Sometimes more."

"You should have said something."

"I had to deal with it myself. Sometimes no matter who you talk to, it doesn't help. The only thing that seemed to help was the booze." She sighed. "Like I said, I had to deal with it. I'm *still* dealing with it."

They spent another half an hour in the coffee shop

before Dani decided to make her way home.

It was a short drive from the town centre and she turned her CD player up as loud as she could stand as she drove, eighties rock music thundering out from the speakers (another legacy of her marriage). As she drew closer to her own home she eased the volume to more manageable levels and glanced at the properties on either side of her, finally looking at the house opposite.

There was a white car parked in the small driveway and Dani could see the estate agent's name and logo emblazoned on the side of the vehicle.

She parked her own car then walked briskly across the street towards the house opposite, moving towards the front door when she saw no one sitting in the white car.

Perhaps the estate agent was inside even now, she thought. Perhaps the new buyers were with him. If so then she could meet them. Or, if they weren't around, maybe she could find out some information about them.

Dani knocked lightly on the front door, surprised when it opened slightly.

She pushed the wooden partition gently with one index finger and it opened further.

She poked her head into the hallway and then stepped inside, looking around, her ears alert for any sounds or movements within the building.

It was silent.

Dani stepped further into the house, finally moving past the bottom of the wide staircase towards the nearest room.

She pushed the door open and peered into what she assumed was the sitting room. There wasn't a stick of furniture inside. No carpets and no curtains either. The room was bare. So too was the kitchen which she moved to next. No reminders of the last householders and no clues to the identity of the new ones. What she did see however puzzled her.

There was a secondary door between the hall and the kitchen that reminded her of a castle drawbridge.

It was metal (and new too by the look of it) and resembled long steel struts joined at the top, bottom and middle by cross pieces of thicker metal which seemed to hold it together.

She closed her fingers around the downward-facing slats wondering what the hell the door was for and who would want it in a beautiful new abode like this.

She was still wondering when she heard creaking and realised that it was coming from above her. It seemed that there was someone inside the house and, as she made her way back into the hallway, she saw a figure descending the stairs.

The estate agent was in his early thirties and he looked quizzically at her as he drew closer.

"Can I help you?" he asked, sharply.

"I noticed that someone was here," Dani explained. "I thought I'd just pop in and say hello."

"To who?"

"The people who've bought the house."

"They're not here, and you shouldn't be in here anyway. This is private property."

"I know that. I was just trying to be friendly. This is a close-knit community and I thought I'd just welcome them. Who are they, anyway?"

"That's really none of your business." He was already ushering her towards the door, almost pushing her in his haste to get her out of the building.

"You don't have to do that," she snapped. "I'm going."

"They won't be happy if they know you've been in here," the estate agent assured her. "Now get out."

As they reached the door he pulled it open and almost shoved Dani across the threshold. The movement caused one of her earrings to come loose and it fell to the floor just inside the house.

She was about to protest when the estate agent slammed the door behind her, shutting out her calls.

He retreated back upstairs, ignoring her shouts and banging on the door, watching as she finally retreated across the street to her own house. Only when she'd gone inside did he reach for his phone. His hand was shaking as he found the number he sought.

***

Dani awoke with a start.

As she woke she knocked over the bottle of wine on the table next to her, some of the contents spilling across the polished surface. She muttered under her breath and hurried off to the kitchen to get a cloth, wiping up the mess she'd made. As she returned to the sitting room again after getting rid of the cloth she moved across to the window and looked out.

Just go to bed.

She sighed, annoyed at herself for what was rapidly turning into an obsession about the house across the street and the new residents.

Does it matter who they are?

Dani continued gazing at the house opposite, her mind turning the questions over and over as she stood there.

It's none of your business.

Almost unconsciously she reached up and touched her left earlobe, and as she did she remembered her lost earring.

Lost inside the house opposite.

She wondered again why the estate agent had been so anxious, so aggressive in his efforts to get her out of the house. What was he hiding?

Probably nothing. It's just your imagination working overtime.

She touched her ear again, remembering how much those earrings meant to her. She wasn't going to give one of them up so easily. Who the hell did that estate agent think he was, anyway? Her questions had been harmless enough and he'd caused her to lose a piece of personal property. She wanted it back.

Dani pulled on a pair of trainers, retrieved a torch from the kitchen and set off out of the house and across the street towards the house opposite.

The street was quiet at this time of night. Almost oppressively silent, in fact. She heard the occasional barking of a dog coming from somewhere in the distance, but other than that there didn't seem to be any noises at all. Lights were out in most of the other houses nearby indicating that the residents were already in bed and Dani was beginning to wonder if she might not be better off tucked up under her duvet rather than trekking across to the other house in what was probably going to be a vain attempt to retrieve her earring.

After all, she thought, as she walked up the driveway towards the building, how was she going to get in? They wouldn't have left the doors unlocked and cat burglary wasn't prominent on her list of skills. There was an ornate metal gate leading to a path that ran along the side of the building and Dani made for that, reasoning that she would be less visible at the rear of the house than the front. The gate was unlocked and she moved briskly towards the back garden where she carefully tried the back door.

Not surprisingly, it was locked.

You mean they didn't leave it open so you could walk straight in? How inconsiderate.

There was a small shed about halfway down the garden and Dani moved towards it, hurrying across the wide-open lawn. She pulled gently at the shed door, delighted when it opened. She peered inside and saw an array of garden implements and tools hanging from a rack on the far wall, illuminated by the torch light as she shone it inside the small structure.

Dani turned and headed back towards the house then, using the thick base of the torch, she broke a window, knocking away enough glass to enable her to reach through the gap and flip the handle there. The window opened easily and Dani smiled, relieved that there was no alarm when she pushed the window further open.

What the hell are you doing? Breaking into a house just to get an earring back?

Dani hesitated a moment, hoping no one had heard her, then she pulled herself up and over the windowsill, sliding across the worktop beyond until she was inside the kitchen.

Happy now? Now you're a burglar.

She looked around in the gloom, getting her bearings, then she hurried out into the hallway and across to the front door where she was sure she'd lost her earring. She shone the torch around briefly and the beam caught something glinting on the far side of the vestibule.

The earring was still lying there, close to a corner and forgotten, but she smiled and snatched it up, pushing it into the pocket of her jeans.

Right, you've got what you came for. Now get out.

Dani hesitated, her gaze drawn to the wide staircase. She knew she should get out but her curiosity was now out of control. Here inside the house with no one to disturb her, she could take the chance to have a good look around.

For what? What the hell are you expecting to find, anyway?

She climbed the stairs quickly and quietly and made her way to the nearest door that led off from the landing.

Like every other room in the house she'd seen so far it was empty. Nothing to presage the arrival of the new tenants and nothing to show that anyone had ever lived there before. Even the floor was nothing more than bare wood. She moved to the next two rooms and found them in exactly the same condition.

She checked the bathroom too and moved towards the rear of the building.

Consequently, she didn't see the car pull up in the driveway.

Didn't see the two figures clamber out and head towards the front door.

Dani pushed open another door and looked in, surprised to see that there were thick metal bars on the windows. She stepped into the room and crossed to the sturdy looking restraints. She closed her fingers around the cold steel then backed away slightly.

What were they for?

She was still turning that question over in her mind when she heard the key in the front door.

Dani gasped, realising that someone was entering the house.

She moved out onto the landing, peering down into the darkness of the hallway, watching as the front door opened. Two figures walked in, a man and a woman. They were followed by two smaller individuals. Children. No older than three or four. They bounded in excitedly, hurrying across the wide hallway before being rebuked by their parents who told them not to run.

Dani moved cautiously back into the room from which she'd come, wishing there was somewhere to hide, hoping that the visitors would be quick so she could merely sneak out again.

And what about the broken kitchen window? As soon as they find that they'll call the police.

Dani looked around and noticed that there were large built-in wardrobes running the length of the far wall. She moved across to them, pulled a door open and slipped inside. If she could remain hidden until the people left the house then no one need ever know she was here.

As she eased the wardrobe door shut she heard

footfalls on the steps and realised that someone was coming up the stairs.

The slatted doors of the wardrobe enabled her to see out but she hoped that they didn't also give her presence away but, she reasoned, who would be looking for her? Who would be expecting her to be hiding there? She swallowed hard and waited as the footsteps drew closer.

It was one of the smaller figures that moved into the bedroom first.

A little girl, Dani thought as the individual ran into the room followed by her father. He was a tall, slightly built man who seemed to be wearing a suit but it was difficult to make out details in the gloom and from her restricted viewpoint. When she saw them both turn back towards the door, Dani thought she might actually get away with what she was doing. However, the child suddenly turned and stood motionless in the doorway, face turned towards the far wall.

Dani felt her heart beating faster and she tried to control her breathing, aware that the child was now walking slowly towards the wardrobe where she was hiding.

She tried to press herself further back into the gloom within the cabinet.

Dani heard the child sniffing loudly. As if she was picking up a scent.

Her scent.

The door was wrenched open and Dani screamed.

She was about to say something as she stumbled from the confines of the wardrobe but before she could speak she felt a crashing impact on the side of her head and she dropped like a stone.

Dani had no idea how long she was unconscious for, but when she finally woke she was in a different room. A smaller one. One that had bars at both windows and also at the door. One that was pitch black apart from the tiny sliver of natural light creeping in from outside through a crack in the curtains.

Dani felt bare floor beneath her fingertips as she sat up, her back against one wall.

"Why did you come here?"

The voice was close to her but she couldn't see its source in the gloom.

"Why can't you just leave us alone?"

"Please let me out," Dani said. "I'll call the police if you don't."

The figure laughed and held up one hand. Dani could see that hand was grasping her mobile phone.

"Call them with what?" the figure chided. "With this? Besides, you're the one who broke in here. You're the one who damaged our property. You're the criminal."

"If you let me go I'll just go home. I won't report you."

The figure chuckled.

"*You* won't report *us*," it repeated, mockingly.

"Please, just let me go," Dani persisted.

"People always have to interfere. We only want to be left alone to live our lives." These words came from a second figure. A woman who had joined the other and was standing beside him just beyond the metal doorway that ensured Dani was imprisoned in the room. "They can't help the way they are."

"Who?" Dani asked.

"Our children," the second figure murmured. "Don't you think we'd help them if we could?"

Two smaller shapes now joined the others and Dani squinted in the gloom to see that the children were standing between their parents. She could also see that their faces were obscured by what appeared to be plain white masks. They covered the children's heads from neck to scalp, obscuring their features and only their eyes were visible through the holes in the front of the mask.

"It's a degenerative disease," the first figure told her.

"It affects the skin, the muscles." He sighed. "It wouldn't bother us but people can be so cruel. And it isn't as if they've done anything to deserve the way they look."

As he spoke, the figure gently pulled the masks from the two children, exposing the features beneath.

Dani swayed and, for a second, thought she was going to faint.

She didn't know whether to scream or vomit.

It was difficult to tell which parts of the children's faces were the worst. They seemed to be covered in growths and tumours, some of which had grown over the eyes or, in the boy's case, over the upper lip creating a protuberance that hung down an inch or two like the beginning of a trunk. The girl's skin was also covered by gleaming pustules, one of which was dripping yellowish liquid even as Dani watched.

The rest of their bodies seemed to be normal enough. It was as if someone had placed the most vile, twisted and monstrous visages on the shoulders of two perfect specimens just to emphasise the horrific contrast.

Dani felt her stomach contract as they moved closer to her.

"The condition can be arrested but not halted completely," the second figure said, gently opening the door and ushering the children towards Dani.

"And you can help with that," the first figure added.

Dani shook her head, watching as the children advanced upon her.

"We've found that when they eat human flesh it helps them," the second figure announced, smiling.

Dani gasped and continued to back off.

"We don't know why it helps but it does and that's all that matters," the first figure added, warmly.

"We have to do our best for them," the second figure intoned. "I'm sure you agree. Children are so important. They're the future."

Dani couldn't back up any further, she was standing against the wall now, the small figures still advancing.

And then, they were upon her.

PORTENTS

Donald Cranston thought he was dead.

He could hear voices whispering around him, figures bending over him. For a moment he thought it was the angels welcoming him into heaven. Especially when he saw one of the most beautiful faces he'd ever seen in his forty-three years of life. Beatific was the only word he could think of to describe her. Her skin was flawless, her eyes large and bright blue and the smile that she wore was perfection itself.

Only as Donald blinked a little harder did he realise she was also wearing a nurse's uniform.

It was around that time that he also caught sight of the tall, dark-haired doctor standing next to her also looking down at him, but with a far more quizzical eye.

Donald was delighted to realise that he wasn't in fact dead but in his hospital bed inside his private room. The effects of the anaesthetic would take a while to wear off, and he was enjoying this state of euphoria if he was honest. He felt as if he were floating. It was a wonderful feeling and, although he'd never done any kind of drugs in his life, Donald imagined that this must be the kind of effect they gave to their users. He smiled up at the medical staff around him and tried to sit up but the tall, dark-haired man restrained him, easing him back onto the pillows that were propped up behind him.

Donald put a hand to his throat and felt the heavy bandaging there. He trailed his fingertips over the dressing there, swallowing gently.

"I would ask you how you're feeling, but I know you can't tell me yet," Doctor Wallingham said, smiling.

Donald touched his bandaged throat again.

"You'll be delighted to know that the operation was a complete success," Wallingham went on. "With it being the very first of its kind we were all rather pleased too, as you can imagine."

Donald nodded then reached for the small pad and the pencil on his bedside table. He scribbled something down and held it up so the doctor could read it.

WHEN WILL I BE ABLE TO SPEAK?

"Well, as this operation is the first of its kind I can't give you any hard and fast rules," Wallingham began. "The transplantation of a voice box from one patient to another has never been successfully attempted, let alone completed before, so we're all a little in the dark about a prognosis."

Donald reached for the pad and wrote another short message that he also displayed for the doctor to see.

CAN I TRY NOW?

Wallingham frowned but, encouraged by the look on Donald's face he relented.

"If there's no pain or discomfort and you feel up to it then, by all means," he said, quietly.

Donald nodded and opened his mouth slightly, his lips fluttering. Wallingham watched anxiously, fearing that his patient was trying a little too hard but when he heard the words he relaxed slightly.

"My name is Donald Cranston."

"Any pain?" the doctor asked, but Donald merely shook his head. "You mustn't overdo it," Wallingham insisted.

Donald nodded enthusiastically.

"Count slowly from one to ten," the doctor instructed and Donald did it. Just as he recited his address and several other sentences all without any apparent difficulty or pain.

When he'd finished he was beaming, propped up in

bed like a monarch surveying his domain.

"I know the temptation is to continue," Wallingham said. "But I must stress that you shouldn't overtax yourself. The tone and intonation of your voice will change over the coming days as the voice box settles down and assimilates with your own body, but as long as there's no pain then you'll be fine."

"Is it okay if I speak to the other patients here?" Donald asked, massaging his throat gently.

"Of course it is but, as I just said, don't overdo it. You've made fantastic progress but I don't want you to jeopardise that by trying to do too much too soon."

"Thank you, doctor."

"You can thank me by making a full recovery," Wallingham told him, gently squeezing his shoulder. "Now rest."

Donald watched as the doctor left the room, closing the door behind him. Donald spoke his own name again, smiling happily. The nurse in the room also grinned but reminded him not to over-exert himself.

She re-dressed his throat and gave him his medication and Donald slid further down in the bed, more relaxed than he'd felt for a long time.

"It'll be nice for your family to hear you speak again," the nurse said.

"I think she preferred it when I *couldn't* talk," Donald said, both of them chuckling.

She left him alone in his room and Donald dropped off to sleep quickly and slept for more than ten hours without waking up. When he did wake the sun was pouring through the window of his room and he realised that a new day had dawned. He smiled as if he were greeting an old friend, gently touching his bandaged throat.

He'd dreamed during the night, that much he could remember. Tortured visions of how he had come to be in hospital.

The car crash.

Donald closed his eyes tightly, trying to drive the thoughts and images from his mind.

The other vehicle hurtling out of a side street and straight into his car. The searing pain in his upper body and throat. The taste of blood in his mouth. He grunted loudly and shook his head, looking up when he saw the door open.

The nurse who walked in saw the concern on his face and moved across to him.

"Are you okay?" she wanted to know.

He told her about the nightmare.

"It could be your medication," she announced. "We'll keep an eye on that."

Donald nodded, sitting obediently as she attached the inflatable cuff to his arm preparatory to taking his blood pressure. As she inflated it he looked at her, a chill running up his spine.

"Your daughter," he gasped, grabbing her hand. "Your daughter will die on July the twenty-first."

The nurse looked shocked.

"What are you talking about?" she said, the colour draining from her face.

"Your daughter, Laura, will die in a train crash on July twenty-first. Two days from now."

"How do you know her name?" the nurse said, pulling away from him.

"I don't know," Donald protested.

"Why would you say that?" the nurse went on, spinning around and running for the door.

"Wait, please," Donald called after her. He hauled himself out of bed and hurried after her but by the time he reached the corridor beyond there was no sign of her. He stood motionless for a moment, looking both ways up and down the corridor, his head spinning. What had made him say what he'd said to her? He didn't know her. He didn't know her daughter. He sucked in a deep breath and decided he needed some fresh air.

Donald headed out into the gardens of the clinic, the sun pleasingly warm on his skin. He made his way over the neatly manicured lawns and between the well-tended flower beds, finally spying a wooden bench ahead of him. He moved towards it, not bothered by the fact that someone was already sitting at one end of it.

The other man was in his fifties, his hair greying, his face full and jowly. He was wearing a striped dressing gown over his orange pyjamas and he smiled as Donald sat down beside him.

"Beautiful day," Jack Rollins said.

Donald nodded.

"It's lovely here, isn't it?" Jack went on. "I came here last year for my first operation."

Donald asked what the other man had done and was told he'd had a small tumour removed from his left lung.

"So why are you back again?" Donald asked.

"They thought they'd got it all but it came back," Jack informed him. He pointed at Donald's bandaged throat. "What happened to you?"

Donald told him about the car crash. "They re-built my voice box using tissue from a donor," he went on. "It was a revolutionary process. Never been done before."

Jack nodded. "Well, good luck with that," he said, smiling.

Donald was about to answer when he suddenly began to shake. It was a barely perceptible motion at first but then he felt his breathing becoming faster too. He shivered as if his entire body had suddenly been wrapped in a cold blanket.

"Are you okay?" Jack wanted to know, seeing his new companion's reaction.

Donald put out a hand and gently touched the older

man's arm.

"Your cancer," he said, softly. "They didn't remove it all. It'll come back and it'll spread. To your brain, your liver and your bones. You'll die on March fourteenth next year."

"Who the hell are you?" Jack snapped. "Why are you saying that?"

"I'm telling you what's going to happen. I'm sorry. But there's nothing you can do to stop it." Donald's tone was apologetic.

He watched as Jack got unsteadily to his feet.

"You're sick in the head. Keep away from me," rasped the older man, moving away from the bench.

"I'm sorry. I can't help myself," Donald protested, watching as the other man walked away.

Donald put a hand to his throat then he too got to his feet and hurried back inside the clinic, seeking the sanctuary of his room. He rushed in and shut the door behind him, his breath coming in gasps. He walked across to the mirror and began pulling the bandages around his throat away, opening them until he could see the cuts and incisions on his throat. He peered at the stitches there, his hands shaking as he gently touched them.

"What the hell is going on?"

Donald turned as he heard the voice behind him and he saw doctor Wallingham standing there, his face set in an expression of annoyance. That expression deepened when he saw Donald examining his stitches. "I've got a nurse in tears and another patient in shock because of things you've said to them."

"I didn't say anything," Donald protested.

"You told a nurse her daughter was going to die. You told a patient he had terminal cancer and–"

"I didn't say those things," snapped Donald, cutting across him.

"Then who did?" Wallingham demanded.

"I don't know. I said them but I don't know what they mean. I don't know *why* I said them. You've got to believe me." He sat down on the edge of the bed, his face milk white.

The doctor crossed to him, seeing how bad his distress actually was.

"I had no idea what I was saying," Donald went on, his head bowed. "It was as if the words were put there by someone else." He looked almost imploringly at the doctor, realising how ludicrous his words must sound. "You have to believe me."

Wallingham sucked in a deep breath and was about to speak again when Donald suddenly froze.

"At 1.46 today, an American Airlines plane will crash at Heathrow airport," he said, evenly. "Everyone on board will be killed. Two hundred and thirty-two people will die."

"For God's sake. Why are you saying these things, Mr Cranston?" snapped the doctor.

"I'm not saying them," Donald shouted. "It isn't me."

"But it's your voice," Wallingham protested.

"It's the voice you put *inside* me. Put the television on. The news is on. Put it on."

Wallingham hesitated for a moment then crossed the room and turned on the TV there. It was already tuned to a news channel and the newsreader was already in full flow. Both men gazed raptly at him as he spoke:

"Eyewitnesses said that the plane burst into flames as it touched down," the newsreader said. "Repeating the breaking news that an American Airlines plane has crashed on landing at Heathrow airport. Early reports indicate that all two hundred and thirty-two passengers and crew have perished."

"It's a coincidence," Wallingham said, softly. "It has to be."

"The voice was correct," murmured Donald. "Even down to the number of people killed."

"It was *your* voice, Mr Cranston."

"No it wasn't. Who was the donor? Whose voice have I got now?"

"I'd have to check. That sort of information is…"

"I need to know. Please," Donald said.

Wallingham looked helplessly at him for a moment then Donald spoke again.

"Tomorrow morning at 3.14 Greenwich Mean Time there will be an earthquake in Durango, Mexico. Five thousand people will die. I have foreseen this."

Donald looked horrified as the words reverberated inside the room. He grabbed at his throat, wanting to silence the sounds.

"Stop this," he roared. "Stop it."

Wallingham lunged towards him as he fell, collapsing across the bed.

When Donald woke again the doctor was still standing over him. He touched his throat to find that it had been re-dressed, the bandages wound tightly around.

"How long was I out?" Donald asked.

"I thought it best to sedate you," Wallingham told him. "You were very distressed. You've been out for nearly twenty-two hours."

Donald sat up abruptly. "The earthquake that the voice foretold…" he began.

"It happened," the doctor told him. "Five thousand died."

"Oh Jesus," Donald gasped, sinking back on his pillows.

"It's a coincidence," the doctor insisted.

"Like the plane crash?"

"Mr Cranston, modern medicine is a marvellous thing but giving someone the power of prophecy is beyond even *my* capabilities."

Donald wasn't impressed. "Did you find out anything about the donor? The man who supplied my voice box?"

"His name was Titus Finlay. He was a fortune teller and a medium. Probably a fake. Apparently he had a large following on social media. People would consult him about future events and he furnished them with answers. The man was obviously a charlatan."

"How can you be sure?"

"People like that make lots of predictions. It's a scattergun effect. If they say enough is going to go wrong then they usually get one or two things right."

"But he got *everything* right about the crash and the earthquake."

"This is coincidence, Mr Cranston. The prophecies. The voice."

"No. It's too detailed. How can you just dismiss it? I want you to remove the voice box. I don't care if I never speak again. I want it out."

"I'm not removing it," Wallingham snapped. "You're overreacting."

"I've heard of mediums channelling their thoughts through people. What if that's what's happening to me?"

"This is ludicrous."

"I'm the one with this... this inside me. If you won't help me then perhaps someone else will." Donald dragged himself out of bed and began dressing.

"I'm not letting you leave, Mr Cranston. You're not in a fit state either physically or psychologically."

"And I'm not going to sit around and wait for more of these prophecies to come true. They've all been true so far."

"Not all of them. What about the things you said to the nurse? To the other patient? We don't know those are going to actually occur."

"The plane crash. The earthquake. The details of those were correct even down to the number of people who died."

"If there is any truth in these… prophecies then stay here. Let me help you."

"No. I can't. I've got to get out."

He pushed past the doctor, hurrying into the corridor beyond. Wallingham pursued him, seeing that Donald was heading for the main doors of the building.

He dashed across the paved area in front of the clinic, desperate to be away from it, wanting to be anywhere other than inside it.

He never saw the speeding ambulance that hit him.

Wallingham gasped as he saw the emergency vehicle plough into Donald.

It struck him with such force that he was catapulted ten feet into the air, his body somersaulting before slamming back down on the tarmac.

The doctor ran to him, looking down at his blood-spattered face. Somewhere nearby, someone was screaming but Wallingham ignored the sounds, concerned only with helping Donald.

And now others were rushing to help, both uniformed staff and others and, together they managed to get Donald's broken body inside and to an operating theatre.

Five hours later they were still working on him, but Wallingham finally stepped back and let out a long sigh.

"That's it," he said, shaking his head. "He's gone."

The surgeon who'd been assisting nodded slowly.

"His injuries were appalling. No one could have saved him. It's a wonder he even lasted as long as he did."

Wallingham was gazing blankly at Donald's body.

"He was one of your patients, wasn't he?" the other surgeon asked.

Wallingham nodded and pulled a small piece of paper from beneath his surgical gown, glancing at it.

"What was the time of death?" he murmured, his gaze now fixed on the piece of paper.

"Eleven thirty-two," the other surgeon confirmed, catching sight of the piece of paper.

Wallingham handed it to him.

"I found that in Cranston's room this morning," he breathed.

Written on the paper were the following words:

AT ELEVEN THIRTY-TWO A.M. TODAY DONALD CRANSTON WILL
DIE ON THE OPERATING TABLE.

THE LEGACY

Emma Grayson rolled onto her stomach and lifted her bare feet up behind her, rocking gently back and forth as she lay on her bed.

All around her, the walls of her room were covered with posters and photographs, just as the bedroom walls of millions of other eighteen-year-old girls were. But it wasn't those images that concerned her now, it was the face of her best friend that she could see on the screen of her laptop.

The picture shuddered, broke up then returned and Emma sighed irritably.

"The signal here is rubbish," she groaned.

"Mine's the same," Sophie Turner told her from the other side of the screen.

She was a little older and, unlike her friend, she had dark hair instead of blonde. She was wearing a white vest t-shirt over a pair of ripped jeans, and she too was barefoot in the safe domain of her own bedroom. Sophie paused to scratch at a spot on her chin.

"Don't do that," Emma snapped, seeing her friend rubbing at her skin.

"Bloody spots," Sophie muttered.

"Don't worry. Pete will still want you."

Sophie looked momentarily perturbed but then she smiled.

"He should be grateful for what he gets," she chuckled. "Like Josh."

"God, that is so over. I'm not seeing him any more."

"Since when?"

"Since he told me I was putting on weight. Cheeky

fucker. He's not exactly built like a cage fighter, is he?"

"You're not putting on weight. You look great."

Emma smiled.

"Thanks, babes," she beamed. "I think it's the smoking that keeps me slim."

They both laughed.

"My mum would go ape shit if she knew I smoked," Sophie offered.

"So would mine," Emma confirmed.

No sooner had she finished speaking than there was a loud rapping on her bedroom door, and from the other side of the partition she heard a familiar voice.

"Emma."

"Yes, Mum," she called.

"Are you getting ready?" her mother continued. "We've got to leave soon."

"I'm not going, Mum. I don't feel well."

"You *are* going. I want you downstairs in five minutes."

"I can't get ready in five minutes." There was desperation in Emma's voice.

"Yes you can."

And she was gone. Leaving Emma sitting on her bed, legs crossed and irritable.

"What did your mum want?" Sophie asked from the screen of the laptop.

"We're supposed to be visiting my nan in hospital. Fuck knows why. It's a waste of time."

"Isn't she dead yet? She's been in hospital for ages."

"Nearly two months. I *hate* going. It's so depressing. Loads of other old people and my nan never says anything. She just *lays* there and we just *sit* there. It's horrible."

"They all smell the same, don't they? Hospitals I mean." Sophie made a face that aptly summed up her disgust.

"My mum says my nan has got something to give me,

something she wants me to have," Emma offered.

"Like what? Money?"

"I hope so."

"Perhaps she's got a fortune hidden away somewhere and she wants to give it to her beloved granddaughter before she dies." Sophie giggled.

"No way. My little brother would get most of her fortune if she had one. She thinks the sun shines out of his arse."

"When we both know it shines out of *yours*."

Emma giggled.

"You should find out what she wants to give you," Sophie went on. "It might be valuable."

Emma raised her eyebrows and sighed, startled a moment later when there was another round of banging on her bedroom door.

"What?" she yelled.

"You'd better be ready, Emma," her mother called back. "I'm telling you. We're leaving for the hospital in five minutes and you're coming with us."

"What's the point?"

The door was pushed open and Michelle Grayson strode in, glaring at Emma.

"The point is, that your grandmother is in hospital and she likes to see visitors, especially her grandchildren," Michelle snapped. "So, unless you're ready to go in five minutes I'm taking that bloody laptop away *and* your phone and you're not getting them back for a week."

Michelle stormed out of the room again.

Emma muttered something under her breath.

"Mate," Sophie said from the screen of the laptop. "I think you're going."

As the car sped along the dual carriageway towards the hospital, Emma contented herself with either gazing out of the window or looking at her phone. Either exercise did nothing to alleviate her boredom and she caught sight of her reflection in the glass and thought that the phrase "bored shitless" might have been invented for her at this precise second in time.

She sighed theatrically, attracting the attention of her mother who glanced at her briefly and shook her head.

In the back seat, Emma's eight-year-old brother, Jack, was periodically banging his feet against the back of her seat, knowing that it was likely to irritate her and gaining a small measure of delight from that knowledge.

"Can't you sit still?" Emma finally snapped, glancing over her shoulder in the direction of her sibling.

Jack kicked the seat again.

"For fuck's sake, Jack," Emma snapped.

"Language," Michelle said. "Don't talk to your brother like that."

"Well tell him to stop kicking my seat then," Emma protested. "Little mong."

"I said don't talk to him like that," Michelle continued.

"Yeah, don't talk to me like that," Jack echoed from the back seat.

"God, he's so irritating. You should have had him aborted."

She returned to looking out of the side window.

Michelle merely shook her head, as if the effort of responding to her daughter was simply too much for her. Instead she concentrated on the road. It was badly lit and wound through the countryside before it got to the approaches of the next town and the hospital itself. The sodium glare of the street lights sometimes didn't seem enough to penetrate the darkness and a strong breeze had sprung up, occasionally sending leaves and other natural debris flying across the carriageway like confetti. Michelle flicked on the wipers as she saw the first spots of rain hit the glass.

"Did you say Nan wanted to give me something before she died?" Emma finally asked.

"So you're interested now, are you?" Michelle muttered.

"What is it?"

"I don't know. You'll have to ask her."

"But she never speaks to me."

"You don't exactly talk her ear off, Emma."

"I don't know what to say to her. What am I supposed to ask her? If she used the bedpan today? How many other people in her ward died?"

Michelle shook her head.

"You'll be her age one day, Emma," she said. "You'll realise how much other people mean to someone old like your nan. She's got no one else."

"Grandad went mad, didn't he? She went downhill after that."

"No, he didn't go mad. He had Alzheimer's."

"Yeah, Emma," Jack chimed from the back seat. "You're so stupid."

"Shut up, retard," Emma hissed, glancing back at her brother.

"I've told you," Michelle interjected.

"Why doesn't Dad visit her, she's *his* mum," Emma went on.

"Dad's working."

"Dad's *always* working."

"And you should be grateful for that. That's how we afford little extras like food and light."

She glared at her daughter.

"You should get yourself a Saturday job, then you'd have some money of your own," she went on.

"If Nan gives me some money then I won't have to get a job," Emma said, smiling.

***

There were eight beds in the ward, four of them

occupied.

Exactly where the other four occupants were Emma could only guess. People were constantly going on about how few beds the NHS had well, here were four that were vacant right now she thought, suppressing a smile.

She was carrying a beaker of hot chocolate in one hand and a coffee in the other, although coffee was rather a grand term for the dark-brown rancid water that was spewed out by the vending machine in the corridor beyond the ward. However, all Emma cared about was that if she was fetching hot drinks then she wasn't sitting dumbly around her grandmother's bed, staring at the walls and listening to her stomach rumble.

The other old people in the ward were all in their eighties, like her grandmother, and Emma had actually smiled at the white-haired man in the bed nearest the window when he'd waved at her.

He was, she'd decided, probably a paedophile or would be if he could still get it up, but, as he was a safe distance from her and not likely to leap out of bed and molest her, she thought it safe to spare him the smile when she passed. He waved again as she returned then turned his attention back to the book of word puzzles that he was engrossed in.

Emma handed the coffee to her mother and sat down on one of the plastic chairs next to her grandmother's bed, sipping her own hot chocolate and wishing that it was time to leave.

"So there's nothing you want then, Mum?" Michelle asked the older woman.

Elizabeth Evans shook her head slightly.

"I got some more cat food," Michelle went on. "Your neighbour said she'll carry on feeding them until you get home."

"If I do," Elizabeth said softly.

"Oh don't start that again," Michelle told her. "You'll

be out of here soon enough. Back home."

The older woman merely gazed into empty air.

Emma glanced at the wall clock. They'd already been here nearly two hours. It felt like two days to her. She stifled a yawn and sipped her hot chocolate.

Michelle got to her feet and straightened her clothes. "Well, Mum, we'd better be going," she said, not particularly surprised at how quickly her two children jumped to their feet preparatory to leaving. She leaned forward and kissed the older woman on the forehead. "I'll pop in again tomorrow and see you." She looked at Emma and Jack. "Say goodbye to your gran."

Emma waved a hand disinterestedly in the air.

"Bye, Gran," she said, turning away from the bed.

"Say goodbye, *properly*," Michelle demanded.

Emma sighed and planted a kiss lightly on the older woman's wrinkled forehead.

Elizabeth suddenly shot out a hand and clasped Emma's wrist.

"It's lovely to see you again, Emma," the older woman exclaimed. "You're such a beautiful girl. I'm so proud of you."

The sudden explosion both of emotion and also of speech startled Emma and she could only nod.

"You remind me so much of myself when I was your age," Elizabeth went on.

"Right then," Emma said. "That's cool."

Elizabeth kept hold of her hand, gripping it like someone who is dangling from a high ledge and has only that one limb keeping them from a lethal drop.

The strength and the duration of the grip were beginning to make Emma feel uneasy.

"Thanks," Emma said, trying to move away but Elizabeth held her fast.

"There's something I want you to have," the older woman said, nodding now as if to add weight to her words. "Something of mine. It's very valuable so I want you take good care of it."

"All right," Emma said, again trying to pull free.

"It cost lots of money."

"You can give it to her yourself when you get home, Mum," Michelle added.

"No," Elizabeth continued. "I want her to have it now." She looked at Michelle. "You know what I mean."

Michelle nodded.

"I want her to have it tonight," Elizabeth insisted.

"Mum, it can wait until–" Michelle said but she was interrupted by the older woman whose tone darkened considerably.

"No," she snapped. "I want her to have it tonight. I want you to go to my house when you leave here and get it for her. Do you understand?"

Michelle nodded.

"Promise me," Elizabeth continued, her eyes narrowed now as she spoke.

"I promise," Michelle breathed.

Elizabeth looked at her and then at Emma, finally releasing her hand.

"You must take care of it," she breathed. "You *must*."

***

The wind that had been blowing earlier had grown much stronger as the night had progressed and now Emma Grayson glanced towards the window of her bedroom as the panes rattled in the frames. She listened to the powerful gusts for a moment longer then turned back to her laptop, seeing the image of Sophie Turner on the screen.

"So you don't know what it is yet?" Sophie asked.

"No," Emma told her. "My mum's gone to get it from my nan's house but she's not back yet."

"If it's valuable then you can sell it."

"I hope it's money."

"It's probably like a family photo album," Sophie chuckled. "With pictures of your relatives right back to the Middle Ages or something."

"That's not valuable," Emma protested.

"But old people say that don't they? They say something is valuable because it's valuable to *them*."

"Oh God, I hope not. I hope it's something worth having."

"And worth selling," Sophie added and both girls laughed.

Emma turned again as she heard a sharp rapping on her bedroom door. She had barely managed to look in the direction of the door when it opened. Her mother walked in, glancing around the room as she did.

"Mum," Emma protested. "This is my room. You're not just supposed to walk in like that. It's private."

"It's not private until you start paying the rent," Michelle told her, moving across to the small desk by one wall. She moved some books and pieces of paper from one corner to make some space and then dug in her pocket for something that Emma couldn't yet see.

She padded over to where her mother was standing, watching as she laid something on the desk. An object that was, as yet, still wrapped in several layers of thick tissue paper.

"This is what your nan wanted you to have," Michelle announced, pulling the tissue open.

Emma moved closer as her mother finally removed the last of the paper to reveal a large brooch.

"That's it?" Emma said, disappointment etched on her face. "That's what she says is so valuable?"

"It's been in the family for years," Michelle said.

Emma looked more closely at the piece of jewellery. It was yellowish metal, about the size of her palm and it looked like a hedgehog or some other small animal. The eyes were two grubby red stones and the overall effect was tacky, Emma thought. She prodded the brooch with one index finger.

"What is it?" she grunted.

"A brooch," Michelle said. "You put it on your jacket."

"I know it's a brooch. I mean what is it supposed to be. What kind of animal?"

"Does it matter?"

"No. Because I won't be putting it on any of *my* jackets."

"You should wear it next time we go to visit your nan. She'd love that."

"Yeah, right," Emma sighed, turning away from the desk and the brooch.

"You could try being a bit more grateful, Emma," Michelle said, wearily.

"I'll send her a text and say thanks."

"Very funny. You know she hasn't got a phone."

"All right, I'll e-mail her then."

Emma raised her eyebrows. She sat down on her bed and stretched out her slender legs, tapping her bare feet together agitatedly. Michelle glanced around the room again and shook her head.

"You need to tidy up in here," she said, briskly. "It's *your* room. You're responsible for it."

Emma nodded.

Michelle hesitated a moment longer then turned back towards the door.

"I'll leave you to finish your conversation," she said, sharply.

Emma had already turned away and was looking at Sophie's image on the laptop screen. Michelle closed the door behind her, the sound of her footfalls echoing away on the stairs as she descended.

"Let's have a look at it then," Sophie said. "Let's see

your valuable prize." She chuckled.

Emma retrieved the brooch and laid it on the bed, adjusting it so it was in view for her friend.

"God it's horrible," Sophie said. "How could your nan say that was valuable?"

Emma prodded the brooch with one index finger.

"I wish those jewels in the eyes were rubies," she murmured.

"Yeah, right," Sophie giggled.

Emma prodded the brooch again, a smile spreading across her lips.

"I know what we can do with it," she breathed.

***

The town centre was usually busy on a Saturday morning. This particular day seemed to be an exception.

As Emma and Sophie made their way along the main street they were both struck by how few people there were out shopping or even just browsing in the windows of shops. Like so many small towns over the last few years, increased rents and the rise of online shopping had led to many businesses that had previously flourished simply closing. The empty shops in the high street stood out as a painful reminder, vying for space with the only kind of venture that did seem to be profitable, the restaurant or cafe. The main street of the town seemed to have an eatery every few doors, Emma observed. Outside many, chairs and tables had been arranged and there were people sitting at some of these, determined to enjoy a little cosmopolitan fun even if it did require wearing a coat and scarf. Emma had never seen the point of eating outside unless the weather was good and this particular morning it was chilly to say the least. And yet, people still sat sipping coffee and chatting, trying to eat pastries with their gloved hands shaking in the chill.

The two girls walked past a newly opened Starbucks, the shop they sought just ahead of them now.

"Are you sure about this?" Sophie asked.

Emma nodded.

"Your mum's going to go mad when she finds out," Sophie continued.

"My nan said the brooch was mine," Emma told her friend. "That means I can do what I want with it, right?"

"I thought your nan said you had to take care of it."

"She's not going to know, is she?"

The two girls looked up at the window of the shop. PAWN SHOP.

Displayed in the window there were rows of phones, tablets and laptops vying for space with guitars, games consoles and several record players.

"Will they be able to help?" Sophie wondered, gazing into the window.

"They buy stuff for cash. Why not?" Emma said, pushing the door of the shop open.

As they walked in, the bell over the door tinkled invitingly and the two girls walked in, glancing at the glass-fronted cabinets that seemed to fill the shop. They displayed other items like cameras, watches and other jewellery. Sophie ran appraising eyes over the array of rings and bracelets.

Emma was gazing at a number of electric guitars hanging up behind the main counter at the rear of the shop.

"You could swap the brooch for a guitar," Sophie chuckled. "Or a camera."

Emma joined her, looking down at the items inside the display case. Every one of them seemed to be more presentable than the brooch she had in her pocket, Emma thought.

She was still considering that when the door towards the rear of the shop opened and a large man with a ponytail emerged. He was enormous, the black t-shirt he wore stretched across his voluminous belly to the point where it looked as though it might split. He pulled up his jogging bottoms and wandered over in the direction of the two girls. Emma noticed that he was also wearing flip-flops.

Nick Cutler was about half a stone from being morbidly obese. He knew it and he'd tried to lose weight but it had proved easier said than done. As he placed his hands on the counter, the silver rings he wore seemed to dig into the flesh of his fingers, the skin piling up around the knuckles. The earrings he wore matched the rings and Emma could see that he had small silver skulls dangling from his lobes.

"Can I help you?" he asked.

"I want to sell something," Emma told him.

"Is it yours? I mean, it's not stolen or anything. You can prove it belongs to you?"

"It was my nan's. She gave it to me but I don't want it. I need to know if it's worth anything."

"Let's have a look then," Cutler urged, watching as Emma reached into her pocket, carefully pulling out the brooch. She laid it on the counter and the big man leaned closer. Emma looked at his expression and saw it change from one of indifference to one of interest. He moved nearer then reached into the pocket of his jogging bottoms and pulled out a loop which he placed over the brooch, inspecting the details more closely now.

"Where did you say you got it?" he wanted to know.

"From my nan," Emma told him.

"Any idea where she got it?"

Emma could only shrug.

"My mum said it had been in the family for years," she told him.

"It's just cheap shit, isn't it?" Sophie offered.

Cutler shook his head.

225

"No, I don't think it is," he murmured. "I've seen something like this before."

"Where?" Emma wanted to know.

"I can't remember," Cutler admitted, still inspecting the brooch.

"That's not good, is it?" Sophie snapped.

Cutler looked at her then returned his attention to the item before him.

"How much were you hoping to get for it?" he wanted to know.

"I don't know," Emma admitted. "What do you think it's worth?"

"I need to get this checked out. I'll speak to a friend of mine who specialises in antique jewellery. If you come back in an hour I should have it all sorted by then."

"An hour?" Sophie gaped.

"I need to check some things," Cutler insisted.

"As long as you don't try to steal it," Sophie told him.

Cutler regarded her with something close to contempt then looked at Emma once more.

"It's pretty rare, I'm sure of that," he announced. "But let me check it out more and I'll give you an answer when you come back."

Emma nodded and turned towards the door, pulling Sophie with her. Cutler watched them as they walked out then he wandered over to the door and placed the CLOSED sign in full view, also pulling down the blind there. Then he returned to the counter, picked up the brooch again and hurried back into the room at the rear of the shop, his heart thudding faster now.

***

Nick Cutler sat back from the laptop and ran a hand through his hair, noticing that hand was shaking slightly in the process.

He looked down at the brooch lying beside the device, transfixed by it. Finally he reached out and gently touched the piece of jewellery but there was a reluctance, a wariness in his movements now.

The conversation he'd just been part of hadn't exactly helped his frame of mind.

As he'd initially suspected, the brooch was the same design as something he'd seen before. Identical to a piece he'd once encountered five or six years earlier. That fact had been confirmed by the conversation he'd just had. The man he'd spoken to, the man he'd shown the brooch to, was an expert in these matters and he'd identified it immediately as Cutler had held the ornament up to the screen, turning it over and around as the watcher had requested.

As he'd held it he had been sure that the metal itself had become hotter. Almost impossible to touch by the time he'd finished but, he told himself, that could not be. He prodded it again and felt only cool bronze beneath his fingertips.

He was still looking at it when he heard the bell over the shop door ringing, signalling that someone had entered the building.

"Oh, for God's sake," he murmured. "Can't you read?" Then he turned slightly on his seat. "We're closed," he called. "Can you come back in an hour or so?"

Silence.

Perhaps, he considered, the two girls who had brought the brooch in had merely returned earlier than he told them to. He listened again, the sound of the tinkling bell now almost completely faded.

Cutler nodded to himself, satisfied that whoever had heard him call had now left the shop once again.

Or was that footsteps he heard?

"I said I'm closed," he called again, getting to his feet now and heading for the door that would lead him back out into the shop beyond. When he emerged from the small back room he could see immediately that there was no one in the shop and he frowned.

Had the wind blown the door open momentarily, causing the bell above it to ring?

It was the only explanation he could think of. He walked across the shop to the front door and locked it this time, tugging on the handle to ensure that it was actually sealed. Satisfied with his security precautions, Cutler made his way back into the room at the rear of the shop once again, sitting down and fixing his attention on the brooch.

Where the hell had that girl got it, he wondered. Or, more to the point, where had the relative who'd given it to her acquired it? These were some of the thoughts whirling around inside his mind as he looked again at the brooch, reaching for his mug of coffee as he considered the item.

He didn't even hear the door of the back room open slightly.

Cutler was too pre-occupied with the brooch to hear the toolbox on the work top behind him being opened.

Too distracted to hear the claw hammer being pulled gently from it.

The heavy hammer was lifted high into the air behind him, hovering there for a moment before being brought down with incredible force. The first thunderous blow caught him on the crown of the skull, the sound of cracking bone reverberating inside the small room and immediately eclipsed by the second strike. And the third.

As Cutler slumped forward onto the desk before him, more blows rained down with dizzying force and stunning ferocity. Blood exploded from the wounds, spattering the wall, the laptop and also the brooch as the attack continued. Lumps of bone came free and, as the assault intensified, the greyish pink of brain matter began to well from the largest of the rents in the skull. Cutler had tried to raise himself, attempted to fight back against the attack but it was useless and, when the assailant turned the hammer and began slamming the clawed side into his skull, there was no chance for him.

Pieces of cranium came free every time the hammer was dragged free, blood beginning to spread across the floor beneath the desk and what remained of his head. His left eye was now dangling from its torn socket by the tendril of the optic nerve. A confetti of shattered teeth and fragments of bone had also fallen into the puddle of crimson oozing across the floor of the room.

Only when the body fell to the ground did the attack end. The hammer was dropped close to the body, the handle slick and impossible to hold any longer it was so drenched in blood and pulverised bone.

The skull now resembled a battered boiled egg. Jellied brain and blood having spilled out over the remains of the cranium. Cutler's body was still twitching slightly, the one eye that remained in its socket gaping wide despite the blood that filled it.

The brooch was still on the desk top.

Footsteps moved swiftly through the shop, heading towards the other door which led up to the first floor of the building.

There was a small storeroom up there and also a one-bedroom flat, owned not by Cutler but by the landlord of the building.

The sound of footsteps filled the stairwell.

***

"He was so fat," Sophie giggled. "Gross."

She wiped froth from her top lip and set her cappuccino down on the table once more.

"*And* he was wearing flip-flops," she added, grunting.

Emma also laughed, looking at her watch yet again, checking the time against her phone.

"I bet he's a right weirdo," Sophie went on, warming to her subject. "Probably spends all day watching porn and wanking." She giggled. "I mean, how would a guy like that ever get a girl to go to bed with him?"

"Some girls would," Emma told her.

"Would you?"

"God, no. Never."

Both girls laughed.

"He must have got money though if that shop is his," Sophie decided. "I wonder what he's worth."

"As long as he gives me something for that brooch," Emma murmured, taking another sip of her coffee. Again she checked her watch. "It's been an hour now, hasn't it? Let's go back and see what he's got to say."

She drained what was left in her mug and swung herself off the seat.

"He said he thought he'd seen one like it before, didn't he?" Sophie added, finishing her own coffee.

"He was probably just saying that," Emma grunted, pushing open the door and stepping out onto the street.

The two girls set off back up the main street towards the pawn shop.

"You could always take it somewhere else for a second opinion," Sophie suggested. "There's that 'Cash for Gold' place up by the cinema."

Emma nodded.

"If this guy doesn't offer me much we'll take it there," she announced.

They both paused before the door of the pawn shop then Emma pushed it, surprised when she found it wouldn't open. She tried again, frowning when she also saw that the blind was pulled down. She banged on the glass and waited.

"Maybe he's run off with the brooch," Sophie offered.

Emma shook her head and banged again.

There was still no answer.

"Oh come on," she groaned. "He said come back in an hour, right? And it's been an hour."

"We could try around the back," Sophie offered.

Emma hesitated for a moment then followed her friend towards a narrow passageway that ran between the shops in this part of the main road. It led between the pawn shop and a bakery, finally emerging into a private car park and revealing the high walled yards that backed onto both shops. There was a battered wooden door that was badly in need of painting blocking the route into the yard at the rear of the pawn shop but, as Emma pushed against the door she was delighted when it swung open. She walked through and straight up to the back door of the shop. She banged hard on the door, stepping back when it opened an inch or two. She glanced at Sophie who took a step forward.

"He needs to up his security a bit," she murmured, pushing the door further open.

Emma peered into the small hallway that led off from the rear door of the shop. There was a bicycle leaning against one wall and piles of cardboard boxes stacked up in other places making it hard to actually enter the narrow space, but the two girls managed to slip through the door.

"Should we be doing this?" Sophie whispered.

"Why not?" Emma countered. "He's got some of my property. I want it back."

She moved further into the hallway.

"Hello," she called.

Only silence greeted her.

There were two doors leading off from the hallway and Emma pushed the first of these, peering into a storeroom beyond. More boxes, piled high but no sign of Cutler.

"Hello," Sophie shouted. "We're here about the brooch."

Again there was no reply but silence.

Emma opened the second door and saw that it led through into another vestibule with more doors leading off and a staircase to the right leading up to the first floor of the building. She glanced towards the stairs, wondering what lay up there but becoming more impatient with each passing second. Where the hell was he? Followed by Sophie she made her way past the steps and through the door that emerged into the shop itself.

It was empty.

The door to the rear office was slightly ajar and Emma moved towards it, tapping lightly on it. When there was no answer from within she pushed it.

"Oh my God," she gasped, clamping a hand to her mouth.

Sophie moved closer, also seeing what lay within the room.

There was blood everywhere. It covered the floor of the office and had also sprayed up onto the walls and the desk that was jammed into one corner of the room.

"Jesus, what's happened?" Sophie breathed, her stomach somersaulting.

Emma had no answer but she hurriedly moved into the room, snatched the brooch from the desk and headed back out again.

"Come on," she urged. "We've got to get out of here."

Sophie nodded but remained motionless, her gaze fixed on the crimson puddles on the floor before her.

"Come on," Emma snapped, her tone more forceful now. "If the police come they'll think we had something to do with this."

Sophie allowed herself to be pulled from the room, following her friend back into the hallway beyond. They ran past the stairs, desperate to be out of this place now.

Had they slowed down they might have heard the heavy footfalls from above them. As it was, they rushed through the building and out into the yard, dashing through the battered old wooden gate towards the car park beyond.

From inside the pawn shop, curious eyes watched their flight.

**

"Someone will know."

Sophie stood at the end of Emma's bed and almost shouted the words.

Emma shook her head and looked down at the brooch with a combination of fear and curiosity.

"He must have had CCTV cameras in there," Sophie went on. "Someone will see us."

"We didn't do anything wrong," Emma reminded her friend.

"What if no one believes us?"

"We didn't *do* anything. We took the brooch in there for him to look at. That was it."

"So where was he when we went back in? Where did all that blood come from?"

"I don't know but it wasn't down to us, was it?"

"The police might not agree."

"If there were CCTV cameras in there like you said then they'll see what happened. They'll see it was nothing to do with us."

"But you took the brooch."

"I just took back what was mine in the first place. I didn't steal it. Stop worrying. Besides, that was hours ago. Someone must have found him by now. If the police were coming to get us they'd have been here by now."

Sophie didn't look convinced. She let out a long sigh and sat down on the bed beside Emma.

"Stop worrying," Emma told her, squeezing her hand.

"We should have told your mum," Sophie murmured.

Emma shook her head.

"She's got enough to worry about with my nan," she said, quietly.

The change of subject seemed to make Sophie a little calmer.

"Are you going to tell her when she gets back from the hospital?" she wanted to know.

"What's the point?"

Sophie sucked in a deep breath.

"What do you think happened?" she said, finally.

Emma could only shrug.

"Someone broke in," she suggested. "That's probably why the back door was unlocked. Someone got in, tried to rob him. He fought back and they legged it."

"But what about the blood?"

"It must have been his or the person who broke in."

Sophie didn't look convinced. The two girls sat in silence for a moment then Emma checked a message on her phone.

"It's from my mum," she said. "She's at the hospital now."

"Is it your nan again?"

"The hospital called my mum and said that she'd had a fall or something when she got out of bed to go to the toilet. She's taken my brother with her."

"At least she didn't find out about you trying to sell the brooch."

Emma raised her eyebrows and set the phone down again.

"What are you going to do now?" Sophie wanted to know.

"Take it to that Cash for Gold place, like we said. See what they say about it," Emma announced.

"You on your own in the house until your mum gets

back then?" Sophie enquired.

"Yeah, my dad's working late again. Do you want to watch something on Netflix or what?"

"I've got to go. My mum's picking me up in about ten minutes. Facetime when I get home, yeah?"

Emma nodded.

She glanced again at the brooch.

The two girls walked down the stairs and stood chatting at the door until a car pulled up outside, then Sophie ran out to clamber into the vehicle, waving happily from the passenger seat as it pulled away. Emma waved back then closed the door and made her way back up to her bedroom. She sat down on her bed again and switched on the TV, searching for something suitable to watch. If she was honest, her mind wasn't really on it. She had too many thoughts whirling around inside her head to concentrate on a film or television programme. As she laid back on the bed and closed her eyes the only thing that appeared behind her eyelids was the memory of the blood-spattered room she'd seen earlier. Emma sat up quickly, wanting to banish the vile images.

She looked again at the brooch.

For interminable seconds she sat gazing at the old piece of jewellery then finally she grabbed it and pushed it into one of the drawers of her bedside table.

Out of sight, out of mind.

Again she settled herself on the bed and glanced blankly at the TV screen.

And then her phone rang.

***

Michelle Grayson gazed intently at the face of Elizabeth Evans for a moment longer, watching the muscles in the older woman's face twitching, studying the closed eyelids as they flickered occasionally.

She moved her seat closer to the hospital bed, careful not to scrape it on the floor and make too much noise.

There were visitors at a couple of the other beds too. They were all gathered around conspiratorially, trying to keep their voices low for fear of disturbing the other ward occupants. All seemed anxious to be anywhere but where they actually were.

Next to Michelle, Jack Grayson was flicking through a comic she'd allowed him to bring in to alleviate the boredom. Michelle realised that a trip to the hospital to see a sick relative wasn't exactly the most exciting way for an eight-year-old to spend their evening but she felt it was important for her children to attend. If she could have made Emma come too she would have but she knew that the boredom threshold of an eighteen-year-old girl was even lower and, she thought sadly, there probably wouldn't be the need for too many more visits such as this.

Again she looked at the older woman in the bed before her. The pale skin, as thin and almost translucent as old parchment. The lank, uncombed hair. The curled fingers with grubby long nails. Michelle suddenly looked away, as if she were silently rebuking herself for gazing at this old woman and finding fault with her. She hadn't asked to be in this place, had she? She hadn't wanted to be ill. Perhaps, she reasoned, visiting old people in hospital was so unpleasant because it reminded the visitors of their own mortality. It offered a glimpse into a possible future they themselves might have to endure, and who the hell wanted to see that?

Michelle looked at her watch and decided it was time to go. Elizabeth hadn't said more than ten words since they'd arrived nearly two hours ago and there didn't seem much point in prolonging this particular agony. She nudged Jack who looked up gratefully from his comic and nodded.

Michelle got slowly to her feet, looking down at Elizabeth again, not wanting to disturb the old woman but not really wanting to leave without saying goodbye. She leaned forward and kissed her gently on the forehead.

As she prepared to back away, Elizabeth suddenly shot out a hand and grabbed Michelle by the wrist.

The grip was far more powerful than Michelle could have imagined and she tried to pull away, shocked by the sudden movement.

"Has she done it yet?"

The words came from Elizabeth but they were spat out with such venom that Michelle shuddered. The soft lines of the face that had been there earlier when the old woman had been resting had disappeared now. The features were hard. Almost furious.

"Has she?" Elizabeth hissed.

"I don't know what you mean," Michelle told her.

"The brooch I wanted her to have. Has she tried to sell it yet? All she wants is the money. She doesn't care about anything else. I knew the first time I spoke to her what a selfish little bitch she was."

Michelle looked shocked.

"She's no good," Elizabeth went on. "She never has been and she never will be."

"Don't say that," Michelle protested.

"She's a little bitch. A greedy, unfeeling little bitch. I knew that the first time I spoke to her."

"Then why did you want her to have the brooch?"

"To teach her a lesson."

"What do you mean?"

"The brooch wasn't a gift. It's a curse. A test. My mother found that out and so did I."

Michelle finally managed to pull free. She stepped back, glaring down at the old woman.

"And your daughter will find that out," Elizabeth

continued. "Her greed will undo her." The old woman sat bolt upright, her eyes blazing.

The other visitors in the ward were now looking around, aware of the commotion that was coming from the other bed. They tried not to make it obvious that they were listening but they still gazed curiously.

"What the hell are you talking about?" Michelle snapped. "What have you done?"

"It's already begun. There's no way to stop it now."

Michelle felt anger building inside her for this old woman now. Part of her felt guilty for reacting that way but she could not control her irritation.

"What have you done?" she repeated.

Elizabeth merely smiled, slumping back on the piled-up pillows. She watched as Michelle reached for her phone.

"It's too late for that," Elizabeth told her. "There's no point trying to warn her. It's too late."

Michelle grabbed Jack by the arm and hauled him along with her as she bolted from the ward.

Elizabeth watched her go, a smile on her face.

***

Emma held up the brooch before the screen of her laptop, ensuring that Sophie could see it.

"So," she began. "How much would you bid for this ancient piece of shit? Five pounds? Five pound fifty?"

Both girls laughed.

"Can you imagine that in an auction?" Sophie added. "God, who would want it?"

"Someone else old. Old people seem to have really bad taste when it comes to stuff like that."

The girls laughed again.

With her back to her bedroom door, Emma didn't see the wooden partition open an inch or two.

"Did you check it out on Google like you said you were going to?" Sophie asked.

"Yeah, I took a picture of it and searched the image to see what came up," Emma explained.

"And?"

"The brooch was one of a pair like that guy in the pawn shop said."

"Where's the other one?"

"Don't know."

Behind her, the door opened a little more, the hinges creaking in the process. Emma heard the sound and spun around. She got to her feet and padded across to the door, aware that it was open slightly. She popped her head out, glancing over the landing beyond then she closed the door once again and wandered back to her bed, sitting down opposite her laptop and Sophie's image.

"What was that?" Sophie wanted to know.

"I thought my dad was home," Emma told her. "He should be back soon. I don't really like being in the house on my own."

"Chicken," Sophie chuckled.

"Oh shut it. You'd be the same. Especially after what happened this afternoon. I keep thinking about all that blood we found."

"It was pretty fucked up, I admit that."

"Do you think we should have called the police?"

"Stop worrying about it. It's not our problem."

Emma considered that for a moment then nodded.

"What else did Google say about the brooch?" Sophie wanted to know.

"Not much," Emma told her. "It just said that they were probably made in the seventeenth century to ward off something called a hex, whatever that is."

"Sounds creepy. Wasn't a hex something to do with witchcraft?"

"How do you know that?"

"I'm sure I've heard it in a film or something."

Behind Emma, the door opened a fraction once again.

"Where is your dad now then?" Sophie went on. "You said he was due back soon."

"He's been working away. He should be here soon."

The door opened a little more but this time the hinges didn't squeak. Emma didn't turn as it moved another inch or two. Instead, she just looked at the brooch again, concentrating on the two red jewels that it sported for eyes.

Even in the subdued light within the bedroom they seemed to be more lustrous than normal. When Emma reached for the brooch it felt warm to her touch. She frowned, thinking that her mind was playing tricks.

"Emma."

The shout came from Sophie and Emma glanced at her laptop screen now, seeing that her friend was pointing, gesticulating wildly towards her.

Emma looked puzzled.

"Emma," her friend shouted again and then her shouts became screams.

Of warning. Of terror.

"Behind you!" Sophie screamed.

Emma turned and, as she did, the door burst open fully as a large figure stepped into her room.

What it was she had no idea. All she saw was something large and dark looming over her, the mouth open, the eyes blazing red like pools of boiling blood.

She managed one scream and then it was upon her. Slashing at her. Closing impossibly long, clawed fingers around her throat. Dripping yellowish saliva onto her face as it bore down upon her.

A vile, choking stench filled her nostrils and she felt something against her skin that felt like fur. Thick, matted, reeking fur. Like that of some kind of animal.

It was her last thought.

SOFT CENTRE

The board room at Carrington Confectionery was huge.

Dominated by a massive polished oak table that sat in the centre of the space it was thickly carpeted and every sound seemed to be absorbed by the expensive floor covering.

The walls were adorned with pictures of the company's origins (a small sweet shop in Kent back in the 1890s) and photos of their products (everything from jelly babies to boxes of chocolates).

When people came together in the board room it had a kind of sepulchral quality to it. The stilted sound adding to the reverence with which the place was treated. Every sound seemed muffled except the sound of James Grant's voice. Grant was a thick-set man in his late forties and he was pacing agitatedly back and forth beside the table, a bar of chocolate held almost accusingly in his hand. He would periodically lift it into view so that the others in the room could see the pink wrapping and gold embossed words upon it.

There were more chocolate bars laid out on the table, like exhibits in a trial. Bars of chocolate, boxes tied with pretty ribbons. And, behind them all, a banner that read:

ONCE YOU'VE TASTED IT YOU'LL NEVER WANT ANYTHING ELSE.

Another banner proclaimed:

IT'S THE TASTE OF HEAVEN.

Grant held up the bar of chocolate.

"It might be the taste of heaven to them," he grunted. "It'll be the taste of redundancy for us if we don't find out more about this bloody company." He tossed the chocolate bar to one side contemptuously. "Morton's Chocolates," he grunted.

"They're new, Jim," Nick Ridley suggested. "People are buying their stuff because it's new on the market. The novelty value will wear off."

"They're selling six times as much product as we are," Grant snapped. "They're even outselling Cadbury by four to one. Fucking Cadbury."

Ridley retrieved a bar of chocolate from the display before him and slid it from inside the wrapping.

"It must be their secret ingredient," he murmured, studying the wrapper and its contents with the same kind of eye a bomb disposal expert reserves for a pile of C4. He sniffed the bar and smiled.

"I'm glad *you* think it's funny," Grant hissed. "The last set of figures I saw showed that they had almost seventy percent of the market. That's unheard of. They're the only ones selling and they have been for the past two months."

"The fact that they've spent next to nothing on marketing makes it even crazier," Jo Temple added, also regarding the wrapping on the chocolate. "It's like they just 'popped up', started selling chocolate and suddenly became the most successful company on earth."

"I want to know why," Grant snapped.

"Perhaps it really *is* their secret ingredient," Jo offered.

"Then find out what it is," Grant told her.

"That'd be like asking KFC for their special spices recipe," Ridley said. "Or McDonald's for their special sauce ingredients. It's not going to happen. Our marketing department and every one else has analysed this product," he waved a bar of chocolate before him. "They can't find anything different to the same ingredients we use and the same ones Cadbury, Hershey or anyone else use."

"Well they're doing something to their product to make

it so bloody irresistible," Grant persisted. "I want to know what." He pointed at Ridley and Jo. "I want you two to go to their factory. Find out what they're about. Find out what they're doing."

"It's only a small family firm, isn't it?" Jo offered.

"They pride themselves on that," Ridley added. "It's one of their selling points."

There was a large poster lying on the table too. Grant glared down at it and read the slogan aloud:

"Every mouthful is like coming home," he said, his tone heavy with sarcasm and scorn.

"What do you want us to do if we get inside their factory?" Ridley asked. "Poison the chocolate? Blow up the machines that make it?" he grinned.

"Either one would be fine with me," Grant said, without a trace of irony. "I mean it, Mr Carrington has got a real problem with Morton's. He doesn't like competition, you know that. Someone's going to get it in the neck if he doesn't get the answers he wants. And I think it's going to be me. And if *I* get it in the neck then *you'll* get it in the neck. Shit rolls downhill." He sucked in a deep breath. "Find out what they're doing. Find out what that fucking secret ingredient is." He sighed heavily. "And if you can't, don't bother coming back because there might not be a job for you to come back to."

***

Nick Ridley sipped at his drink and looked around the bar. Beside him, Jo Temple was nursing a gin and tonic in one hand and a bar of Morton's chocolate in the other.

Behind them, the barman busied himself with various tasks, returning to polishing glasses after he'd served another customer.

Jo broke a square of chocolate off and popped it into her mouth.

Ridley watched as she chewed, a beatific expression on her face.

"It is bloody good," she said, smiling. "What do you think is their secret ingredient?"

"There isn't one," Ridley told her. "It's just marketing."

"It's a pity our marketing department couldn't come up with something as good," she said, still chewing softly.

"That's *your* department, Jo," he reminded her.

She merely raised her eyebrows slightly.

"The taste of heaven?" Ridley said, grinning.

"Pretty damn close," Jo cooed.

Ridley sighed and shook his head.

"Right," he said. "What do we know about Morton's Chocolates?"

"Small family company in the west of England," Jo began. "Based on a farm somewhere in Wiltshire. No one knows much about the owners, a Mr and Mrs Morton. They've had the business for about three years. No one knows how many employees they've got. They've got no social media presence which is unheard of in this day and age."

"Not everyone wants publicity and attention, do they?" Ridley mused. "But how the hell they've managed to avoid it with such a successful business I don't know."

"Would you recognise the CEO of McDonald's?"

Ridley shook his head.

"There you go," she went on. "Perhaps they just don't like the limelight."

Ridley sipped at his drink.

"So how do we play this?" Jo wanted to know.

"We drive to their factory, have a look around. See what we can find out from the locals. Get inside if we can."

"That could be easier said than done."

"Jo, we work for a confectionary company, not MI5," Ridley reminded her. "This is product research, not espionage. We get a couple of days away from the office, put it all on expenses. Let's enjoy it."

"But what about our jobs? Grant said we might lose them if—"

"He's talking bollocks," Ridley said, cutting across her. "They're not going to sack us just because we can't find out what a rival puts in their bloody product."

"I hope you're right."

She chewed another square of the chocolate, offering the bar to Ridley. He shook his head, called the barman over and ordered another whiskey.

"Really?" she said.

"What? It's just a drink," he protested.

"That's what you used to say. You had a problem with booze, Nick, you know that."

"Well, it's not your concern any more, is it?" he told her, ignoring the hurt expression on her face. "It stopped being your concern when we split up."

"Thanks," she said, flatly.

"Look, we had fun for eight months but then we just outgrew each other, didn't we?"

Jo shook her head dismissively. "Thanks for that fascinating overview of our relationship," she added.

"I wouldn't call it a relationship," Ridley grunted. "We fucked a few times. That was it."

Again Jo looked a little hurt by his words. She got to her feet and picked up her handbag.

"I can see the next two days are going to be a real treat," she grunted.

"Stay. Have another drink. We don't have to leave until tonight."

"No. I've got a bag to pack."

She turned and walked out.

Ridley waited a moment then signalled to the barman and ordered himself another drink. This time it was a double.

***

The darkness closed in around the car, in places it seemed as if it was so dense that even the headlights wouldn't penetrate it.

As they got further off the main roads and were forced to drive on country thoroughfares, Jo switched the headlights to full beam in an effort to guide her.

"I could have driven," Ridley told her.

"You've been drinking, remember?" she said, her eyes fixed on the narrow road ahead.

Ridley glanced out of the side window in the direction of the fields around them. High hedges framed the roads, some of them so tall it was almost impossible to see beyond the narrow verges. Every now and then the low hanging branches of trees would scrape against the car's roof.

"I hate the countryside," Ridley grunted.

"Not enough pubs?" Jo asked, the sarcasm clear in her tone.

"It always smells like a shithouse," he informed her. "And the people are a bit inbred sometimes."

"Nothing like a good stereotype, eh, Nick?" She smiled to herself, swinging the car around a sharp bend. It rattled as it passed over a cattle grid. They drove a little way in silence then she spoke again. "So, what do we do when we get to the hotel?"

"Check in," Ridley said. "Find out what we can about Morton's chocolate. Talk to the locals. How long before we get there?"

Jo glanced at the satnav. "About ten minutes," she informed him.

"It feels as if we've been in this bloody car for weeks," Ridley said, peering into the gloom.

Jo nodded silently and drove on.

When she finally saw the lights of the building that marked their destination, she was relieved.

The whitewashed structure looked like a classic cliché of a country inn. A throwback to another age. It was like something out of a guide book. If that guide book was fifty years out of date.

Jo parked outside the building and they clambered out, walking towards the main entrance. Spots of rain were falling now.

Ridley had to duck slightly to get through the doorway into the reception area. The paint was peeling off the door frame.

They emerged in a small reception that featured an open fire off to the left. However, it seemed to be producing more smoke than flame and Jo waved a hand before her as she breathed. They walked across to the small reception desk and noticed that there was a little brass bell on it. Ridley picked it up and rang it a couple of times, the tinkling chimes filtering through the air.

To the right they both noticed a small poster for Morton's Chocolate. There was even a box on the counter with bars of it on display.

Ridley rang the bell again and a woman in her forties emerged from a doorway behind the reception counter. She had a huge mop of dark hair that was pulled back and held in place by a thick navy-blue ribbon. She smiled brightly at them and Jo could see she was wearing a badge with the name CLAIRE on it.

"Can I help?" she asked, cheerfully.

"We're checking in," Ridley told her. "Mr Ridley and Miss Temple." He watched as she retrieved a large leather-bound book from beneath the counter and ran a finger down the list of names there until she found theirs.

"No computer?" Ridley asked, smiling.

"It's on the blink," Claire told him. "We like to do

things traditionally here." She ticked off their names and fumbled behind her for two large keys.

"Is their factory far from here?" Jo asked, pointing towards the poster for Morton's chocolate.

"About four miles north of here," Claire informed her. "Near the church."

"What do you think of their chocolate?" Ridley wanted to know.

Claire smiled warmly.

"It's lovely," she cooed.

"A taste of heaven," Ridley said under his breath.

"My son works there," Claire went on.

"Really?" Jo said. "What does he do?"

"He loads up the lorries and that. He loves it there. Lots of local people work there. They've done so much for this area. They're nice people, the Mortons."

"How well do you know them?"

"They've lived around here for years," Claire trilled. "They only started their chocolate business about two years ago though. They've been very successful."

"Yes, they have," Ridley breathed.

Claire ran appraising eyes over her two newest guests.

"Where have you come from?" she asked.

"London," Jo told her.

"What have you come here for?" Claire went on and Jo wasn't slow to catch the edge in her voice. "You seem very interested in the Mortons."

"We work for a confectionary company," Ridley confessed, smiling. "You could say we're rivals."

Claire didn't return the smile.

"We want to speak to them about their chocolate and—"

"They won't talk to you," Claire snapped, interrupting him.

"Well," Ridley continued. "We just want to know—"

"You're wasting your time," Claire snapped, cutting

across him again. "They've done nothing but good for this area. Why can't you just leave them alone? People are always coming around and…"

"What people?" Jo wanted to know. "Have other people come here to see them?"

"Bloody newspapers and TV have tried," Claire told her. "Nosey buggers. Trying to cause trouble."

"People love their chocolate," Jo explained. "They just want to see how it's made."

Newspapers always cause trouble for people," Claire snapped.

"I won't argue with that," Ridley said by way of mediation.

Claire glared at them both again then peered over the counter.

"If you've got any luggage you'll have to take it to your rooms yourself," she informed them. "My husband is busy."

"We can manage," Ridley assured her.

"Can we get something to eat?" Jo asked.

"Dining room through there," Claire told her, pointing. "Someone will take your order shortly."

Jo nodded.

Claire looked at them once again, her mop of black hair waving as if it had a life of its own, then she turned and disappeared back through the door behind the counter.

"Welcome to Wiltshire," Ridley said, quietly.

***

The meal they ate was better than either of them had expected.

They were the only ones in the small dining room and Ridley looked around at the paintings on the walls. They all showed some aspect of country life. Ploughing, collecting the harvest, picking apples and that kind of thing. All the paintings seemed to have been done by the same artist. They all had the same look and style. Ridley got to his feet and looked at each one more closely.

"It makes you wonder how they make a living, doesn't it?" Jo said, also glancing around the empty dining room. "It looks as if we're the only guests in the place."

"Maybe the others are in bed," Ridley said, his gaze on the array of pictures.

"I suppose they could sell up and go and work for Morton's Chocolate," Jo added, sipping at her drink.

Ridley nodded, his attention fixed on a larger painting that showed a church and graveyard around it.

"Can I get you anything else?"

The voice made him turn and he smiled as he saw the waitress who had served them walk back into the dining room. She was barely sixteen, he guessed. A slim, willowy girl with long blonde hair, dressed in a white blouse, an impossibly short black skirt and black tights. Ridley knew she was young but he couldn't help but look more intently as she cleared their table, his eyes travelling up and down her slender legs.

Jo saw him and shook her head gently, dismissively. She knew what he was thinking.

The waitress asked if everything had been okay.

"Beautiful," Ridley said. "Like you." He smiled as the girl's cheeks turned red.

"Ignore him," Jo said.

"Is it always this quiet in here?" Ridley asked the young girl.

The girl shook her head and continued to clear the table.

"You'd be better off working somewhere busier," Ridley continued. "Like Morton's Chocolates."

"My boyfriend works there," the girl said.

"Does he like it?" Jo enquired.

"He doesn't talk about it much," the girl informed her.

"They're not allowed to. The people who work there aren't allowed to talk about the factory or what goes on inside. They have to sign something when they start working there."

Jo and Ridley exchanged a brief glance, both of them now sporting slightly furrowed brows.

"Perhaps they're guarding their secret ingredient," Ridley said.

"Their chocolate is so good, isn't it?" the waitress said then she turned and headed off towards the kitchen carrying their dirty plates.

Ridley nodded.

"Not allowed to talk about what goes on in the factory?" Jo murmured. "What the hell is all that about?"

Ridley finished his drink.

"Let's find out in the morning," he said, holding her gaze.

***

The watery sunlight pouring into the car caused both of them to shield their eyes momentarily.

Despite the fact that they were parked among some trees, the sunlight still seemed to penetrate into the car and Jo reached for a pair of sunglasses from the glove compartment.

They were at the top of a small rise overlooking several small buildings in the shallow valley below. The trees were planted thickly all the way from the crest to the bottom of the valley, providing good cover. There was an area of open ground about twenty feet wide between the trees and the high mesh fence that formed the perimeter of the land owned by Morton's Chocolate.

Beyond the small complex of buildings they could see the dark outline of a church just beyond. It too was surrounded by trees.

Even from where they sat, they could see several signs on the fencing that read:

MORTON'S CHOCOLATE

"So how the hell do we get in?" Ridley murmured, shielding his eyes from the sun. "Climb the fence? Batter the gates down?"

"Or we could just drive in, say we made an order but it hasn't been delivered," Jo said, her gaze also fixed on the buildings below.

"And when they ask for proof?"

"We'll worry about that when it happens."

She swung herself out of the car, slamming the door behind her. Ridley followed, reaching in his pocket for his cigarettes.

They set off along the narrow dirt path that led to the road which snaked down towards the complex of buildings below them. The whole area seemed silent, not as they'd expected. There seemed to be very little activity for a place that was the hub of a successful business.

As they reached the bottom of the hill they found themselves heading towards the high fence and two large metal gates.

"And tell me again why we left the bloody car up on that hill?" Ridley said, breathing heavily.

"The exercise will do us good," Jo told him, smiling.

Ridley shook his head and continued walking.

As they approached the gates they slowed down a little, expecting to be challenged by a security guard at least but there was nothing to interrupt their steady progress. Ridley pushed the gates gently and was a little surprised when one of them opened wide enough to allow access.

He looked quizzically at Jo then they both walked through, following the badly tarmacked driveway towards the closest of the network of buildings.

Jo saw the sign first.

Next to the door of the first building was a hand

painted sign that proclaimed:

RECEPTION

"Are you fucking kidding?" Ridley murmured, looking at the sign. "This lot are selling more product than *us*?" He shook his head.

They both walked towards the door and Jo pushed it open. It gave them access to a small room that reminded Jo of a doctor's waiting room. The yellow painted walls were also adorned with posters for Morton's Chocolate. The banner that trumpeted THE TASTE OF HEAVEN, almost seemed like some kind of taunt.

There was a small desk on one side of the room and seated behind it was a woman who looked to be in her early seventies.

She peered at them through thick, round glasses and then smiled welcomingly.

"Hello," she cooed. "Welcome to Morton's. Can I help you?"

They both said their hellos and moved closer to the desk.

"We hope so," Ridley said, smiling. He looked around the office and then back at the older woman. "We've got a bit of a problem. We made an order with you but it seems to have been… lost. I've got the details but I'm sure you must have a record of it. It wasn't a particularly big order but…"

"That's all right," the old woman said. "Don't you worry about that. If you've not had your order we'll replace it."

She pulled open one of the desk drawers and hauled out a huge black lever arch file. She began flipping through the pages, some of which looked yellowed with age.

"It'll be in here somewhere," she said, happily. "If I didn't take the order them my sister did."

"This is a family firm, isn't it?" Jo offered.

"Oh, yes," the woman said, looking up from the file. "We think that's very important."

"The lady at The Black Stag told us that lots of local people work here too," Ridley added.

"That's true." The woman's smile broadened. "Is that where you're staying? With Claire at the Black Stag?"

"She's like you, she keeps all her records by hand," Ridley said, nodding towards the file.

"Everyone's like that around here," the woman chuckled. "We don't like all this new-fangled stuff. You have to trust the older ways in some things."

"You must have hundreds of orders," Jo said. "The business is very successful, isn't it?"

The woman sighed wistfully. "Yes, we've been very lucky," she announced.

"How long have you worked here?" Jo enquired.

"About three years but we've lived here all our lives, myself and my husband," the woman went on. "We've always lived on this land you see. We own it."

"Are you Mrs Morton?" Jo asked, trying to conceal the surprise in her voice.

"Yes, dear," the woman chuckled. "For my sins. Myself and my husband own this land and this factory. We're the keepers, you see."

Jo frowned.

"The keepers?" she murmured, watching as the old woman got to her feet and crossed to a large metal filing cabinet behind her. She slid open the topmost drawer and began rummaging through it, occasionally pulling out files and opening them.

"Keepers of what?" Ridley added.

"All our records are kept in here," the woman said, ignoring his question.

"Mrs Morton," Jo said. "Could you tell us something about your chocolate?"

"It's nothing to do with us really," the old woman said,

her back still to the two newcomers.

"You make it," Jo reminded her. "I'd say it had quite a lot to do with you."

"We're just the keepers," the old woman said, slamming a filing cabinet with a loud crash. "We found it here, you see. Found it on this land."

"Found what? This factory?" Ridley asked, his patience running out.

"What name was it again?" the old woman said. "Your order must be in here somewhere but I promise you we'll replace it. You can watch while we do if you like." She turned to look at them, beaming broadly.

"You'd show us inside your factory?" Ridley asked, hopefully.

"Of course," the old woman announced.

"That would be wonderful," Jo interjected. "We'd love that. We promise not to give away any secrets." She and Ridley laughed.

The old woman smiled and nodded.

"Come on, then," she said. "Follow me." She bustled towards the door that led outside. Jo glanced warily at Ridley then they both followed her out into the open beyond.

As Jo and Ridley followed Mrs Morton, Jo pulled up the collar of her coat. The air seemed chillier than before. The watery sun had disappeared behind some thick banks of cloud.

"Snow coming," said Mrs Morton looking up. "You can tell by the clouds."

Ridley smiled sceptically.

"You can tell that just from looking at the clouds?" he said.

"Oh yes," the older woman informed him. "I learned that from my father. I learned a lot from my father. He owned this land before us, you see. He was a diviner."

"What's that?" Jo asked.

"He could find water or minerals using a divining rod," the old woman announced.

Jo looked at Ridley who shrugged and tried to hide a smile.

"Amazing," Ridley said. "The ways of the countryside, eh?" he added, not too careful to hide the scorn in his voice.

"We have our ways," Mrs Morton told him without looking around. "You shouldn't mock them."

"I wasn't," Ridley told her. "I wouldn't dream of it."

"My father used to help the farmers around here, you see," Mrs Morton went on. "He'd find water for them, for their herds. Or he'd find food for them to feed their animals with. He was the one who found it."

"What did he find, Mrs Morton?" Jo wanted to know but she cursed as one of her shoes stuck in the increasingly thick mud that formed a perimeter around the building they were approaching. Perched on one foot, Jo reached down and pulled her shoe free of the sucking ooze, pushing it back onto her foot, wincing when she felt how wet it was now.

"You need a pair of these, dear," Mrs Morton chuckled, pointing to her own Wellington boots. "Not those flashy shoes of yours. They're only any good for walking around in cities." She laughed loudly.

Jo nodded and managed to force a smile, despite the fact that the thick mud was practically pulling her shoes off. Jo muttered irritably as she saw how the mud was clinging to her shoes, coating them. There was a certain irony that the liquid dirt looked like melted chocolate.

Up ahead there were two large buildings that seemed to be built of nothing more than corrugated iron.

It was towards the closest of these buildings that Mrs Morton now led them.

"Do you get many people coming out here to see you?" Ridley wanted to know.

"Not so many now," Mrs Morton told him. "But we do get people asking questions." She looked back and smiled. "Like you."

They trudged on.

"But I still don't understand why you had to build the factory out here," Jo grunted, sighing as the sucking mud finally claimed one of her shoes. Balancing precariously on one foot she attempted to pull it free, hoping that she didn't overbalance. She managed to drag the shoe from the mud and slipped it back on, wincing when some of the oozing filth trickled into it. She could feel it beneath her foot as she walked on.

"We had to build it out here," said Mrs Morton. "This is where we found it."

"Found what?" Jo asked, almost toppling over again.

Seemingly untroubled by the thick mud, Mrs Morton strode on, finally coming to the locked door of a large corrugated iron building just ahead. She took a set of keys from her pocket and unlocked the large padlock, pulling the chain free.

"Lots of people want to know our secret," she murmured, pushing the door open. She laughed to herself.

Nick looked at Jo and raised his eyebrows quizzically, following the old woman into the building.

It was pitch black inside. Jo blinked hard, unable to see a hand in front of her and Nick almost stumbled as the thick mud they'd been walking on gave way instead to cracked stonework beneath them.

They flailed about in the impenetrable blackness for a moment longer, wondering what the appalling stench was that assailed their nostrils. It was so powerful it was almost palpable and Jo felt her stomach somersault as the vile smell seemed to seep into her very pores. She put a hand over her mouth in an attempt to mask the odour.

From somewhere inside the building there was a

deafening roar. A sound that reminded Nick of an animal in pain. It reverberated inside the metal structure, bouncing off the walls and drumming in his ears.

He swallowed hard.

Mrs Morton flicked on some lights, banks of dull bulbs flickering into life high above them, bathing the interior in a sickly yellow glow.

Nick looked around, his brow furrowing.

The interior of the huge shed was filthy. The floor was cracked. Weeds poking through the gaps in the riven concrete. Everything seemed to have a patina of dirt upon it and, Nick noticed with disgust that the large trough that they were standing close to even had green mould growing on parts of it. The rest of gleaming metal receptacle was filled with dark brown fluid that was coursing past slowly.

He watched as Mrs Morton crossed to the trough and dipped one finger into the thick brown stream.

She lifted the finger to her mouth and licked it clean.

"Tastes like heaven," she said, smiling. "We collect it from here."

"Collect what?" Jo said, swallowing hard.

"Taste it," the old woman urged, pulling Jo gently towards her. "You'll see how beautiful it tastes."

Jo looked down into the brown depths and, almost in spite of herself, she dipped a fingertip into the liquid.

It was warm.

She looked startled but she scooped some of the dense matter up and tasted it, her eyes rolling with pleasure.

"Oh God, it is *so* good," she purred.

"We wanted to say it was sweetness from corruption but bloody Tate and Lyle had already used that for their treacle," Mrs Morton chuckled.

Nick joined them and tasted some of the oozing brown fluid, also letting out a deep sigh of approval as he sampled it.

"I still don't understand why you built the factory here," Jo said. "Right out in the middle of nowhere."

"It had to be near to the church, you see," the older woman explained conversationally. "It's been living here for hundreds of years. It feeds on the bodies, you understand."

Nick and Jo looked at her in bewilderment.

Somewhere nearby they heard the dull roaring sound once more.

"What the fuck *is* that?" Nick demanded.

"It feeds on the bodies then it... it excretes the waste into here," Mrs Morton told them, tapping the trough. "Corruption into sweetness." Again she smiled.

"Oh Jesus," Nick grunted, his stomach contracting.

"They know, then."

The voice came from behind them. Jo and Nick turned to see a man in his seventies approaching. He was carrying a double-barrel shotgun over the crook of his arm.

"Yes, I told them," Mrs Morton explained.

"Why can't people just mind their own business?" the man said, swinging the shotgun up to his shoulder.

And again that loud roaring sound came but, this time, it was accompanied by something else. A soft sucking sound. As if something very large and very wet was being dragged along a stone floor. The stench too intensified. Jo vomited, staggering across the broken concrete.

"You can see it if you want," the old man told them. "You will in a minute anyway."

Nick turned and looked towards the exit, desperate to escape this place. He spun around and began to run.

He'd barely taken three steps when the old man fired.

The blast hit Nick in the back just below the nape of the neck, tore through him and exploded from his chest. He pitched forward on his face and lay still on the cold broken concrete, blood spreading out around him in an ever-widening pool.

Jo screamed.

The old man swung the shotgun around in her direction.

"Some secrets should never be shared," he murmured then he fired again.

Jo was dead before she hit the ground.

The stench and the awful sucking sound grew.

The old man dipped his finger into the trough and tasted some chocolate.

"It'll get rid of these," he said, grinning, gesturing to the bodies of Jo and Nick. "With them being fresh it might change the flavour a bit."

"Sweetness from corruption," Mrs Morton intoned.

They both laughed.

And the sucking sound grew louder.

THE CHAMBER

Motes of dust turned slowly in the beams of sunlight pouring into the office.

Neil Chamberlain sat at his small desk in that equally small office and blew out his cheeks as he read and re-read the printed material and the e-mails before him.

On the other side of the desk, Carl Chamberlain, a year younger than his forty-two-year-old brother, sat watching helplessly.

"We've lost money every month for the last seven months," Neil sighed. He ran his hand through his greying hair. "And there's no sign of that changing." He dropped the letters and accounts back onto his desktop and sat back in his chair.

"We've got so much competition," Carl offered. "It was different when Dad was running this place. People didn't have so many... distractions. They didn't have box sets and YouTube and Christ knows what else. They had the cinema, TV and the pub and that was it. We're way down on the list of things people want to do now. How many kids under eighteen have even *seen* a bloody wax museum, let alone been inside one?"

"Madame Tussauds still do good business," Neil reminded him.

"In the centre of London with thousands of tourists passing through every day," grunted Carl. "We're in a poxy seaside town that's dead for six months of the year when the season finishes." He got to his feet and began pacing back and forth.

"Perhaps we need to update some of our figures," Neil suggested. "The last ones we had in were the

Kardashians."

"People don't want to look at models of celebrities when they can see the real thing on TV or on the internet," Carl sighed.

"We just need some more... current ones. Some of these people from Strictly Come Dancing or Love Island or something."

"We're supposed to have models of celebrities," Carl said. "Not nobodies."

"But most of them are nobodies these days. It's what people want. Christ, every other person on the planet is a so-called celebrity. Anyone with more than twenty-five followers on Twitter thinks they're a celebrity." He sighed. "How many followers have *we* got on social media? The museum, I mean?"

"Forty-seven on Instagram. Fifteen on Twitter and twenty-six on Facebook," Carl proclaimed.

The declaration was greeted by a moment of silence.

"So what do you suggest?" Neil muttered eventually. "Sell the place?"

"Have you got a better suggestion?" Carl intoned.

The two men remained silent for a moment then Neil sat forward slightly in his seat.

"We need a gimmick," he said. "Something to get people in. If could generate some publicity, just to make ourselves more relevant, just to let people know we're still here. If we could do that we might be able to survive."

"What kind of gimmick?" Carl asked.

Neil could only shrug.

"We'll have to think about it," he said. "We could ask the staff as well. See if anyone's got any ideas."

"The staff? All four of them?"

"Oh come on, Carl. I'm not letting this place go if I can help it. This wax museum has been run by our family since 1924. I'm not going to be the one who sees it run into the ground." He sucked in a deep breath and glanced at some of the framed photos on the wall opposite him. A number were sepia tinted they were so old. One showed the front of the building the day it opened for business. There were others that depicted it through the other years it had been standing and operating. Black and white and colour. Scenes from the twenties right through to the nineties. The photos hung there like accusations. Reminders of when business had been good.

There was one of himself, Carl and their father and mother standing outside the main door, arms linked, happy smiles spread across their faces.

It seemed like a very distant memory now.

"What do you think we could get for it if we do sell?" Carl wondered.

"Christ knows," Neil sighed. "We've got no chance of selling it as a going concern. Whoever buys this place will demolish it and start up some *other* business here and I don't want that."

"Neither do I but it beats going bust," Carl reminded him.

Neil began tapping lightly on the desktop with the end of his pen.

"How about getting people to pay to get the celebrity of their choice added to our collection?" Carl offered.

"Who's going to pay money for that?" Neil answered. "What does one figure cost? Three thousand? And knowing our luck we'll get some joker wanting to pay to have Tommy Robinson and Katie Hopkins put in here. That would go down well." He rolled his eyes.

"We could do a blitz on our social media platforms but not enough people follow us to make a difference, even if every one of our followers turns up here at the same time," Carl went on.

"What about cutting the staff wages?" Neil suggested.

"We did that four months ago," Carl reminded him.

"Wait a minute," Neil said, a smile spreading across his face. "What about offering a cash prize for something."

"What cash?" Carl grunted. "We've got no cash to offer."

"We do a publicity splurge," Neil went on, warming to his subject. "We advertise outside the building, on flyers, in the media, on the internet. Everywhere we can think of."

"What exactly are we advertising?" his brother wanted to know.

"Years ago, Madame Tussauds used to pay a hundred pounds to anyone who could spend the whole night in their chamber of horrors," Neil announced. "No one ever managed it."

"A hundred pounds? Are you kidding? You can't get a meal out for two for that."

"Well, we make it more than a hundred obviously," Neil went on, the enthusiasm in his voice more noticeable now. "Ten thousand. We offer ten thousand."

"We haven't *got* ten thousand," Carl gaped. "If we had ten thousand we wouldn't be talking about having to sell the business."

"Ten thousand for anyone who can stay the night in our chamber of horrors," Neil went on, smiling broadly.

"And when they do how are we supposed to pay them? We haven't got ten thousand to give away."

"We won't have to give it away because no one will last a night down there."

"How the hell do you know that?"

Neil got to his feet.

"Come on," he said, heading for the office door. "I'll show you what I've got in mind."

Carl hesitated a moment then followed his brother.

Neil walked out of the office and down a flight of wooden steps to another door that opened out into a thickly carpeted corridor beyond. Opposite him was a figure of Cristiano Ronaldo. It was standing in the middle of figures of Lewis Hamilton and Mohammed Ali. Behind them three members of the England World Cup winning team of 1966 were standing triumphantly in front of a football that, Neil noticed, needed some air in it.

He and his brother passed through the sporting section and moved down a narrow stairway to another part of the building.

It was in the basement. Bare stone walls and a stone floor that led towards a bare brick wall built into an archway.

To the left of the arch there was a brightly lit area containing fruit machines and amusement arcade games. Over the archway a sign had been hung that read:

ABANDON HOPE ALL YE WHO ENTER HERE.

A smaller, free-standing sign to the left read:

Anyone not wishing to view our Chamber of Horrors can leave via this exit now.

Neil walked on towards the archway, passing beneath it into a darkened stretch of corridor lit by just one single, unshaded bulb hanging from the ceiling.

He and his brother moved cautiously down four more stone steps, emerging into another narrow corridor with black painted walls and, on the right-hand side, a series of glass-fronted display cases each one featuring a tableau involving a famous murderer from the past.

John George Haigh stood over an acid-filled bathtub containing the remains of his latest victim.

John Christie was crouching beside his latest victim, the rope he'd used to strangle her still dangling from his hands.

Charles Manson stood with his arms outstretched, his hands blood stained.

The Yorkshire Ripper, gripping a bloodied screwdriver, stood over the body of a woman.

Neil Chamberlain smiled as he looked at the exhibits, happy with how they looked.

He waited until his brother caught up with him then they both descended three more stone steps into another area lit by dull yellow lights. It was bare brick walls again but there were bars across the subterranean room separating visitors from the figures beyond, all of which were bathed in deep shadows, some of them barely recognisable.

There were torture devices on show, too. An iron maiden, its door open to reveal the victim inside. A rack, the unfortunate on it open-mouthed in agony. A brazier, glowing red due to the lights within it, with a torturer pressing a red-hot iron against the face of a victim. Someone being skinned alive. The catalogue of atrocities was large, each embodied by figures spattered with blood.

Neil turned to look at a small compartment in the wall behind that featured a severed head.

Next to it was another exhibit showing a flight of steps upon which was laying a woman with her throat cut. At the top of those steps, knife in hand, was Jack the Ripper.

Neil smiled and extended a hand towards the models.

"So we offer ten thousand for anyone who can spend the whole night in here," he said.

"And what if they get halfway through the night and decide they want to get out?" Carl asked.

"We leave the side door open for them," Neil told him. "I mean, we need them to be running out before they get to the morning anyway. We don't want anyone lasting the whole night or we'd have to pay them."

"And how do we ensure they *don't* make it right through until morning?"

Neil walked through into the next collection of exhibits. It featured Burke and Hare skulking behind some gravestones, victims of the Inquisition being disembowelled or burned and figures of Dracula, Frankenstein and the Wolfman, all sculpted to look like their film counterparts.

"We scare them," Neil said.

"How? Aren't they supposed to be scared enough just by being down here?" Carl asked. "What can we do to make sure things get worse?"

"How about if one of the exhibits came to life?"

Carl looked at his brother flatly for a moment then shook his head, turning away.

"So this problem has finally pushed you over the edge, has it?" he grunted. "You've lost your mind."

"Look, you've been down here for a couple of hours," Neil explained. "Your imagination is working overtime, it's dark. You're hearing noises. And then, one of the figures starts moving about. Are you going to sit around wondering what's happening? No. You're going to run for the nearest exit."

Carl shook his head.

"If that actually happened then yes but Neil, these are wax figures, they don't come to life," he gaped. "Get a grip."

"Let me explain how it will work," Neil told him, smiling.

***

Neil Chamberlain closed the house door and leaned against it for a moment before making his way into the sitting room beyond.

His wife was sitting on the sofa glancing at her iPad but she looked up when Neil walked in, smiling warmly as he approached her, kissing her lightly on the lips before seating himself beside her.

"You're late," she told him.

"Sorry," he sighed.

"And you've been drinking," she noted, raising her eyebrows.

"I needed it," he told her.

Melissa Chamberlain eyed her husband warily for a moment.

"Are things really that bad?" she wanted to know.

He nodded.

"Anything *I* can do?" she offered, smiling.

"Not unless you know how to work miracles," he said, getting to his feet. He crossed to the drinks cabinet, took out a bottle of Jack Daniel's and poured himself a large measure which he swallowed almost in one gulp. He re-filled his glass, poured his wife one too and then wandered back to the sofa. He told her what was going on with the wax museum. He told her the plan to save it.

Melissa listened to the entire story with the same emotionless expression. Even when he got to the part about the ten-thousand-pound prize for anyone who lasted a full night inside the chamber of horrors. When he'd finished he sat back, eyes closed, as if the effort of telling the story had been too draining for him.

"When do you start?" she asked. "When do you launch the challenge?"

He looked at her and smiled.

"You don't think I'm crazy?" he asked.

"I think that you're doing everything you can, Neil," she told him. "I think that ever since I've known you, you've never walked away from anything. You've never given in. You've always been a fighter. That's one of the things I love about you."

"You don't think I'm fighting a losing battle this time?"

"You won't know that yet."

"You mean I won't know that until I go bust."

"And Carl thinks it's a good idea?"

"He's going along with it because he's got no choice,"

Neil grunted. "His only solution is to sell the place. I can't do that."

"So you offer ten thousand pounds," Melissa said, quietly. "Someone agrees to be locked in the torture chamber for eight hours. If they get through, they get ten grand. If they leave before the time's up, they get nothing."

"That's about it," he told her, running a hand through his hair. "We contacted every newspaper, media outlet and social media platform we could think of before we left tonight. If we're going to get any response at all it should start in the next couple of days. Then we might have a clearer idea of where we are."

"So all you've got to do now is hope that no one who wants to stay down there for eight hours has got nerves of steel," she mused.

Neil raised his eyebrows.

"I think we've got that covered," he murmured.

"But how? You can't be sure the people who volunteer to be shut in there for eight hours are going to get scared. If they survive for eight hours you're screwed."

"All right, let me explain why they won't last."

He moved closer to Melissa who listened raptly as he spoke.

When he'd finished she merely sat gazing silently at him.

Neil smiled.

***

The first person to volunteer for a night in the Chamber of horrors saw the advertisement on social media.

At least that was what he told Neil and Carl Chamberlain.

He was a tall, pale-looking individual in his early twenties and, he assured the attending media, he loved horror films and was interested in serial killers.

This prompted questions about his state of mind from two or three of the journalists gathered around but Neil and Carl didn't care about his state of mind. All that bothered them was that someone had decided to take up the challenge.

It created the publicity they craved. They hoped that the rise in takings would now follow.

News crews from most of the large networks were in attendance on the night the challenge took place and dozens of newspapers and magazines had sent representatives to a press conference that turned out to be so big that the brothers decided to host it in the area outside the front of the wax museum.

This gave additional coverage for them and enabled them to make constant reference to the museum.

A large table had been set up in front of the building and Neil and Carl took up their positions on either side of Lewis Price.

"Would you take on the challenge yourself?" one of the journalists asked Neil.

"No," he said. "Definitely not. I haven't got the courage for that."

The assembled media laughed.

Lewis Price grinned broadly.

"Aren't you worried about what you've got to do, Lewis?" a reporter from Sky TV asked.

"No," the young man answered. "They're only waxworks, aren't they? It's not like they can hurt me."

Neil smiled more broadly.

"Mr Chamberlain," a reporter from the BBC called, raising a hand. "What happens if Lewis wants to get out of the chamber before the eight hours are up?"

"There'll be security guards to release him when that happens," Neil announced. "We wouldn't leave him in there longer than we had to."

"I won't be coming out before the time limit is up," Lewis added, defiantly. "I want that ten grand."

The assembled media laughed.

So did Neil Chamberlain. His brother remained impassive.

"You've had more than fifty applications for this task," a reporter from MTV called. "It could cost you a fortune if they all succeed."

Neil smiled more broadly.

"We're confident they *won't* succeed," he said.

"Is it true that Lewis has had to sign a contract absolving you and your brother of responsibility if he dies of fright while he's inside the chamber?" asked someone from Capital Radio.

"That's perfectly true," Neil said, smiling. "We've ensured that all legal loopholes have been covered."

"Do you honestly believe he won't be able to last eight hours in the chamber?" a woman from Channel 4 wanted to know.

"If we didn't, we wouldn't be offering ten thousand pounds," Neil chuckled.

"Lewis will enter the chamber at midnight," Carl interjected. "He'll be locked in there until eight the next morning. If he leaves or wants to leave before that deadline, he gets nothing."

There were more mutterings and murmurings from the assembled throng and then Neil stood up.

"Well, ladies and gentlemen," he called. "It's now 11.30. I'm sure you'll allow Lewis some time to himself to prepare for his ordeal."

Lewis Price laughed mockingly then followed Neil and Carl back inside the wax museum. They led him to the chamber where he turned over his mobile phone to the security guards present. Once that was done the brothers led him into the chamber of horrors, shook hands with him, wished him the best and announced that he would be collected again in eight hours.

Lewis nodded, glancing around briefly at some of the exhibits.

It was one minute to midnight when he was left alone in the darkened chamber.

The metal door was slammed shut and locked, the sound reverberating within the stillness of the chamber.

The only sound Lewis could hear now was the slow, steady thumping of his own heart.

He checked his watch and seated himself on the stone floor.

***

"You realise that if anyone finds out what we're doing we'll probably get locked up."

Carl Chamberlain looked at his watch and then at his brother who was seated behind his desk.

"Why?" Neil wanted to know. "We're not breaking any laws."

Carl didn't look convinced.

He glanced at his watch again and saw that it was almost 1.36 am. He got to his feet and began pacing the office slowly.

"Go home," Neil told him. "I can manage here."

"There's no point. I wouldn't be able to sleep anyway."

"So, stay and watch the show," Neil said, smiling. He opened his laptop and pressed a couple of keys.

The image that appeared on the screen was split into four. Each portion of the screen showed a different part of the chamber of horrors.

Clearly visible on one was Lewis Price.

"What the hell is this?" Carl murmured, standing beside his brother now, his gaze fixed on the footage.

"I had CCTV cameras installed," Neil murmured, his own eyes on the images.

"You didn't tell me," Carl protested.

"I don't tell you *everything* I do," Neil grinned.

"Are you just going to sit and watch him for the next seven hours?"

"I don't think it'll be that long. I had the cameras installed for our sakes. Just to ensure that he hadn't sneaked another phone or device in there with him. He has to endure the experience in full. Solitude. Alone with just his own thoughts and fears. No outside help."

He tapped a key and changed the angle of two of the cameras.

"I'm trying to safeguard our money," Neil murmured.

The time signature in the top right-hand corner of the screen showed 2.06 am now.

Lewis Price was still sitting on the floor of the chamber but his head had lolled forward onto his knees. He seemed to be sleeping.

Neil adjusted the focus of the camera and zoomed in on the younger man.

"That's how scared he is," Carl sighed. "He's gone to sleep. Another six hours and he'll be wanting his money."

Neil didn't answer. He was too intent on watching Lewis Price.

The younger man had lifted his head and was glancing around, blinking myopically as he emerged from his temporary torpor. He continued looking around, his head sometimes jerking back and forth.

"Isn't there any sound on this?" Carl asked, also seeing the movements.

Neil shook his head, never taking his eyes from the images before him.

He watched as Price got slowly to his feet, still looking around. The younger man walked back and forth a couple of times then made his way into another part of the chamber, looking closely at each of the exhibits in turn.

"What the hell is he doing?" Carl mused.

Once again, Neil remained silent.

On the screen they both saw Price jerk his head around once again, turning to hurry back into the first area of the chamber that he'd just vacated.

When he zoomed in on the younger man's face, Neil could see that Price looked agitated.

Frightened?

He turned sharply two or three times as if attracted by something that was just out of shot.

Then both men watched as his eyes bulged wide in the sockets, his mouth dropping open.

He bolted for the door of the chamber, crashing into it, hammering on the partition with both fists, his mouth still open but this time in a silent scream.

"What the hell is going on?" Carl asked, leaning closer to the screen.

As he watched he saw the door being opened, the two security guards being pushed aside as Price blundered past them, desperate to be out of the chamber now.

Neil Chamberlain smiled thinly and closed the laptop.

"Come on," he said, getting to his feet. "We'd better get down there."

The two men hurried out of the office, down the stairs to the corridor and then down again to the lower level.

They found Lewis Price sitting in the small amusement arcade with one of the security guards. The younger man was milk white, his entire body shaking uncontrollably.

"He looks as though he's in shock," Carl observed, his forehead wrinkling.

"What happened?" Neil wanted to know, looking first at the security guard.

"We had to get him out, Mr Chamberlain," the uniformed man said. "He was banging on the door."

"What happened, Lewis?" Carl enquired, trying to place a comforting hand on the younger man's shoulder.

Price looked at him blankly, his mouth still hanging open.

"It moved," he said, breathlessly. "It fucking moved."

He began to cry.

"What moved?" Carl went on.

"One of the fucking figures," Price roared at him, tears now coursing down his cheeks. "It moved. I saw it."

"Listen, Lewis," Neil said, his voice reflective. "Don't tell anyone about this. Don't tell anyone what you thought you saw."

"What do you mean *'thought'*?" the younger man blurted. "I *did* see it. I saw the fucking thing move."

"I know what you thought you saw but it might be best to keep that to yourself," Neil went on. "If anyone asks why you left just tell them you got too scared to carry on. If you say something about the figures moving they'll lock you up."

Price suddenly stood up, turning angrily on Neil.

"What's in there?" he gasped, motioning in the direction of the chamber. "What the fuck is in there? I saw something move. I'm *not* imagining it. Don't treat me like a fucking idiot."

"All right, all right," Neil murmured, stepping away from the younger man. He motioned to the security guard to join him on the other side of the room, content to leave Carl with Price.

"What did he say to you when he came out?" Neil asked the uniformed man.

"He started banging on the door screaming for us to let him out," the security guard said. "He kept on about one of the figures moving."

"You keep this to yourself, right?" Neil instructed. "He's probably been drinking or he's on drugs or something. If anyone asks he just got scared and wanted to come out."

The security guard nodded.

"I thought it might be drugs," he agreed. "His eyes were like saucers when we let him out of there. We called an ambulance. It should be here any time."

"Drugs," Neil echoed, his voice low. He patted the uniformed man on the shoulder and nodded.

Outside, the ambulance siren echoed in the stillness.

***

By the end of the third week they were getting over a hundred applications daily for people wanting to brave whatever horrors the chamber might hold.

With the attendant publicity came a sharp rise in attendance for the wax museum.

By the end of the first month they were well into profit again.

By the end of the second month they raised the prize money to twenty thousand pounds for anyone who could remain for eight hours inside the chamber of horrors.

The number of those wanting to try grew exponentially.

The longest anyone had lasted was four hours. No one, it seemed, was able to go the full eight hours.

The imaginations of those temporarily imprisoned within the chamber had played havoc. Many of those who had fled had spoken of some of the figures moving but these declarations had been met with scorn by the media as the products of disturbed minds. Or, more often than not, the result of a heavy drinking session before the door of the chamber was slammed shut on them.

Even when a man in his early fifties suffered an almost fatal heart attack due to shock and fear, the numbers of those volunteering to try and win twenty thousand only increased.

And so did attendances.

"Up for the third month running," Neil Chamberlain said, smiling. He held up the sheets bearing the information and waved them momentarily. "We'll need to take on extra staff if the attendances keep rising like this."

"The fewer staff, the bigger profits," Carl intoned.

Both men laughed.

"Dad would have been proud," Neil chuckled.

"Who's the next one into the chamber?" Carl wanted to know.

"A young woman," Neil told him. "Tanya Best. Age thirty-three. Single. Part time model."

"I wonder why she wants the money," Carl mused.

"Why does *anyone* want twenty thousand?"

"Same routine?"

"It hasn't failed us yet, has it?"

Both men laughed once more.

***

Melissa Chamberlain looked at the dashboard clock and smiled to herself.

Ten thirty.

She had plenty of time.

She could be there in less than an hour should the need arise. There was no need to rush.

She saw the headlights in the rearview mirror, wondering why the car behind was flashing her. Melissa glanced at the oncoming vehicle in her mirror and eased to one side slightly. The other car was within a hundred yards of her by now and closing rapidly.

What the hell was he playing at? Why didn't he just overtake?

She moved further towards the side of the road, encouraging the other vehicle to move around her but it still continued to hang back, lights flashing occasionally.

The road they were on was flanked on both sides by a wide grass verge and then lines of trees that masked the fields beyond. Every now and then she would pass an isolated house but, for the most part, the darkness of the night was unbroken.

At last the car behind accelerated, drawing up alongside her momentarily, allowing her to see inside it.

The driver and his three passengers were all young. No more than twenty she guessed and, as one, they waved and gestured at her as they drew level with her. Melissa tried to ignore them, keeping her eyes on the darkened road. Even when the driver hit the hooter, she refused to acknowledge them. She could hear them jeering and shouting.

Melissa was relieved when the other car sped away, disappearing into the gloom.

She slowed down, wanting to ensure that the other vehicle was well and truly gone.

When her phone rang she slowed the car slightly, finally pulling over onto the grass verge before answering it.

The caller ID told her it was her husband.

"Hello," she said, cheerfully, not bothering to mention the other car and its occupants.

"When you get here, come in the back way," Neil Chamberlain told her. "There's lots of media around tonight."

"Well, it's the first night with twenty thousand at stake, isn't it?" Melissa grinned. "Is the... contestant there yet?"

"She's with Carl. She asked if she could have a look around the rest of the museum before she goes down into the chamber. He's giving her the guided tour now." Neil chuckled.

"I'll be there before eleven," Melissa told him.

"Like I said, just come straight in the back way, don't

284

come up to the office first, like you usually do," Neil repeated.

"Okay," she said. "Love you."

She hung up.

Melissa turned the key in the ignition.

Nothing.

Not a sound. Not a flicker. She tried again and, this time, the engine let out a low whirring sound then died.

"Oh Christ," Melissa hissed, banging the steering wheel.

She turned the key again.

Once more there was nothing, not even the whirring sound.

Melissa sat back in the driver's seat and let out a sigh of frustration. There was no point in looking beneath the bonnet because she wouldn't have a clue what she was looking for anyway. She reached for her phone and dialled the RAC but, as she did, she noticed with horror that her battery was almost dead. After she'd been told that no one would get to her for another hour she called her husband.

There was no answer.

"Come on," Melissa said, her concern beginning to overcome her frustration.

Still no answer.

She got out of the car and began pacing back and forth beside the stricken vehicle. And it was then that the battery died.

"No," Melissa gasped, staring at the blank screen. "Oh God," she murmured.

She looked anxiously at her watch.

Ten fifty-seven.

***

It was almost eleven forty-three by the time Neil Chamberlain joined his brother and Tanya Best just outside the chamber of horrors.

He shook hands with Tanya, wished her all the best and the three of them chatted happily about the museum, about the challenge she was about to undertake and assorted other subjects that were effectively killing time before Tanya was due to be shut into the subterranean chamber.

"I'm definitely going to do this," Tanya said, confidently.

"Doesn't it put you off that so many others have tried it and failed?" Neil asked.

"No, it just makes me more determined," Tanya said, smiling.

"And you're not scared?" Neil went on.

"No," she beamed.

"Well, see what you feel like in a couple of hours," Carl added and all three of them laughed.

The two security guards joined them, one of them escorting Tanya into the chamber.

As Neil and Carl walked away Carl looked at his brother.

"Did you tell Melissa to come in the back way?" he asked.

Neil nodded. "I warned her there were lots of media about tonight," he said.

The two men continued walking, making their way up the stairs towards the office.

"I wonder what those reporters would say if they knew that your wife was the reason no one can stay in the chamber without being frightened off?" Carl chuckled.

Neil also laughed. "I know, it's amazing what a bit of make-up and an overactive imagination can accomplish. I don't know if any of them actually stop long enough to look closely before they run out."

"We'd better hope they don't," Carl added. "If anyone had realised that it wasn't a wax figure coming to life but your wife in a costume, then we'd have had problems."

"She was happy to help us," Neil told him. "She didn't want this place to go under any more than we did."

"She's a fine woman," Carl said, grinning.

Both men laughed.

"A little subterfuge never hurt," Neil said.

They made their way back up to the office where Neil opened the laptop and both men sat around watching the feeds from the CCTV cameras.

Through those they could see Tanya Best in the chamber. She was walking around. Moving from one part of the room to another, sometimes pausing to look at the wax figures more closely, other times just walking back and forth as if she was out for a stroll on the seafront.

Neil slid open one of the drawers of his desk and took out a bottle of Jack Daniel's and two glasses. He poured a measure of the liquor into each then offered one to Carl who took it gratefully.

"A toast," Neil said, raising his glass. "To... subterfuge."

"To the tricks the mind can play," Carl added.

Both men laughed and drank deeply.

On the screen of the laptop they could see that Tanya Best was now standing close to the bars in the larger part of the subterranean room. She was leaning against them as if trying to get a better view of something in the shadows beyond. Neil watched raptly as he sipped his drink.

He checked his watch.

"Here we go," he said, smiling.

Both men saw the young woman turn quickly and then bolt for the locked door behind her. She began hammering on it, sometimes looking over her shoulder, her eyes now wide with terror.

Even without the benefit of sound on the laptop, the

two men could see that her mouth was wide open as she screamed for help. Shouted for someone to get her out of the underground rooms.

She continued to bang on the doors, occasionally looking around, tears of uncontrollable terror now coursing down her cheeks.

"We'd better go down and meet her when she comes out," Neil said, closing the laptop.

By the time the two men got down to the area outside the chamber, Tanya Best was rocking back and forth like a child while one of the security men tried to comfort her.

"I want to go," Tanya blurted. "I want to get out of here. Let me out."

"All right, all right," Neil said, trying to calm her. "Perhaps you'd better calm down a little first. What happened?"

"I was in there and something moved," she told him, still breathing heavily. "One of the figures. It moved. I swear to God. I saw it. It was walking." She began to shudder even more violently.

Carl nodded, delighted that the ruse had worked once again.

"I saw it," Tanya said again, her voice cracking. "It was coming after me."

"Just sit for a minute," Neil said, patting her shoulder reassuringly. "Try and calm down."

"One of those fucking figures walked," she shrieked, pointing in the direction of the chamber. "What the hell is going on in there?"

"It was your imagination," Neil said, softly.

"I saw it," she roared.

"Do you want to show me?" he offered.

"No," she snapped. "I wouldn't go back in there for a *million* pounds let alone twenty thousand. I just want to go home."

"All right," Neil breathed. He nodded to the nearest of the security guards who supported Tanya as he helped her towards the exit.

When she was gone he turned to his brother and smiled broadly.

"Fancy another drink before we close up?" he asked and Carl also smiled. They headed back up to the office and Neil poured them fresh drinks.

They were about to make another toast when the office door opened.

Melissa Chamberlain walked in, her face flushed.

"I tried to phone but my bloody battery died," she grunted.

Both men looked at her blankly.

"The RAC guy managed to fix my car temporarily but I've got to get it to a garage tomorrow," Melissa went on.

"I'm not with you," Neil said.

"My car broke down on the way here," Melissa told them. "I tried to ring but I couldn't. What happened with the girl in the chamber? Is she still in there?"

"No, she ran out screaming about twenty minutes ago," Carl breathed.

"She said one of the figures moved," Neil added. "She said it came after her."

"That's impossible," Melissa snapped. "I've only just arrived here. I haven't been near the chamber."

Neil opened the laptop and hit the necessary keys.

"Play the footage back," Carl snapped.

"That's what I'm trying to do," Neil rasped, hitting the keys harder. "It won't play. There's nothing but a blank screen."

"So she said she saw one of the figures move?" Melissa asked, her face pale.

"She said it walked," Neil informed her, his own voice low. "But if you weren't in the chamber, if you weren't pretending to be one of the waxworks like you usually do, then what did she see?"

The words hung on the air like dust in a ray of sunlight.

PORTRAITS

The sunshine pouring through the large windows of the office made it unbearably warm inside the room.

Even with the air conditioning turned up, the heat inside the room was uncomfortable and Dani Porter used her hand to fan herself, trying to create a small cool breeze, however fleeting.

Beside her, Jake Wells pulled at the collar of his t-shirt, moving the material, feeling the perspiration beneath the fabric. At twenty-nine he was a couple of years older than Dani and they'd worked together two or three times before. The last time under more distressing circumstances. They'd been covering a gig by an American band and, during that time, a fire had broken out in the venue which had spread with incredible speed and ferocity and resulted in the deaths of six audience members. Instead of photographing a rock band, Dani had found herself taking pictures of dead and injured music fans while Wells had tried to interview those closest to the blaze. It had been a harrowing time for both of them.

Now, Wells glanced to the far end of the large table that dominated the centre of the room, looking at the laptop set up there but also at the prints and posters on display. Each one bore images of monstrous creatures and looked as if they had been freshly ripped from some fevered and possibly warped imagination. The figures that populated the posters, prints and album sleeves were the stuff of nightmares. Wells sipped at his can of Sprite then got up and walked to the end of the table, sifting through the illustrations.

Dani joined him.

The other person in the room, a squat, burly man in his forties dressed in faded jeans and a worn black t-shirt with the legend "Appetite for Destruction" on the back, glanced at each of his colleagues in turn. He took a hefty drag on his electronic cigarette then pointed at the screen of the laptop where a slide show was exposing more of the fearful images already on display.

"Joshua Barton," murmured Wells, his eyes fixed on the laptop screen. "The man who draws what others are afraid even to imagine." He smiled broadly.

"I think he's genuinely insane," David Charlton said, taking another drag.

"He's just gifted," Dani offered, her own gaze fixed on the images.

"You call being able to draw things like that a gift?" Charlton grunted. "I wouldn't want those thoughts and images in *my* head."

"Supposedly he has terrible nightmares," Dani went on. "He paints what he sees during those."

"Didn't H.R. Giger used to do that too?" Wells added. "The guy who designed the monster in '*Alien*'."

"There was a story that Barton had been in a psychiatric hospital too," Dani said. "Didn't he have a mental breakdown a few years back?"

"After his wife's suicide," Charlton confirmed. "I'm not surprised she killed herself living with a nutter like him."

"Just because he's creative it doesn't make him crazy," said Dani.

"All truly creative people have at least one screw loose," Charlton proclaimed. "It goes with the territory. It's that instability that puts them ahead of everyone else."

Dani chuckled.

"When was the last time he gave an interview?" she wanted to know, lifting one of the prints and inspecting it more closely.

"He's *never* given an interview," Wells told her. "He's been working for more than forty years, most of that time at the top of his game but he just won't do interviews. He lives like a hermit. None of the bands who he's done work for have ever met him. He never turns up to exhibitions. He won't have his picture taken. Everything is arranged through a team of personal assistants. No one ever meets him or discusses his work with him. He just gets on with it and presents it when he's finished."

Dani shook her head.

"You have to admire him a bit for that," she murmured. "Everyone wants to be a celebrity these days. Everyone wants their photo taken or wants to share their private life and this guy just keeps away from all that. God knows how he does it."

Charlton shrugged. "Every rock band in the world wants Joshua Barton artwork on their album covers," he said.

"I don't blame them," Wells offered. "His work's like a trademark."

"Why was his exhibition at The Tate Modern shut down last year?" Dani wanted to know.

"Some of the artwork showed child abuse, child murder," Wells said. "People accused him of being a paedophile. There was all sorts of outrage on social media. People started protesting outside the building, they had several threats. People saying they'd burn the building if the exhibition went on. The Tate didn't have any choice, they closed it down."

"A private collector bought every single exhibit," Charlton interjected. "Paid a fortune for it."

"No such thing as bad publicity," Dani mused, looking at the laptop screen and one of the other examples of Barton's art. It showed a creature the size of a man with a very prominent erection holding a screaming baby up in one hand while, with the other, it dragged a naked woman along behind it like so much luggage. Just as a single maggot was dragging itself from the urethral slit of the creature's organ, there was a bloodied, worm-like monstrosity emerging from the woman's vagina, its lips spread wide to reveal teeth that resembled stiff penises.

"I want to know how he works," Charlton said. "I want to know how he thinks of these bloody images. I want to know everything you can find out about him."

"And lots of pictures?" Dani grinned.

Charlton nodded.

"I want every part of his creative process documented," the older man said.

"He's not the only artist who's ever created controversy with what he paints," Dani observed, her gaze still fixed on the succession of images before her. "Why has Barton had so much flack over the years?"

"It's because of the realism of what he paints," Charlton explained. "This isn't some spotty teenager scribbling away in his bedroom, trying to be controversial, drawing with one hand and wanking with the other. This is one of the richest artists in the world."

"So why give an interview now?" Wells asked. "After all these years?"

"He's dying," Charlton explained. "Alzheimer's. Motor neurone disease. Fuck knows what else. His PA said he wants to talk now. Before it's too late."

"Like a confession?" Dani murmured, looking at a picture of a monstrous image that showed an impossibly pale white skinned apparition, eyes wide, huge mouth spilling dog excrement and maggots down its chest.

"That's what I want you two to find out," Charlton said. "And if Barton's as sick as we're led to believe, you'd better get your arses in gear. He's expecting you."

"Why us?" Wells asked.

"I don't know and I don't care but he asked for you by name," Charlton said. "Both of you."

***

"Why do you think he asked for us?"

Dani sipped her Starbucks and gazed out of the passenger side window as Wells guided the car through the busy streets.

"He's obviously aware of our reputations as the undisputed masters of our chosen crafts," he said, smiling. "Well, of *my* reputation anyway, not so sure about *yours*."

She punched him playfully on the arm and smiled.

"He probably just got his PA to print out a list of journalists and photographers and then stuck a pin in it," Wells said. "Who cares? We got the gig, that's all that matters."

"He could have done the last interview on TV or online and reached even more people," Dani offered.

"Who knows how his mind works? I'm sure he's got his reasons for doing it this way."

"Imagine knowing when you're going to die. How does he manage to carry on like that?"

"It's a case of having to, isn't it?"

"But I wonder why he wants to make it so public after all these years of living so privately?"

"Fuck knows. Perhaps he really has got something to confess. Everyone's got secrets, haven't they?" Wells looked at her and smiled. "You must have got a few of your own."

"Like I'd share them with you?" Dani grinned.

"I'm the soul of discretion," Wells assured her.

"Yeah, right. You'd sell your own mother for a good story. Speaking of which, has Barton got any family?"

"He was married a couple of times. His first wife died,

the second one committed suicide. He's got a daughter by his first wife. She's in her twenties. She's his PA. It was her who got in touch with the magazine in the first place."

"Why did his second wife kill herself?"

"No one knows."

Dani reached for her phone and began scrolling through more images created by Joshua Barton.

"The detail he creates is incredible," she murmured.

"He is handy with a paint brush I'll give you that," Wells offered, slowing down at a set of traffic lights.

Dani finished scrolling through the images and was about to sit back in her seat when her phone rang. She glanced at the caller ID and sighed irritably. What the hell did Tom Cassidy want now? For a moment she considered answering it and then thought better of it, pushing the phone into her jacket instead.

Wells glanced at her questioningly.

"You could have answered it you know," he told her. "I wouldn't have listened in."

"It isn't important," Dani told him. "Just a loose end."

"Who is he?"

"What makes you think it's a guy?"

"Journalist's intuition," he said, grinning.

"It was a mistake," Dani told him. "I should have known better."

"Want to talk about it? I'm not asking because I'm caring, just because I'm nosey."

Dani smiled. "I met him at a party," she said, quietly. "We hit it off. Things happened. But now it's over. It's just that he doesn't seem willing to accept that. I think we were both a bit vulnerable at the time. We sort of fell into each other's arms. I'd just split with my boyfriend and he was having problems with his daughter."

"His daughter? How old is he?"

"Fifty-eight."

"Jesus."

"He's a very young fifty-eight."

"You got a thing about older guys then?"

"Not usually but there was something about him."

"What was it? His pension book?"

"Oh fuck you. He was very charming and respectful."

"If you say so."

"Anyway, it's over now."

"Maybe you should tell *him* that."

Dani gazed out of the side window again, watching the buildings hasten by.

"I knew a photographer who tried to get inside Barton's studio," Wells said, his voice lower, more earnest now. "This was five or six years ago."

"Did he manage it?" Dani wanted to know.

"I don't know. He disappeared a few days afterwards. Him. His equipment. Everything."

"Do you think Barton had something to do with it?"

"It's a hell of a coincidence, isn't it?"

Dani nodded slowly.

"What could he have been hiding that was so important?" she murmured.

Wells had no answer and they drove the rest of the way in silence. When he finally brought the car to a halt in the quiet Fulham street, Dani glanced out at the houses surrounding them.

Large, well-kept town houses seemed to be the order of the day in this affluent part of London and Dani could only guess at the cost of property here. It was a different world. Even as she stepped from the car she could see curtains twitching in a house across the street. She smiled to herself, wondering who was watching them. Dani had the feeling that very few people came and went in this neighbourhood without the locals knowing about it. She checked her camera, waiting for Wells to join her on the pavement.

"Which one is Barton's?" she enquired.

Wells pointed to an imposing whitewashed edifice about a hundred yards away.

"He owns the houses on either side too," the journalist added. "He's lived here for years."

"I was expecting some big rambling place in the country," Dani murmured, snapping off some pictures of the exterior of the large house. "It's easier to live like a hermit when you're not surrounded by people isn't it?"

Wells raised his eyebrows quizzically then he glanced at his watch.

"Come on," he urged. "We'd better not be late. Apparently he hates people who aren't punctual."

They set off towards the privet hedge that marked the perimeter of the property and Wells pushed open the black painted metal gate that led to the pathway up to the front door.

"What about Barton's staff?" Dani asked, looking up at the house. "Has anyone ever come forward with any strange stories about him?"

"You must be joking," Wells grunted. "He ties them to contracts slightly less stringent than the Official Secrets Act. If anyone has ever worked for him and had stories to tell they've never dared come forward for fear of legal action against them. They all have to sign non-disclosure agreements when they work for him."

"Maybe he's just a perfect employer," Dani grinned.

Wells muttered something under his breath, taking the first of the stone steps that led up to the black painted front door of the house. He rang the doorbell and waited.

He was about to ring it again when the door opened.

The young woman standing inside the hallway was in her mid-twenties. She looked immaculate in an expensive black two piece and a white blouse beneath. Behind the spectacles she wore, her eyes were of the brightest blue and Wells found himself gazing into those wide orbs. She ran appraising eyes over the two newcomers and smiled efficiently.

"Can I help you?" she said.

"I'm Jake Wells, this is my colleague Dani Porter," the journalist told her. "We're here to see Joshua Barton."

The young woman smiled happily at them and ushered them inside, closing the door behind them.

"I'm Imogen Barton," she announced. "My father is expecting you."

She shook hands with both of them and Wells was surprised at the strength in her grip.

Dani raised her camera and prepared to take some shots of the inside of the huge hallway but Imogen put out a hand and waved it in front of the lens.

"Not in here please," she said, her smile still fixed in place.

"I just wanted to give a feel of your father's environment," Dani told her.

"*This* isn't his environment," Imogen said, flatly.

Dani shrugged and nodded.

"If you say so," she muttered.

"If you could both follow me, please," the younger woman asked, beckoning to them. "I'll take you to him."

Dani looked around the hallway. The walls were dark green and bare. Not one single picture or painting in view.

"It's strange that a man who's made his name and his fortune by painting has no artwork on his walls," she mused.

"Would you expect a surgeon to have pictures of internal organs around his house?" Imogen asked. "My father doesn't need to remind himself what he does for a living."

Dani looked at the younger woman for a second then

returned her attention to the vast open hallway that they were crossing. The floor was completely covered by thick carpet that absorbed the sound of their footsteps and the dark painted walls too seemed to be sucking in the extraneous noise. Dani saw a wide flight of stairs to the left and wondered what lay up there in the higher reaches of the house. Was that where Barton worked? Or was it within one of the rooms that Imogen was now leading them towards? There were three dark wood doors ahead of them and the younger woman headed to the one on the left.

Dani could smell the odour of polish but assumed that a team of cleaners kept the house in its immaculate state. She couldn't imagine Imogen with her sleeves rolled up and a duster in her hand. The younger woman opened the door to reveal not a room beyond it but another set of doors. Metal partitions that reminded Dani of lift doors. Indeed, beside these there was a small panel bearing buttons very similar to those outside an elevator and, when Imogen used one perfectly manicured finger to press the topmost button, the doors slid open to reveal the small cubicle beyond.

Imogen stepped into the elevator and signalled for the journalist and photographer to join her, which they did.

The inside of the small elevator car smelled of polished wood like the hallway. The dark oak panels that lined the walls seemed to make the confined space even more constricted. Imogen pressed a button inside and the elevator began to descend very slowly.

"It's a beautiful house," Dani offered.

"Thank you," Imogen answered.

"It must have been wonderful growing up here," Dani went on.

Imogen smiled thinly.

"It's just a house," she said, without looking at Dani. "My father bought it more than thirty years ago."

"It must have been great having him around when you were growing up," Dani continued.

"I didn't see any more of him than if he'd worked in an office," Imogen revealed, the smile now completely gone. "I was never allowed near his studio. No one was."

"How long have you worked for your father?" Wells wanted to know.

"Two years," Imogen informed him. "I wasn't sure what to do when I left uni so working for my dad seemed to be the perfect solution for both of us." .

"What did you study at uni?" Dani enquired.

"Psychology and forensic medicine," Imogen said.

"Not art?" Wells continued.

"One artist in the family is enough," Imogen announced. "And my father always tried to guide me away from his line of work."

"Why?" Dani asked.

"He knew the sacrifices it called for," murmured Imogen. "And the pain it could bring."

Dani looked at the younger woman for a moment, aware of the darker expression that had settled on her finely chiselled features.

"Does your father have trouble getting around?" Wells interjected. "I wondered why the lift had been installed."

"No, he's still pretty mobile," Imogen explained. "But some of the tunnels are very deep."

"Tunnels?" Dani murmured.

"Does your father work in the basement?" Wells wanted to know.

"There *is* no basement," Imogen said as the lift bumped to a halt. She looked at each of her guests in turn, her face expressionless. "I must ask you both to stay close to me when we leave the elevator. It's very dark down here. And please don't touch anything. Also, can I ask for your mobile phones and any other electronic devices please? My father hates them. He's a bit of a technophobe."

Wells and Dani hesitated for a moment then handed over their devices, watching as Imogen slipped them into the pockets of her jacket. She then reached for the control panel close to the doors and hit another button.

The lift doors slid open and what lay beyond those doors was like an open sewer.

The stench was the first thing that hit Dani and she raised a hand to her face, covering her nose and mouth as best she could in a desperate attempt to keep out the vile stink that filled the air like invisible smoke. The terrain outside the doors looked like a passageway, but only as Dani stepped into it did she realise that the floor, sides and ceiling of the conduit were little more than bare, oozing mud. The tunnel was about six feet across, the same again in height and, as she glanced up in the almost impenetrable blackness she could see that there were droplets of moisture falling from the roof of the walkway. Some of those were dripping into the puddles of reeking water that had accumulated on the floor of the tunnel, and that sound created a persistent tattoo as Dani and Wells moved out into the chamber.

However, now, as her eyes gradually became accustomed to the almost palpable darkness, Dani realised that there were small lights arrayed along the uppermost reaches of the walls. They looked like blinking fairy lights in such overwhelming gloom and several of them had already failed or were in the process of dying.

"Your father works down here?" Wells said, incredulously.

"He rarely comes up to the house now," Imogen said, walking ahead of them, her feet squelching in the sucking ooze beneath. There were several lengths of wood in the centre of the tunnel, designed to make the walk along it easier but these too had sunk into the mud and been virtually submerged in the black slime. "He's more comfortable down here."

"Some people think he's insane," Wells offered. "If they could see this they'd probably be even more convinced."

"Some people are idiots, Mr Wells," Imogen said softly, walking on, seemingly untroubled by either the darkness or the noxious odour that filled the tunnel. "My father has never been troubled by the opinions of others."

"How the hell does he stand it?" Wells continued. "The smell..." He allowed the sentence to trail off, more concerned with covering his mouth and nose with his hand, attempting to shut out the rank fumes.

"You get used to it after a while," Imogen announced. "Like the darkness. But it has to be dark."

"Why?" Dani wanted to know.

"Some of them are sensitive to light," Imogen said.

Dani felt something cold against her fingertips and she gasped loudly, the sound echoing through the tunnel.

"What is it?" Wells said, moving towards her.

"Something cold," Dani said. "I touched something."

"It's a door," Imogen told her.

"To what?" Dani gasped.

"One of the cells," Imogen called, still walking.

"Cells?" Dani said, her voice cracking.

"What do you keep inside them?" Wells wanted to know.

"They're necessary," Imogen told him, her tone untroubled. She disappeared around a bend in the tunnel and both Wells and Dani hurried to catch up with her, desperate not to be left behind in this subterranean maze. She finally turned to face them, holding up a hand to slow their advance. "I must ask you both to wait here," she said. "My father's room is just ahead. I'll tell him you're here." She looked at the journalist and photographer more earnestly now. "Please don't move from this spot while I'm gone. If you wander off down one of the tunnels you could get lost. Please stay here. It's for your own safety."

Imogen walked a little further on and then tapped four times on a large metal door set into the wall of the tunnel. She hesitated a moment and then pushed the door which swung back on well-oiled hinges. Imogen stepped across the threshold into the chamber beyond, disappearing from sight. The door swung shut behind her.

"Let's get out of here," Dani said, grabbing Wells' arm.

"Not until we find out what's going on here," the journalist told her.

"I don't think I *want* to know," Dani snapped.

"It's all part of the charade. Barton's just trying to build up the atmosphere."

"Well he's doing a good job of it. What the hell is that awful smell?"

"It could be methane gas, maybe."

"But who made these tunnels?"

Wells could only shrug.

"Give me your lighter," he said, holding out a hand as Dani rummaged in her pocket. She finally pulled a Zippo free and handed it to him.

"If that smell is methane, is lighting that a good idea?" Dani muttered.

Wells smiled.

"Don't worry about it," he grunted. "Methane smells like rotten eggs. This smells more like rotting meat."

He flipped the lid open and worked the small wheel, watching as sparks and then a flame burst from the device. He held it up, the sickly yellow light spreading out in a broad puddle inside the tunnel, cutting through the blackness, illuminating the subterranean area.

In the gloom he saw something standing behind Dani. The shape loomed up, as if it had detached itself from the shadows or from the wall of the tunnel itself.

For a split second, Wells wasn't sure if he'd actually seen it or not as it rose up behind Dani.

He blinked hard, wondering if his eyes were playing tricks on him. Had he actually seen the man-like figure? It was about five feet tall. Deathly pale. Its skin reflecting the sickly glow as it swayed there behind Dani, one hand outstretched towards her. The fingers were hooked and twisted, covered in mud and something darker. Indeed, there were splatters of dark matter all over its body and, in that split second, Wells realised that it was naked, its skin looking as if it was coated with some gleaming substance that dripped from it here and there. Its wide mouth was gaping open but no sound came forth. Its eyes were disproportionately large, glistening and swollen in the sockets. Almost grey, they looked as if they were afflicted with cataracts. There was no pupil.

And in that split second Wells gasped in shock and revulsion, lifting the lighter higher, wanting to see this monstrosity more clearly.

A gust of air blew the lighter out and the entire tunnel was once more plunged into blackness.

"Oh, Jesus," Wells gasped, struggling to re-light the Zippo, forcing his hand into the air once again when the flame sprang forth.

The creature was gone.

Just he and Dani stood alone in the tunnel, his own heart now thudding uncontrollably against his ribs.

"What's wrong?" Dani asked, seeing the contorted expression on his face. "What did you see?"

"I think my imagination is playing tricks," he gasped. "This darkness. These tunnels." He sucked in a deep breath, not caring that it was tainted by the vile stench hanging in the air.

"I'm beginning to think Barton's critics are right," Dani said. "He must be crazy to work in surroundings like this."

The sound that now rattled through the tunnel was unlike anything either of them had ever heard before.

A long, high-pitched caterwaul that thrummed in their ears and bounced off the walls and ceiling of the tunnel, finally degenerating into what sounded like many harsh, asthmatic breaths before dying away as rapidly as it had arisen.

"What the fuck was that?" Dani gasped, turning to her left and right. Part of her wanting to know what had made the sound but most of her not caring if she ever discovered its source. She could feel the hairs on the back of her neck rising. In fact, the skin all over her body puckered at the sound and she felt herself shaking uncontrollably for a second as the keening ululation died away in the blackness. "Let's get out, now." She grabbed Wells' arm and tugged hard, desperate now to be out of this place. "Do you still think he's just building the fucking atmosphere?" she snapped, angrily.

Wells hesitated then nodded.

He was about to set off back down the tunnel when he heard the large metal door ahead of them swing open once again.

Imogen Barton stepped from inside the room beyond and looked at them both.

"My father will see you now," she said, cheerfully.

"What's down here with us?"

Dani's words echoed inside the tunnel.

She glared at Imogen who merely met her gaze evenly.

"You must have heard that sound," Dani persisted. "What made it?"

"My father will explain," Imogen told her, stepping back and motioning them forward towards the room beyond the door.

"No, *you* explain," Dani snapped. "I'm not staying down her a second longer until I know what the fuck is down here with us."

"Come inside. You'll be safer in here."

As both Dani and Wells walked into the room, Imogen closed the door behind them.

They found themselves in a large room, again with a floor, ceiling and walls constructed simply of bare, wet mud. There were more of the bare light bulbs inside that had lit the tunnel beyond, each one it seemed flickering uncertainly.

In the centre of the room was a chair and an artist's easel. However, it was so dark inside the room it was impossible to see what was on the easel. There were shapes and figures there but no one could discern their outline without walking right up to the canvas.

"My father will be along in a moment," Imogen told them, motioning towards another door in the far wall. "This is his studio."

She had barely finished speaking when another roar filled the tunnel and the room in which they stood. This one seemed like an unholy combination of rage, pain and madness.

Dani felt herself shaking again.

"What *is* that?" she demanded.

"You still don't understand, do you?" Imogen muttered.

Dani looked helplessly at her.

"The things my father paints," Imogen went on. "He found them years ago."

Dani tried to swallow but her throat was chalk dry.

"No one could imagine the kind of things he does," Imogen went on. "He doesn't dream them up. He paints what he sees. He paints from life."

She gestured towards the canvas in the centre of the room and both Dani and Wells moved closer, trying to get a good look at what was there.

The painting showed a monstrous entity standing over

two human bodies, both of which had been eviscerated. The room in which it stood was identical to the one in which they both were now.

Dani was the first to see the faces of the dead bodies.

One bore her own visage, the other the features of Jake Wells.

Dani shook her head, suddenly aware that Imogen had slipped out of the room through the door at the rear of the subterranean chamber. Dani hurried across to it and pulled at it, trying to get it open, desperate to escape this room and this place.

And now the lights began to go out. Each one dying and leaving darkness behind it. One by one they faded and went out.

Another loud roar came from behind her.

From beyond the other metal door.

And it was drawing closer.

Wells drove a foot against the door, trying to move it, trying to force it open. His own fear was threatening to overwhelm him now, his heart hammering uncontrollably in his chest. And all the time the smell seemed to intensify. Filling their nostrils as surely as the roars filled their ears.

And now the roar was right outside the door.

There were only two or three lights still burning, darkness was filling the room.

The first of the impacts against the metal made Wells jump back in terror.

Whatever was out there was determined to get in and, judging by the power of the blows striking the metal, that would not take long.

Dani looked once again at the canvas. At the images of the torn, bloodied bodies with her own face and that of Wells and she shook her head slowly, feeling tears of fear and desperation beginning to course down her cheeks.

She screamed.

The sound was eclipsed by the newest roar of fury coming from beyond the metal door. The impacts against that door were incessant now.

The last of the lights went out. The darkness was total.

And, in that cloying blackness, another roar sounded that was so loud it almost shattered Dani's eardrums.

Her own scream rose on the rancid air as she realised that whatever had been outside in the tunnel was now inside the room with them.

For the first time that day, she was grateful for the darkness. She didn't want to see what was in the room with them.

And in a few seconds it didn't matter.

"There is no such thing as paranoia. Your worst fears can come true at any moment."
Hunter S. Thompson